ERIE ENDING

The Wildlife Refuge Mystery Series Book One

Christy J. Kendall

Kenmore, WA

A Camel Press book published by Epicenter Press

Epicenter Press
6524 NE 181st St.
Suite 2
Kenmore, WA 98028

For more information go to:
www.Camelpress.com
www.Coffeetownpress.com
www.Epicenterpress.com
www.christyjkendall.com

This is a work of fiction. Names, characters, places, brands, media, and incidents are either the product of the author's imagination or are used fictitiously.

Cover design by Scott Book
Design by Melissa Vail Coffman

Erie Ending
Copyright © 2025 by Christy J. Kendall

Library of Congress Control Number: 2024940288

ISBN: 978-1-68492-244-4 (Trade Paper)
ISBN: 978-1-68492-245-1 (eBook)

Printed in the United States of America

*For my husband Gary, my biggest fan and first reader,
and in memory of my dear friend, Bill Dailey,
Ottawa National Wildlife Refuge Volunteer, RIP.*

Acknowledgments

I want to thank the Petrocellis for their Book Passage Mystery Writer Conference in Corte Madera, CA, and the talented agents and authors who gave their time and efforts to create a high-quality event every year. Book Passage is where my journey began and grew.

A special thank you goes out to my Beta Readers for continuing to read those dreadful, unedited first final drafts and helping me to craft a better story—Fran McTamaney, Suzanne Fellows, Jessica Samuelson, Bob Willoughby, Gene and Cathy Cox, and George and Connie Ziesemer.

Without my developmental editor Jaden (Beth) Terrell and line editor Carol Cartaino, I would be nowhere near the finish line. Your encouragement and help made a big difference and will always be invaluable.

I also want to thank MaryLee Woods (Ashford) and Anita Carter, my Sisters in Crime—the Sparkle Abbey team. You led the way and always helped me step up.

And finally, a thank you to Camel Press for taking a chance, and my agent, Eric L. Miller, for being easy to talk to and making this happen.

ONE

The woman slumped forward over the steering wheel— her blond hair matted onto her face. Blood ran from her head and dribbled down the steering column, pooling around her feet. Outside, the black night was lit by a nearby streetlamp that drained all color from the scene. Blood had splattered the windshield, leaving long black exclamation marks on the glass.

Angela Martin, Refuge Manager for the Ottawa National Wildlife Refuge, glanced up as clouds marched across the night sky. A light fog stretched over the marsh, cloaking everything with a misty gray veil, leaving a light dew on the landscape. Clipboard in hand, she joined her twenty-four-year-old volunteer, Jim Messinger, at the front of the vehicle, where he stood with a thermometer and pocket watch at the ready.

It was Tuesday, the first week of June, and this would be the last survey of the year for frogs. The temperatures were cooler than normal. Adding to the chill was a little breeze blowing in from Lake Erie. While the temperatures were cool, they were still within the range required for surveying frogs. Otherwise, Angela would have postponed the trip.

Although relatively shallow at thirty-five feet at its deepest,

Lake Erie earned its place in the Great Lakes by being large in area, encompassing more than ten thousand square miles. Angela was amazed by its sheer size: fifty-seven miles wide, its northern border is Canada and its southern is the United States. Its length spans two hundred forty-one miles south-westerly from Buffalo, New York, past Pennsylvania to Toledo, Ohio.

Unfortunately, it is one of the most heavily impacted of all the Great Lakes from urban and agricultural development. One of the benefits to humans of having a wildlife refuge on its shores is the slowing and cleaning of run-off before it harms the lake.

Ottawa National Wildlife Refuge, one of over five hundred seventy national wildlife refuges administered by the U.S. Fish and Wildlife Service, is located on the southern shores of Lake Erie, about fifteen miles east of Toledo. The refuge's primary purpose is to protect migratory birds along with all other marsh-loving creatures.

Angela stood ready for data collection. Despite the haze, the night was bright with ambient light. The white paper on Angela's clipboard glowed like she held pieces of the moon. She recorded the current temperature.

"You know the routine—one minute, then three," Angela said.

Jim looked at his watch. "It's 9:32 p.m."

A faint breeze stirred Angela's damp, newly short-cropped hair. She relished the cool, moist air against her scalp and recorded the time. They stood in silence for a minute, allowing the creatures in the area to recover from the disturbance they had created by their arrival. The next three minutes were for data collection. Angela slowed her breathing while she focused.

For a few moments, it was quiet and still.

As the night closed in, small flashes began to float around them. Fireflies began to light up the night. Bullfrogs thrummed their rhythmic grunts, followed by the irregular twang of green frogs.

Sounds became sharper, and rhythms grew in tempo as she concentrated, letting her vision and hearing blend with the night.

She faintly heard Lake Erie, less than a mile away, lapping against a remote levee front. The pair stood together, perched on an interior levee of a diked pool, a smaller man-made body of water that had long since lost the energy absorbed from the wind and sun that day. It stretched peacefully before them, but Lake Erie could not rest so easily.

Jim gestured that the first minute had passed.

The breeze picked up, stirring the branches of willows on an island farther out in the pool. Wood ducks silently glided between water-logged trunks, and the startled croak of a great blue heron echoed across the marsh, setting off the eerie call of a pied-billed grebe.

Green frogs grew more vocal now, and the dull sound of their twangs, like loose banjo strings struck repeatedly, offered an alto contrast to the monotonous bass of the bullfrogs. Fireflies, may-flies, and other gnat-like creatures winged their way around the human intruders, settling on Angela's arms and white datasheets.

Life engulfed her as she stood invisible in it. She counted the number of frogs calling and approximated their locations, marking them within the semi-circle representing a 100-foot radius drawn on the sheet.

For a moment, a full moon revealed itself through a break in the clouds before the wind in the upper atmosphere marched the clouds eastward, obscuring it again.

"Time's up." Jim's voice startled her. When she switched on the flashlight, the mood of the night changed. Fireflies extinguished their lights, the frogs went silent, and crickets hushed their chorus.

When they climbed back into the truck, Angela turned on the cab light to prepare a map sheet for the next stop. Her window, now a black wall of glass, made the world outside distant and alien.

Jim glanced over at her clipboard. "Not bad for the first stop. We already have a higher count than we had on this whole route last month."

"It's the warmer temperatures," Angela said. "Tonight will be our last run for frog surveys this year. Summer is approaching fast."

She looked at her watch. They had to hurry to finish. Jim was getting up early the next morning to help Pearl Zhang, the refuge biologist, with other fieldwork. Angela scheduled a meeting with her Assistant Manager, Gilbert Chavez, to review the property inventory, which could take most of the day.

Gilbert had been away for training over the past week. She and Gilbert would check the list of structures and buildings on the refuge to make notes about any needed repairs. With that information, Angela could prepare a budget to request additional money if needed. She would pay for most of it from her current funds or defer the work. The refuge system was rampant with deferred maintenance projects. There were never enough funds to cover everything.

Jim pulled out a paper tablet from his field bag and sketched a frog holding a fishing pole. He drew it in a small rowboat with its hind feet crossed and propped on the side.

"I like that," Angela said as she finished preparing for the next stop. Jim tore the drawing loose from its pad and placed it under her data sheets on the clipboard.

Angela smiled. She might frame it for her office.

A promising art student at the University of Toledo, Jim had volunteered to assist Pearl with her work when a friend convinced him it might enhance his creativity. He would spend the entire summer with them until school started in the fall. He told Pearl the experience would let him get in touch with warm, fuzzy Mother Nature.

Angela was glad Jim volunteered. He was enjoyable company for such a young guy. Mostly, he did a great job of tracking the time without getting distracted, which allowed her to concentrate on listening.

Ah, if he only knew the reality of biology. It was all about survival. Period. There is nothing warm or fuzzy about wildlife's struggle to live. He'd learn soon enough. In the meantime, Angela enjoyed hearing a different perspective on her world, a view focused only on aesthetics.

"I heard you had a pretty rough day today," Jim said.

Angela blew air out through her lips. "Rough doesn't begin to describe it. I went to a public meeting, and things got pretty heated."

"Pearl said Connie King attacked you—verbally, I mean."

Angela was quiet.

"What did she say?" Jim asked.

"Only that I was a selfish sorehead who didn't want to accept free land." Angela shook her head. "Free land, my foot."

At his questioning glance, she explained. "Some developers are interested in buying a large tract of land near Toledo. The issue is that it's next to a thin strip of property along a creek polluted by historic glassmaking that is also for sale. Connie convinced everyone that she could get the U.S. Fish and Wildlife Service to make the strip part of a national wildlife refuge. She told them that the Service would take over the cleanup of the land, which would increase the value of their investment. There are several things wrong with the promise she made, not the least of which is that Connie King had no authority to make it."

He nodded for her to go on. Angela held up her fingers, ticking each point off as she spoke. "First of all, it's miles away from any other refuge, so it's not connected to any other wildlife habitat. Second, it's next to a little stretch of creek that doesn't have value for wildlife because it's sandwiched between wall-to-wall houses. Lastly, wildlife refuges do not accept land with industrial pollutants because they don't have the funding, staff, or expertise to clean up industrial waste."

She was on a roll now. "Without consulting the Fish and Wildlife Service or me, Connie started a public campaign to make it part of the refuge, knowing that if the public pushed for it, she could probably shove it down my throat, somehow. I know how she works. If she can't make us take the land, she'll give us a black eye with the public. Either way, the refuge will lose. She knows taxpayers shouldn't have to pay to clean up land that industry polluted. She doesn't care. I've been the recipient of her bad deals before. I won't let it happen again."

"So, you yelled at her?" Jim raised his eyebrows, and Angela frowned.

"The woman is trying to dump a piece of worthless land on us." Angela tried to lower her voice. "I told Connie to get the developer to clean it up. They could build a small dog park with a walking trail adjacent to the new homes. Now, *that* is something buyers would want, and it would add value to their homes, which would make up for the cost of cleaning it up. It makes much more sense than making it part of a highly regulated wildlife sanctuary with a long list of restrictions on use. The problem is that people buy into her crap because they don't understand that a wildlife refuge is for wildlife first. People say they love nature until beavers or deer eat their trees or skunks move in under their porches. The biggest issue to me is that the people who polluted that land will profit without lifting a finger to fix what they wrecked. It's just wrong."

Heat rose up Angela's neck as she recalled her argument with Connie. When she looked at Jim, her shoulders slumped. "Geez Louise. I've had enough of that woman."

Angela set her clipboard down hard and started the truck. She'd love to have a look at Connie King's bank account. It was a sure bet someone was lining Connie's pockets.

She slammed the truck in gear. "Anyway, the meeting ended in a loud argument. One I should have avoided. I know better than to rise to her bait." She thumped the steering wheel. "I blew it."

"I like it when you get steamed up."

"Yeah, well, it might be entertaining. My point is, it gets me nowhere."

Conversation ceased, and they wasted no time working through the rest of the stops. When they finished the survey, just after midnight, Angela drove back to the refuge headquarters office while Jim jumped out to unlock and re-lock gates as they passed through them. Taking a back route, Angela swung onto Stange Road, where they saw red and blue flashing lights ahead.

"What the hell?" Angela drove past the back entry gate of the refuge, where they found an Ottawa County Sheriff's SUV and her refuge Law Enforcement Officer, Danny Levin, with his Fish and Wildlife Service truck blocking the roadway. Beyond them, she could see the rear end of a car barely sticking up out of a drainage ditch. The ditch was deep enough that only the tail lights were visible.

"Someone must have driven into the ditch," she said as she stopped.

"Do you think anyone's still in the car?"

She shrugged. Angela didn't want to borrow trouble, but this wasn't the first abandoned car ever found on the refuge. Danny discovered two others within the past few years. Both contained decomposing bodies. The drivers had suffered heart attacks behind the wheel when they crashed into shrubs along State Route 2. On the other hand, remote refuges were favorite dumping spots for stolen and stripped vehicles. Maybe this was the case tonight.

The headlights of the car were still on, creating a soft glow from the water in the ditch.

As they exited the truck, Danny met them carrying a roll of yellow plastic tape. "You guys will have to stay back while I tape off the area." Behind him, Angela could see a deputy from the Sheriff's office dripping wet, wearing only his uniform pants. The deputy sheriff wiped the water from his face and body as he walked to his SUV, reaching down to swipe at his legs.

"What happened?" Angela asked.

"A dead body in the car," Danny said. "Looks like it might be murder."

Two

MURDER. WHOA. "ARE YOU SURE IT'S NOT an accident? Or a suicide?" Angela asked.

Danny shook his head. "Deputy Hill's pretty sure."

She looked past Danny's truck at the red taillights of the car. "Do you know who it is?"

Danny looked at her, then at Jim. "No. Dep. Hill is running the plates. He called a tow truck. When they pull the car out, we'll look for ID."

"How'd you find the car?" Jim asked.

"The deputy found it when he took a shortcut from Jerusalem Township," Danny said. "When he pulled up, the engine was still popping and bubbling in the water. He thought there might be someone in the car, so he jumped in to try a rescue. Too late. The woman was already dead. After I pulled him out, he called for a detective and a forensics team."

Danny lowered his voice as if there were someone else to overhear him. "Dep. Hill says it looks like someone shot the woman driving the car from the passenger seat. At least one of the bullets shattered the driver's side window. You can see glass on the road down there." He pointed past the deputy's vehicle. "That's where he thinks it happened."

Angela grimaced. Jim looked away.

Danny finished, "Ugly, I know. He's leaving her body in the car until the tow truck gets here to avoid disturbing evidence. It'll be easier to assess what happened when the car is out of the water."

Angela sniffed the air. "Do you smell that? Oil and gas are leaking into the marsh. I need to get some baffles in place before it travels too far."

Jim looked at her, and she explained. "We have an oil spill kit with rolls of absorbent materials that float on the surface of the water to capture oil. The rolls prevent oil from spreading throughout the marsh. After they soak up the contaminant, we can dispose of the waste properly." It seemed heartless to think about contaminants at this time, but it was her job. The ensuing habitat destruction would be hell if this spill required a full-blown cleanup, not to mention the paperwork.

Dep. Hill joined them. His Ottawa County Sheriff's Office badge shone bright in Angela's headlights. He'd dried himself off and had dressed. Danny introduced them. "Deputy Hill, this is the Refuge Manager, Angela Martin. Jim Messinger is one of her volunteers. They were out on the refuge tonight doing wildlife surveys."

Dep. Hill nodded at her, reaching out to shake her hand.

"Danny says this just happened," Angela said.

"Yeah, less than half an hour ago, I think." Dep. Hill looked at the ditch, then turned back to Angela. "Which direction did you come from?"

She gestured over her shoulder toward Toledo. "We came in on the back roads from Cedar Point."

"Did you hear anything while you were out there? A gunshot?"

Angela shook her head.

"Driving in, did you see any cars going out? Or anyone walking?"

"No. Didn't see anyone until I turned onto this road and saw your lights. Jim?"

"Nope. I didn't hear anything while we were doing surveys, either. I was snoozing between gates."

"You got here fast," Angela said to Danny.

"I was home when county dispatch called to tell me there was an issue on the refuge. Dep. Hill was still in the water when I drove up. Had a hell of a time pulling him back up that steep slope." Danny wiped at his muddy pants.

"Yeah, it'll be tough pulling the car out." Dep. Hill looked at Angela. "We're waiting for our detective and the coroner to arrive. A tow truck with some divers is on its way." He looked around, taking the roll of tape from Danny. "In the meantime, we can close off the area. I can take some photos."

As if on cue, the car lights went out. The popping and hissing of the hot engine stopped. Headlights from Angela's truck and the deputy's vehicle now lit the black, oily surface of the water, leaving the depths in darkness. Dep. Hill walked to his cruiser to turn the flashing lights off. A couple of pieces of pink tissue and other paper trash floated around the car.

Angela looked at her watch. It was almost one in the morning.

"Danny, I'm going to take Jim back to the office. While I'm there, I'll grab some of our spill gear. Could you help me place it down the ditch when I get back? I think we can do it without disturbing the scene. I need to catch the contaminants from the car as best I can."

"Sure." Danny turned to Jim. "I know this is all kind of strange stuff for you. Please don't talk about this with anyone. We need to notify the next of kin first. Understand?"

"I understand. No problem, man," Jim said.

Backing up the truck, Angela turned into the gate they had passed earlier. They bumped along over the rough, dirt road overhung with tree branches, their lights reflecting back from the eyes of raccoons and other tree-dwelling creatures.

They were almost to the office when Jim spoke, "What do you think happened back there?"

Angela glanced over at him. "I don't know what to think. It's such a dark, lonely road, and it goes nowhere. There used to be a few houses at the end, but we demolished them when we acquired the land. Now, it's just a dark, dead end. A good place to commit murder, I guess."

"Wow." He looked out into the darkness. "Yeah, there could be a lot of stuff happening here at night. No one would ever know about it. Do you think whoever killed that woman is still around?"

Angela glanced out her side window into the darkness. Maybe she should have asked Danny to escort them back to the office. "I hope not. I'm sure the person who did this is long gone," she said, trying to reassure herself as much as him. "Remember what Danny said? We can't talk to anyone about this until Dep. Hill gets the story out."

"Is Danny going to investigate since it happened on the refuge? Why is the Ottawa County Deputy Sheriff here?"

"Murder is a state crime, not federal. We have a written agreement with the County that they take jurisdiction on this type of thing."

"Don't you have to call the FBI? Don't they handle stuff like this on federal land?"

Angela glanced at Jim. How was he supposed to know how things worked on refuges? Most people only know what they see on TV.

"The FBI only gets involved with murder when there is a reason to believe that the crime has violated federal law, like if the murder crosses state lines or something. It sounds confusing, but our federal law enforcement officers enforce wildlife laws. That includes assisting the public, catching poachers, and checking hunting licenses. That sort of thing. We used to call them game wardens."

"Will you tell Danny to help them?"

Angela took a breath. "No, Danny works for the U.S. Fish and Wildlife Service Law Enforcement Division. His primary supervisor is in our regional office in Minnesota. Danny is assigned to this refuge complex and has a desk in my office. He patrols the refuge and assists the state wildlife people and other law enforcement. I supervise his daily activities because I'm the refuge manager. I'm not the final authority to decide how he will assist the County with this investigation. The Regional Chief of Law Enforcement will likely allow him to help them. At least to a limited extent. Danny will make a full report to his Chief by phone and fill out what is called a Serious Incident Report, or SIR, on the computer. After I talk to my supervisor, I have to do the same kind of computer report. The SIRs go to our U.S. Fish and Wildlife Service main headquarters in Washington D.C."

An owl flew across the windshield, and a deer dashed into the brush on the side of the road. Angela gripped the steering wheel. The night was alive with animals. Another deer jumped out in front of them. Angela hit the brakes hard, letting the clutch slip, and the truck stalled.

She took a deep breath. Jim's knuckles showed white as he gripped the dashboard. "I don't know about you, but I'm tired. My nerves are shot, too. Nothing a little sleep won't help, though. Let's get out of here." She restarted the truck. They drove on without difficulty, parking behind the office.

The parking lot light did little to illuminate the shadows around the buildings. The thought that whoever had killed the woman might still be around made Angela shudder.

"Help me load up some oil spill gear. After that, you can go home," she said, glad her voice was steady. "I'll leave a note to let Pearl know you won't be in this morning."

Jim looked relieved. Angela fumbled for her keys. She had trouble inserting them into the lock until she pulled herself up straight and steadied her nerves. Nothing was amiss around the office or its grounds. She was just a little jumpy.

Jim helped with the gear. Once they finished the loading, he lost no time leaving. Was chivalry dead? Ah, youth.

She left the note about Jim and the frog data for Pearl on her desk. She also left a brief message for Kate Barnes, her Administrative Officer, to let her know she'd be late in the morning. After leaving a note for Gilbert to reschedule their meeting, she emailed her boss, giving him as much information about the incident as possible.

Like Danny, Angela's supervisor was also in the Region Three Office in Minnesota. The murder was likely to make the news, and, as the Regional Refuge Supervisor, he'd be pissed if a reporter blindsided him, calling to ask questions.

Carrying a heavy flashlight back to her truck, more for protection than light, she hurried back to the scene to get the spill material into the ditch. An Ottawa County fire engine and pumper truck were there when she arrived, along with a couple more deputies. Two spotlights were positioned over the car in the water, where the fire crew had already set out absorbent rolls to capture the contaminants in the water.

Angela noted the winds had shifted. Small eddies at the surface indicated the water was moving out toward the lake, passing through the wetlands. The crew had set out the spill gear in time, saving Angela a lot of work and worry.

Danny, Dep. Hill and a new guy approached her. "This is Detective Hugh Lane with the Ottawa County Sheriff's Department," Dep. Hill said. "He'll be in charge of this case."

"We're still waiting for the tow truck," Detective Lane said.

"I'd like to check out the spill gear the fire crew put out. Is that okay?"

Dep. Hill led them down the road away from the crime scene, and they crossed over the ditch on an old driveway. Walking back toward the scene on the opposite side of the water, they approached the containment equipment.

Angela was impressed with the fire department's work as she checked the stakes and the position of the absorbent rolls, noting they had full contact with the surface of the water and banks of the ditch. The fire crew had set a second roll twenty feet farther down. The first baffle already captured trash floating from the car through the shattered window. Standing up, she felt better. A minor problem wouldn't become a more significant, long-term disaster. Some oil had leaked out. Thankfully, it wasn't much. She made a mental note to give the fire department special thanks for doing such a great job.

Detective Lane was equally impressed. "The baffles are a pretty handy setup. It'll make collecting any evidence that escapes the car easier when we pull it out."

The tow truck drove up as they walked back. Angela stepped clear as it approached the ditch. Strange to think that just a few yards beyond, a body was still in the driver's seat, buried in the darkness below the surface.

As she watched, brown ripples formed on the dark surface of the water, and it began to churn. Everyone turned to see what was happening.

A gurgling sound erupted next to the car. Bubbles broke the surface, and a prehistoric snout emerged. Clinging to the jaw of the creature was a clump of blond hair.

THREE

THE SNAPPING TURTLE DROPPED BELOW THE surface to dine on its newfound meal. Nature cleaning up what life leaves behind. The blond hair floated on the muddy water for a few seconds before it, too, sank from sight.

Angela called out across the ditch, "You guys better get with it, or there won't be much left of that body. Snappers don't take long to do their job, and there's likely more than one turtle down there."

Another deputy on the scene threw a couple of big rocks into the water. Angela doubted those efforts would help. A red tint rose to the surface, mixing with the brown water. Angela turned away, unable to watch anymore.

She leaned against the front fender of her truck, crossing her arms on her chest. Who was this woman? What had she been doing out here? Danny said she wasn't alone. Who was with her?

Everyone worked under a dome of stark light cast on the scene by the spotlights that shut out the rest of the dark, dead-end road. A deep sadness came over Angela that human life could end like this and become just another matter of procedure. Stomping her feet, she rubbed her hands briskly, trying to shake off the mood.

The divers hooked up the car while Dep. Hill slowly paced the roadway, searching for clues with Det. Lane inside the barrier created by the crime scene tape.

"I've been thinking about the timeline," she said, leaning against the truck again. "It might not be much help, but Jim and I left the refuge through this back gate around nine this evening. There wasn't anyone in the area. I didn't see any other cars or headlights on the road."

"You're sure of the time?" Det. Lane asked as he wrote something in his notebook.

"I'm absolutely sure. We mark the time at every stop. When we finished, I was in a hurry because Jim had to return."

Det. Lane squatted to place a marker on the ground in the middle of the road. He photographed it. Then he took more photos of the car in the ditch and the road itself, placing plastic flagging next to objects Angela couldn't identify before taking more pictures.

An ambulance arrived, followed by a car with Ottawa County license plates. A woman joined Hill, Lane, and Danny. They looked over the scene together as the divers finished hooking up the cables. The tow truck operator stood by, waiting.

Angela pulled out her cell phone to call home. Her boyfriend, LJ, picked up on the fourth ring.

"Hullo?"

"Hi, Babe. Sorry if I woke you. I'm going to be really late tonight."

LJ yawned in her ear. "What's up? What time is it? Is everything okay?"

"It's after two. I'm fine. The sheriff's deputy found a dead body in a car on the refuge."

"My God, Angela." He sounded fully awake now.

"I'm going to stay a little longer to see what's going on."

Dep. Hill gave the signal to pull the car out. Mucky water oozed out of the cracks around the doors as the steel line wrenched the sedan from its watery socket. More water poured out from under the hood, releasing a marshy stench of sulfur into the damp air.

There was no sign now of the snapping turtle, crayfish, or any other creatures that may have been feeding.

"Are you okay?" LJ asked. "Who's in the car? Do you know what happened?"

"I don't know anything yet. I'm okay though."

"I'm glad you called." LJ sounded relieved.

"I thought you might be waiting up."

"Well, actually, I fell asleep in the recliner reading a book." He sounded a little sheepish. "Do you want me to wait up for you?"

"No. I don't know how much longer I'll be. Go back to sleep."

LJ yawned again. "I'll see you when you get here, then."

She hung up just as Dep. Hill approached her.

Angela was looking at the car. It looked familiar. "When will you be able to find out who the woman was?" she asked.

"We have a read on the plate, and we should find her driver's license. The woman who just arrived is the county coroner. She might be able to make a positive ID with that."

The coroner walked around the car, surveying the scene with her head bowed down. Her chin-length brown hair fell across her face. *She's too young for this kind of job.* Angela shook her head. How old did you have to be to deal with dead bodies?

In the glow of the headlights, the deputy's facial features looked chiseled, and there was a hint of gray at his temples. He couldn't be much older than forty. It could be from spending time with Jim, but Angela felt much older than her thirty-six years.

Angela's body sagged, her stomach growled, and a headache started at the base of her skull. She rubbed her neck.

Danny worked with the other deputies to set up another absorbent baffle around the car as they pulled it onto the roadway. When they opened the car door on the driver's side, pink tissue and other trash washed out onto the ground. The coroner walked to the driver's side of the car, taking several photographs of the open door, the interior, and the woman's limp body before the ambulance driver unbuckled her seat belt to pull her out.

Angela saw a bright red jacket. Long, bare legs followed as they placed her on the stretcher.

"Crap." Angela's ears began to ring. She caught her breath as she stood up straight. "Dep. Hill. I think I know who she is." Under the bright spotlights, although she couldn't see the woman's face, she recognized those clothes and the once beautiful blond hair. Now, it was stringy and matted with something black. Angela's knees buckled.

"Sit down." Ducking under the tape, Dep. Hill took her arm, gently guiding her into the passenger seat of her truck. Angela sat sideways in the open doorway, staring at the stretcher as Dep. Hill squatted near her. The ambulance driver pulled a black body bag around the woman, leaving it unzipped, exposing the dead woman's hands and feet.

There was no mistake. Angela could see the red fingernail polish and red high heels. Her feet looked larger now, and her long legs splayed out awkwardly.

"You don't have much dignity once you're dead, do you?" Angela asked no one in particular. *All vanity is gone.* The coroner stopped taking pictures and bent down close to the corpse.

"You said you think you know her?" Dep. Hill prompted.

"Connie King. Her full name was Constance King. Everyone called her Connie." She couldn't pull her gaze from the body. "What is the coroner looking for?"

There was still no response from the deputy. Angela turned her head to look at him. Was he waiting for her to tell him something?

Her mind reeled, and she fought to control her breathing. *Everyone is vulnerable, no matter how tough they act.* She could still hear Connie's voice, and the argument they had earlier in the day ran through her mind.

"If this is her, Connie is a co-director of LECOS, Lake Erie Cooperative Open Spaces. They're a non-profit group working with the city of Toledo to protect natural open spaces throughout the county. They get developers and environmentalists on the same page. I just had a meeting with her this afternoon." She glanced at her watch. "Well, yesterday afternoon." Her voice trailed off.

"I ran the plate," he said. "The car registration lists Constance Elizabeth King as the owner." Angela watched him walk to the car to speak to Det. Lane, who leaned into the vehicle and pulled out a purse. He retrieved the wallet, opened it, and showed it to Dep. Hill, who nodded at Angela.

Angela closed her eyes. She never knew Elizabeth was Connie's middle name.

Connie stood out in any crowd. Her white-blond hair fell in soft sweeps around her face and brushed her shoulders. She was tall, well-proportioned, not too thin. She could have been another Grace Kelly, except for her hardheaded demeanor. Cool, blue eyes appraised you in a snap, often leaving you with the impression they found you wanting. With her perfect skin and finely sculpted features, she was attractive, to say the least, and she had used her looks to her advantage.

The last time Angela saw her, Connie was wearing a red leather jacket over a short pink and yellow shift that rode six inches above her knees. Red high heels, a salon tan, and red polish on long nails completed the look. Connie dressed to be in the spotlight because she always was.

Now, all her glamour was gone. She was just an awkward, gaudily dressed corpse in a black plastic wrapper.

Angela had always felt inadequate around Connie. Angela's dark hair and olive complexion were a far cry from the image Connie projected. She looked down at her not-so-glamorous khaki and brown uniform. Angela had banked on professionalism and credibility as a biologist and manager to garner support. Well, she'd blown that all to hell at their last meeting.

The ambulance driver zipped the bag closed. The sound grated on Angela's nerves. Without ceremony, he then secured Connie to the stretcher and placed her into the wagon. While his movements were respectful, he would have treated a fragile, living person differently. Angela wasn't sure how.

Angela's head spun, and she leaned sideways, resting it on the back of the seat. Ending life as food for a turtle was not such a bad way to go. She could at least bring sustenance to another creature and avoid the inevitable intrusive after-death inspections Connie's body would now undergo.

Dep. Hill came back to check on Angela. "I'm sorry. It makes it very different when you know the victim. Are you okay?"

"I was asking myself why Connie would be driving on this road at this time of night. What was she doing way out here?" She looked at him. "Up until this moment, I believed this might be someone who committed suicide. I can tell you now Connie would never have done that. No way in hell. Are you sure there isn't any way it could have been an accident?"

He shook his head. "No. Not an accident. It was murder."

Angela felt her chest tighten. She had called Connie a bitch. She hadn't liked or trusted the woman, but she would never have wished her dead. "No. It can't be murder. Not on this refuge. Our refuge. My staff, my volunteers. Friends. We're out here every day."

No response from Dep. Hill. She looked into his eyes and could see understanding. She said, pleading, "It was Connie. One of us." She paused. "Sort of." As much as she disliked the woman, she was sorry her last words to her had been so harsh and so public.

"I'm going to send you home in a few minutes," Dep. Hill said. "I don't think Det. Lane will need to ask you anything tonight. When I release you, I don't want you to talk to anyone about this. Don't tell anyone the name of the victim. Not yet. Other than working with Danny, no talking to your staff, volunteers, or friends." Their eyes met. "Not even the kid you had here. Do you understand?"

She nodded. Dep. Hill waited for her to speak.

"Yes, I understand."

He walked over to Danny. After a brief conversation, Danny came over and squatted next to Angela. He offered her his thermos of coffee, which she gladly accepted. Angela wasn't a fan of sweetened coffee. She gulped it down anyway. After a while, he spoke. "Detective Lane is going to handle this case with the deputy. They have a lot of experience with serious crime and know what they're doing. Don't worry."

Danny handed her the detective's card. She looked at it before giving it back to him.

Murder. Not suicide. Not an accident. "It's Connie King, Danny."

He nodded. "I met Connie once." He paused. "As you know, it's their jurisdiction. My Chief will probably want me to help them all I can." As she had explained to Jim, murder was a state crime, not federal. The County Sheriff's office would handle it. Danny could assist but was not a homicide detective.

Angela could tell Danny was a little excited to be involved with this case. He hadn't known Connie as well as she had.

He searched Angela's face. "You look tired. We don't have any questions for you now, so you should go home. Can you drive yourself, or do you need me to take you?"

She sighed. "Thanks. I'm okay now, and the coffee helped. I'm just tired." She stood up. "Could you make sure I get everyone's contact information? I might have questions." It was up to the Regional Office to decide if and how Danny would become involved. Angela wanted to make sure he kept her in the loop. She didn't look forward to calling her supervisor in the morning. Tonight, before she went home, she'd leave him another email to prepare him for the call.

The murdered woman was no longer a stranger. Connie had a connection to the refuge, which meant Angela would have a long conversation with her Refuge Supervisor in the morning. Her boss would want to make sure Angela handled the press correctly.

At this moment, Angela's mind reeled with the implications of Connie's murder on the refuge and the safety of everyone on it. Who killed her? Why here?

Four

A NGELA PULLED INTO THE DRIVEWAY AT HOME just as the sun peeked above the lower edge of the eastern sky, changing the hues from soft gray to salmon pink. Her home was a rented two-story Victorian in Oak Harbor, Ohio, a few miles from the refuge. The owners did a good job maintaining the old house built in 1905.

Stepping through the back door, the smells of cinnamon and fresh-brewed coffee enveloped her. She closed her eyes for a moment, breathing it in. LJ was up, ready for work, finishing a cup of coffee at the sink.

Lawrence James Koenig hated any iteration of his name, so instead, he used his initials. He was a computer programmer. Clean-shaven and dressed in a crisp button-up, long-sleeved shirt he must have just ironed, he had the sweet scent of clean linen on him. His tie matched his gray slacks. He was neat as a pin, as always.

Angela looked down at herself. Quite a contrast. He sniffed the air as he looked over her disheveled appearance. She'd brought the marsh home.

LJ motioned toward the counter. "Cinnamon-pecan waffles and a few slices of crisp bacon. You need a little special treatment after your ordeal last night." He poured her a cup of coffee while she put down her backpack. "Are you okay?"

LJ worked for a software company that developed programs for almost anything, including home design and video games. He did most of the work from home using a high-speed internet connection. He often met with clients to discuss or review a product in person. LJ loved to cook, and his food was always delicious, which was fine because cooking was not one of Angela's talents.

She plopped down at the kitchen table, exhausted. A shower would have to wait. "No. Eating might help. I knew the victim," she blurted out, trying to shake the bad feeling of the scene she had just left.

"Someone close to you?"

"I don't know if I'd say that. Her name was Connie King. She wasn't a friend, but I worked with her often." *We didn't get along,* she almost said. Instead, she swallowed the words and dug the edge of her fork into her warm waffle. The first bite, smothered with butter and maple syrup, evoked gentle memories and satisfying comfort.

"These take me back to our first road trip together on your bike," she said, changing the subject. "Do you remember the little waffle place we found in Cleveland?"

"I remember it well."

She stuffed another large piece into her mouth. "Delicious. Just what I needed." For a few minutes, she ate in silence, stopping to sip black coffee between bites. LJ stood away from her. He leaned in to kiss her forehead to avoid the mud on her cheek and syrup on her upper lip.

Angela had come to Ohio over three years ago to take the job as a refuge manager. She met LJ at a computer store while picking out a new laptop. One thing led to another, and they moved in together. Angela found herself on the back of his motorcycle, riding back and forth across the state every chance they got. On or off the bike, spending time together was something they hadn't done in a while. Lately, things had begun to change for them. Between her job and LJ's new contracts, there wasn't much free time for them to be together now.

LJ prodded her. "Fill me in." He glanced at his watch. "Make it quick. I have to leave."

She laid down her fork. As good as it all tasted and as hungry as she felt, she couldn't eat more. "We found a body on the refuge. It's a woman I argued with yesterday afternoon. I didn't wish her dead." With exhaustion, her speech was becoming disjointed.

She fell silent again, dazed. LJ didn't know anything about who she worked with or the partnerships she forged. She rarely talked about work once she was home.

After a few moments of her silence, LJ put down his cup and put his hand on her shoulder. "You've been through a rough night. We can talk later."

Angela felt relieved. She didn't want to go back over it. After eating, exhaustion overwhelmed her.

He picked up his cup and walked to the sink. "I'm flying into Chicago to meet a client over lunch."

"Will you be back tonight?"

"Maybe. If I can." He rinsed his cup and turned to smile at her again. "Lunch can sometimes run long. When I get home, I'll give you a neck rub. While I do that, you can tell me more about this crazy night of yours."

Angela tried to sound interested. "Which client is this, the Mirilla group again?"

"Yeah."

"Wow, this must be a tough one. This is your fifth meeting with the company in two months. Lots of money involved?" In the past six months, his job had pulled him away from home more often and for longer periods.

"They're just a bit hard to please. I'm meeting with them in person because we can deliver what they want. I have to show them." He kissed her on top of her head before he grabbed his briefcase—rich, black leather, with his name, *LJ Koenig*, engraved on a silver plate—and ducked out the door.

She pulled her cell phone out of her purse and dialed her supervisor's number. He answered on the first ring, and having read her email, Angela was able to brief him quickly. She assured him she'd keep him informed. Satisfied with her responses to his questions, he hung up. At that point, all the energy drained from Angela's body.

ANGELA TOOK A HOT SHOWER BEFORE SHE HIT the sack. She was jolted awake three hours later by two cats chasing each other across the bed. She crawled out of the covers and went downstairs to the kitchen to feed them.

Pete and Poe were two cats her friend and refuge volunteer Jack Dumas had rescued a year earlier. While fishing, he'd found them in a bag on the side of a creek. Someone had tried to drown them, but the bag washed up on the bank, leaving two starving kittens in it, barely alive. Jack took them home and nursed them back to health. However, his old dog, Bowzer, didn't like their company. It made Jack feel disloyal to his old hound friend to keep them around.

He offered them to Angela, who fell head over heels in love with them. Pete was a brown tabby with eyes that could look through your soul. Poe, a black and white tuxedo cat, was a fat little bundle of fluff who couldn't sit still. Between the two of them, they brought joy to Angela's life. For that, she was grateful. Jack rescued the kittens, but he saved Angela, too.

The cats were a responsibility she enjoyed. The three of them needed each other without demanding too much. She watched them for a few minutes as her mind returned to the night before. She still felt anxious, but the shock was gone. Once Danny briefed her, she'd feel better. As a federal law enforcement officer, he would be privy to everything the County Sheriff's office planned to do.

Looking in the mirror as she dressed, she saw a face puffy and drained from a lack of sleep. No cosmetic in the world would set her face to right this morning. She gulped a half-warmed cup of coffee from the microwave and ran out the door, making it to the refuge office just before noon.

A middle-aged woman greeted Angela as she came in. Kate Barnes was Angela's office assistant. A solidly built woman with gray permed hair, she was used to taking charge of most things in what she considered *her* office. Everyone else was only a visitor. She wore her readers low on her nose, so she always looked like she was giving you the stink eye.

Ottawa National Wildlife Refuge was one of three refuges in the Ottawa National Wildlife Refuge Complex. The Complex also included Cedar Point and West Sister Island National Wildlife Refuges. Altogether, over 10,000 acres were protected under this complex. It had ten employees, including Angela. Her job was to manage all the refuges, which included supervising five employees directly, overseeing the restoration of habitat and inventory of wildlife, maintaining infrastructure, and engaging with the public and partners to maintain a relationship with the northwest Ohio environmental communities.

Ottawa Refuge had several non-contiguous units, such as the Darby and Navarre Units. Cedar Point Refuge was a few miles northwest of Ottawa and encompassed 2,500 acres that protected rare plants and nesting black terns. West Sister Island Refuge was nine miles north of Ottawa in Lake Erie. It protected a large nesting colony of wading birds.

"Good afternoon, Kate. Is Pearl in the office, or is she in the field counting something? I need to chat with her right away."

"She's in her office. Gilbert got your note. He said he'd talk to you later." Kate peered at Angela. "How are you? It sounds like you had some excitement last night."

"Excitement isn't quite the word for it." Angela stopped to grab some mail from Kate's desk. "After I hear from Danny, I'll fill you in."

"He left a note for you. He's at a meeting at Ottawa County Sheriff's office." Kate handed her a yellow slip of paper. "While you're talking to Pearl, why don't you tell her to get her timesheet done so I can validate it? If she wants to get paid, that is." She looked up at Angela over her glasses again. "She seems to think I'm her secretary."

Angela poked her head into Pearl Zhang's office. Pearl was tall and thin, with warm brown eyes that sparkled when she smiled. She'd graduated from the University of California at Berkeley only three years ago. The position as a wildlife biologist at Ottawa was her first job with the U.S. Fish and Wildlife Service. "When you get a minute, stop to see me," Angela said.

Pearl came in while Angela booted up the computer and entered her password. She wore the customary uniform cargo pants, hiking boots, and a khaki shirt with the Fish and Wildlife Service shield on its shoulder. Her chin-length haircut accentuated her large brown eyes and cheekbones.

Usually, Pearl was in a cheerful mood, always smiling. Today, her face expressed concern for Angela. "Are you okay? What happened last night?"

Angela waited to answer Pearl as she read the yellow slip of paper on her desk. Danny's note lacked detail, leaving Angela with questions. He was probably worried someone might see the message before Angela did. She doubted he got much sleep last night, if any. She stood up to get coffee, and Pearl followed her to the kitchen.

Angela filled her in, remembering Dep. Hill's warning about sharing too much information.

"It sure was a heck of a way for you to end the day," Pearl said. "That meeting started it out badly enough. Do you know who the woman was?"

Connie had ended her day far worse. "I can't discuss it. The Sheriff's Office will release the news when they can."

Pearl didn't press further. "Is Jim okay? He must have gotten a shock."

"He was okay last night, but don't expect him to come in until tomorrow." Angela poured her coffee, adding a dollop of cream.

"Time. That reminds me, before you go anywhere, get your timesheet done and tell Kate when it's ready."

"Yeah, okay. I know I always forget. Did Kate complain about me again? She thinks I forget on purpose. Such a grouch."

"Walk in her shoes," Angela said as she returned to her office. "Oh, I won't have time to meet with you today about your muskrat trapping program plan."

"That's okay. How about tomorrow morning?"

"Sure. Give me some time in the morning to get in and settled. You'll have my full attention."

Pearl left, and Angela sat down at her desk to call Danny. There was a light knock on the door. Lilly Weathers popped her head into her office. Whenever possible, Angela made it a point to stop whatever she was doing to make time to talk with her volunteers and share some of their lives. Like family, they did a lot of work together. They gave the refuge their time, which was usually easy for Angela to give back.

However, that would not be the case today. Angela glanced back at Danny's message. Still, she couldn't blow Lilly off. Lilly, Jack Dumas, and Ed Spakley had become much more than volunteers—they were her dear friends.

Lilly was a retired legal researcher for the Air Force, well-educated, and recently widowed. Her husband, Harry, had passed away almost a year ago. That's when Lilly stopped many of her social and volunteer activities to take time to heal. Angela knew it was tough for her to adjust to life without him. Angela had visited Lilly at her home several times during the past year. She had missed seeing her friend at the refuge and worried about her. Seeing her return with a smile today as she walked in lifted Angela's spirits and her hopes for Lilly's healing.

"Come on in." Angela stood up to hug Lilly. "Welcome back, my friend. I'm so glad to see you."

Lilly was bubbling with energy. She readjusted the barrette, holding her long blond-gray hair out of her eyes. "I just wanted to say hi and thank you for all the support you and your staff have given me this past year."

Angela started to respond, but Lilly waved her hand. "Oh, no, don't be modest. You all kept tabs on me to make sure I was doing okay. You have the most wonderful people here. I shouldn't have waited so long to come back because I feel alive for the first time in months."

"I'm glad you're back, Lilly. I've missed you." Angela said, glancing at the note on her desk.

Lilly continued. "I can see you're busy. Can we catch up later today?"

Angela smiled. "Thanks, Lilly. I'm slim on time today. How about getting together this weekend?"

"Absolutely. Give me a call." Lilly hugged her before she left.

After Lilly had gone, Angela closed her door and punched in Danny's number.

FIVE

DANNY'S PHONE RANG AND WENT TO VOICEMAIL. *Damn.* She left a message and forced her focus back to the computer screen before her. She answered a few urgent emails, including one from a local newspaper, before she called her supervisor in the Regional Office to assure him that she was handling the death on the refuge appropriately. They spoke for nearly an hour before she hung up. She had given the newspaper minimal information—a woman was found dead in her car on Stange Road. The Ottawa County Sheriff's office was investigating.

Once the sheriff's office released information, she knew she'd have a flood of calls from reporters. She would deal with that when it happened. She had already prepared a written response while on the phone with her boss.

She crafted a letter of thanks to the fire department for their work with the spill containment and glanced at her watch, wondering if it was too soon to try Danny again. She tried anyway.

This time, he answered on the first ring.

"It's Angela. Am I interrupting anything?"

"No. Not at all," Danny said, sounding distracted. "I just left the sheriff's office, and I'm in my truck jotting down some notes. I just sent you an email with everyone's contact information."

"Good. Did you get any sleep last night?"

"A couple of hours. Don't worry. I'm fine."

"Has it been confirmed that the dead woman was Connie King?" Angela asked. "It seems too strange. Was I mistaken?"

"No mistake. It was Connie King. Just a minute."

Angela heard paper shuffling.

"I can't tell you much more about it," Danny said. "Not more than you already know, of course. Someone shot Connie in the face and chest multiple times. No water in the lungs, so she was dead before the car went into the ditch. Her face and chest were a mess, but they positively identified her. You understand this is a murder investigation, and everything we discuss will have to be in confidence?"

"Of course."

Danny continued, "Det. Lane spoke to the Sheriff, and they agreed that you could help us. He wants information about Connie, specifically a list of all the committee boards she sat on. I know she was with Save the Open Spaces—I think you call it SOS. I'm not familiar with the others."

"Sure, I can give him a list. I have another meeting this afternoon with LECOS, the Lake Erie Cooperative Open Space folks." She wondered if she should mention yesterday's blowup with Connie and decided against it. It wasn't as if she had anything to do with Connie's death. Could the argument incriminate her?

"I attended their public meeting yesterday," she continued. "I'll be at a closed meeting with partners and developers today. Connie organized this one." Her voice trailed off as the tragedy hit home again.

"Anything else?" Danny asked.

"Connie was on the board of SOS, LECOS, and a few others. Some groups don't exist anymore. I'll try to remember them. I'll get the entire list to you all at once, no later than tomorrow."

"Tomorrow will work. Give us a list of every board Connie served on the past two years. While you're at this meeting today, take note of anything unusual. Let me know if someone should have been there but isn't or if someone you haven't seen for a while shows up. Or anything strange. Someone will benefit from Connie's death. We need to know who."

"I can do that." As Danny's words hit her, she realized the refuge would benefit. Angela wouldn't have to worry about the land deal Connie had proposed. It was highly unlikely anyone else on the LECOS board would push it forward without her. The tight knot in Angela's stomach loosened from relief. Along with the relief, she felt a little guilty.

Breaking into Angela's train of thought, Danny continued, "Deputy Hill will notify Connie's next of kin today. After that, he'll put out a press release. I advise you to stop any nighttime surveys or activities for a while. There probably isn't anything to worry about, but you never know."

"Not a problem. I don't think there's anything scheduled anyway. I'll notify the staff. Thanks." She picked up a ballpoint pen from her desk, clicking it a few times. "I'll keep an eye open at the meeting. I should be out by four-thirty or five. I'm going to stop for a bite in Oregon City before I go home. It's on your way back from Toledo. Why don't you meet me at Gino's Deli? I can fill you in on anything I learn. I'm buying."

He chuckled. "I'm always in for free food."

Angela smiled. "See you there. Good luck, Danny. Connie's death hits close to home, you know. Keep me informed, at least as much as you can."

"Will do." He hung up before she could say goodbye.

The sky was cloudy, and a stiff, cold breeze ruffled her hair as she stepped out the back door. The northeast wind skimmed across Lake Erie, bringing a fresh, watery scent. The small, wide creeks, or portages as the locals called them, that drained into Lake Erie were filled to the brim as the wind pushed the lake back up into them. When the deputy found Connie's car last night, a light breeze blew off shore, allowing water to drain into the lake. Today, the wind had reversed with force, and the water was much deeper in the portages and ditches. If the conditions had been the same last night, Dep. Hill might not have seen the vehicle at all. Did the killer realize how quickly someone would find the body?

Angela dropped her backpack into the truck and made a detour to the newly constructed greenhouse behind the maintenance shop.

Just outside the greenhouse, she met Lilly and Ed Spakley, another volunteer, coming out.

"Enter at your own risk," Ed said, "Jack's in one of his grumpy moods—the rat bastard. I'm leaving. Have an appointment. I'll see you later." He gave Angela a peck on the cheek and dashed toward the parking lot.

Lilly shrugged. "I'll give you a call later. I'm heading home, too. Jack is a bit tiresome today."

Ed and Jack had practically grown up together. They went to the same schools, played on the same teams, and were almost like brothers. Just like brothers, they didn't always get along. It didn't mean they weren't loyal to each other. Lilly rarely tolerated their nonsense, preferring to leave them to work it out. Angela ignored the warning and slid the greenhouse door open. Warm, humid air hit her full force.

She had a little time to visit Jack, her friend, kitten rescuer, and kayaking buddy. He was a good-looking widower, a retired truck driver in his mid-60s, with stamina and a lean, hard back to go with it. He liked to work and didn't spend much time sitting around.

They hit it off from the first day they met when he made a grumpy, politically incorrect statement about too many women being in charge of things. Angela fired back about how he wouldn't have made it without his mother. And, by the way, didn't he still live with her? He laughed and gave her a high five, sealing their friendship.

Jack was gruff, but his rough exterior hid a kind and compassionate heart. Angela could always count on him. It was more than just his love for nature or animals in general. He did more than most people, and he always delivered, including doing the lion's share of work to build the greenhouse.

Jack put down a bag of acorns, spilling them onto the floor. "What're you doing today? Other than bothering me." He softened his words with a grin.

Angela picked up an acorn. "Are these the trees—no, I mean the forest—you promised me? It looks like I'm going to have to wait a while, huh?"

Jack pulled up the sides of the bag and reached for a dustpan to scoop up the mess he'd made. "These will be my legacy, not yours, young lady. Yours is out back in the grow-out shelter." He stopped to look at her. "I might be dead by the time this all grows into decent habitat. The sweet part is, I'll die knowing I did it."

She smiled, and they said, almost in unison, "If it's gonna be, it starts with me."

"You know it," Jack said. "Now, I'm busy, little Sis. What's up? Looks like you have something on your mind."

Angela was quiet for a moment and leaned against the bench. "No, nothing on my mind. I was glad to see Lilly back with us. It's a sign she's starting to recover from losing Harry. I just wanted to check to see what you were doing. You weren't around last week. I thought you might have decided to take one of your unannounced trips."

Jack frequently took off to kayak rivers in the western U.S. with a geologist friend. He was an enthusiastic kayaker and canoeist who loved to share his knowledge and love of the sport with Angela. She welcomed the friendship of this older man who took her under his wing. They kayaked the portages together at least once each month.

"Not yet. I have too much to do right now. I did some fishing at the creek last week. Luckily, I didn't find any more cats." He smiled, focusing his gaze on her. "You sure nothing is going on?"

He was looking through her. She looked around to avoid it. "No. Nothing. Fill me in on where you are."

He stared at her a moment longer before speaking. Angela picked up an empty pot.

Jack shrugged. "Well, a couple of the folks who pitched in to build the greenhouse have volunteered to help run it. That's a relief. I was worried I'd have to do everything."

She ignored his journey into martyrdom as he turned to clean up the spilled acorns.

He continued, "We'll have about five hundred oak seedlings potted and growing in the greenhouse by fall. That should be enough to start a small woodland, don't you think? Next week, we expect to plant those bigger oaks by the entry road this fall."

He lifted a bag of potting soil onto the bench. "Those bad boys are big enough to survive becoming deer candy, I hope, anyway. About twenty feet tall or so, now. They should have no problem surviving if we put them in right."

He walked to the end of a bench and picked up a rack of cone-shaped plant containers. "Son of a bitch. I told Ed to have them schoolkids wash these containers." He looked over at several buckets full of seeds on the table. "And don't ask me what the hell those are."

He looked over at Angela. "I was gonna spend the day planting acorns. Now it looks like I'm doing dishes instead. Damn. People aren't supposed to leave unlabeled seeds anywhere. Everything is supposed to go into drying pans, be tagged and dated when they bring it in."

Angela looked in the buckets. "Pearl probably knows what they are."

He threw his gloves on the bench. "Pearl would've labeled them, wouldn't she? No, Ed screwed this up. Sometimes, I wonder what the idiot has for brains."

"Stop picking on Ed. He's your best friend." She shook her head and headed toward the door. "Your friends warned me you were in a foul mood. What's up with you?"

"Hold on a minute, little Sis." He grinned at her. "I know, I know. I'm sorry. I'll lighten up. Hey, do you want to go kayaking this weekend?"

"Absolutely." She smiled, glad to see his mood change.

"Sometimes feels like all we ever do is work, work, work." Jack put on rubber gloves, dumped the cones into a bleach and water solution in the sink, and started to brush them clean.

"Yeah. Work." Angela agreed as her mind wandered. Three years and this refuge had become her whole world. She spent a lot of time here, long hours at her desk or late-night meetings. Now, one of the people she worked with, or against, was dead.

How had Connie lived? Did she ever have fun, or did her after-hour activities always involve work? She didn't know much about the woman except that she was a force to be reckoned with.

Jack was smiling now, making short work of cleaning the cones. Angela chuckled.

"Hey, what's so funny?" Jack pulled off his gloves and hung them on the edge of the sink. "The rest of these cones can soak a bit. Now, pay attention. I can tell you need cheering up, so let me show you your forest back here."

He took her arm and pulled it through his to lead her back to the door. "Did I ever tell you the one about the Widow of the Marsh and the Trapper?"

She laughed. "No, Jack. I don't want to hear one of your dirty jokes."

"I would never tell you a dirty joke," he said with a wink.

Angela rolled her eyes. He always offered up a joke. She always turned it down. It was a game Jack enjoyed. He took Angela into the grow-out shelter. "Here it is, as promised. The hardwood forest of the future."

She smiled at his optimism.

"What? No shouts of joy? No waxing poetic?" Jack's eyes sparkled as he teased Angela. "Ungrateful. That's what you are. Look how healthy these buggers are. They're beautiful!" He looked at her and shook his head. "You say you're okay, but you look like you have something on your mind."

She shook her head. He pressed on anyway. "Have you heard from one of your parents? Are they coming out to visit you?"

Angela touched a leaf on one of the oak trees, pretending to examine it. "No. My Dad's in Canada and may stay up there until winter. He says he'll head back to southern California when the snow flies. Mom is in Europe with girlfriends." At Jack's sympathetic wince, she changed the subject. "The trees look great. You're right. They'll be awesome if they can survive transplanting and the deer."

"When's the last time you visited either of them? Maybe give them another chance. People change."

Jack didn't know everything about Angela's family life or childhood, but he'd met her dad once and quickly understood the picture. Angela gave him a brief story of her life over a few beers after that.

She was an only child, which should have resulted in two doting parents with one very spoiled kid. That wasn't the way it played out. According to some of their friends, her parents met in college and had an all-consuming, passionate, fairy-tale love affair that turned to bitter hatred after marriage. Angela didn't know the reason for the change. She couldn't remember a time when they were happy. She suspected things had changed with the addition of a baby to the family and the reality of daily life. Years of unabashed fighting made her appreciate the times she found herself at home alone.

Their divorce, when it happened, came as a relief. Angela spent her last few years in high school living between two homes, listening to the venting that overcame them from time to time. She tried to intervene and quickly learned to stay out of the way, careful not to place herself in the middle. No one had written a part for her in their drama.

She shook off the memories and smiled at Jack. They'd shared so much time together that Jack had become family to her.

"I'm fine. My parents are fine," she said. "I'm just a bit tired. I was out doing surveys late last night. Show me the rest of what you've been up to out here."

Jack put his hand gently on her shoulder. His eyes sought hers, and for a moment, he held her gaze. "I worry about you. I know something's on your mind. Is everything okay with LJ?"

"He's in Chicago now on a business trip. He has some big deal he's working out with a new company." She gave him a bright smile. "We're doing okay. Now, hurry. I have a meeting to get to."

Jack took the hint and backed off. Angela stayed a little longer, listening to his ideas, watching his face. The more he shared, the more animated and passionate he became. For those few moments, Angela was right there with him.

Six

RAIN BEGAN TO FALL AS ANGELA LEFT THE REFUGE. It'd be slow going with wet road conditions. Puddles were everywhere. As Angela drove through them, water splashed her windows and the side of the truck.

Unlike the parched Southwestern desert where she grew up, this landscape south of Toledo was continually bathed in water that saturated the ground, making it unusable. Farmers invented an ingenious yet simple system of dealing with this—clay tile or perforated plastic tubing that they placed a few feet below the roots of their crops. The tubing channeled water off the land before puddles could form, filling deep ditches along every road and highway. Still, nature won out when silt clogged the tubes, and puddles formed again anyway. Farmers replacing tiles was a common scenario on the landscape.

Water, the key element of life on this planet, so rare in other parts of the world, routinely washed the southwestern shoreline of Lake Erie. It was a far cry from running through dust devils and playing dodge-the-tumbleweed when she was a kid.

The weather service predicted the thunderstorms would continue through tomorrow. Pearl would have to cancel her morning surveys for birds. She wouldn't be happy, but that was how it went during the spring and summer when the weather was the least predictable. A three-day survey could sometimes take two weeks to complete. Angela was happy to have finished the frog surveys on time.

She made it to the meeting just before it began and was lucky to find a seat at the back of the room. The main agenda item was the creation of a land mitigation bank for development occurring on the edge of Toledo. It looked like standing room only. This meeting could impact the wallet of a developer or two.

An unfortunate fact of life was that everyone wanted a house with a river view or trees, so builders destroyed acres of healthy natural wildlife habitat to accommodate only one or two homes. To offset the loss of habitat in one area, developers paid money into mitigation banks. A mitigation bank was a fund developers would use to purchase or restore habitats in or around their housing developments. Sometimes, they restored land in a different watershed or county altogether.

Too bad the wildlife occupying those destroyed areas didn't have moving vans. Angela was heartsick seeing healthy, vibrant habitats filled with wildlife replaced with grass lawns and non-native shrubs that provided nothing for nature—not to mention the chemicals needed to maintain the new vegetation that polluted the waterways.

Angela wasn't the only one those decisions angered. Others wanted to keep mitigation within the same neighborhoods where the damage occurred to balance things out or, better yet, prevent it altogether.

Initially, because healthy wetlands and swamps were cheap, they often became mitigation banks themselves. Multiple developers either purchased the land or did restoration in them, driving the cost of swampland to sky-high levels.

Angela attended these meetings to monitor discussions about lands in sensitive areas, particularly those close to the refuge. Housing developments could someday surround the refuge, introducing pollutants as well as cats, dogs, mice, and other pests into the marshes, harming wildlife.

It saddened Angela to call animal control to pick up a dog or cat running loose on the refuge. Considering the alternatives the animal would endure, she knew it was the best thing she could do. Not only did pets kill and harass wildlife, but they were also often targets for predators themselves. Being caught by a raptor or other four-legged hunter wasn't a nice way for a pet to die. However, predators were the least of the worries for animals dumped on the refuge. Unwanted, afraid, and alone, animals more often died slowly from starvation, parasites, or disease.

Susan Worth stepped to the front of the room. She wore a well-tailored beige suit, a pale-yellow blouse, a slim-fitting knee-length skirt, and pumps of the stylish Jimmy Choo variety. For the first time, Angela realized she was a beautiful woman. When Connie had been present, Susan was barely noticeable in her shadow.

The meeting started a little late. Susan introduced herself. "Please take a seat so we can get started quickly. The day is growing short." She smiled and looked at her watch, then back at the door. She was probably looking for Connie.

Susan faced the audience, taking a deep breath. "We are here today to determine which areas along the shoreline of Lake Erie are suitable for development and which are possible mitigation sites. Please look at the color-coded maps on the walls indicating available lands. These are the same as the electronic versions sent to you last week for review."

She scanned the room, making eye contact with Angela for a moment before she looked away. After a quick breath, she went on. "I want everyone to openly discuss expectations. I also want to know how you believe you need to be involved. Open and considerate communication will speed the process considerably. We'll start by discussing the areas for mitigation first. The shoreline areas noted in shades of green are the most ecologically intact."

The maps on the wall indicated by Susan displayed heavily

congested areas along the Maumee River that ran through Toledo. The Ottawa River was on another map, also flowing through urban development. A third map displayed areas southwest of Toledo where there was wall-to-wall farmland. That was Angela's area of concern as it was west of the refuge.

The small areas depicted along the Ottawa and Maumee Rivers were tiny. Even the places highlighted in the farmlands weren't large. There wasn't much land available for development, much less conservation.

Several people burst out, speaking all at once. One developer shouted, "I've already done a hell of a lot of restoration on the Ottawa River. Is that going to count toward this bank? I don't see any part of my work on the Ottawa River on this map."

A woman across the room chimed in. "How much credit do we get, and for what? Does it matter what kind of restoration we do?"

At the back of the room, a man asked, "Who gets to decide what will be mitigation and what isn't? Who decided what to put on your maps?"

Susan put up her hands. "Please, one person at a time. If we discuss each item on the agenda in order, I can answer all your questions." Despite her efforts, the meeting barreled out of control as several more developers called out concerns.

She forged onward. "Let's start with the map along the Ottawa River. We can discuss the areas where we have identified the most severe habitat destruction."

More shouts carried over her voice. No one bothered to look at the schedule or cared about the map. Without Connie leading the discussions, Susan was overwhelmed.

Angela made notes, as she'd promised Danny. Several environmentalists were in the room. They loudly gave the developers a piece of their minds. A developer she hadn't seen for a long time, Ray Silverman, dressed in jeans and a raincoat, his hair wet from the rain, entered the room. He made his way quietly to the back of the room, where he found a seat. Angela also noted two developers who worked closely with Connie over the years. In his standard polyester suit with white patent leather shoes, Dwayne Palmer sat beside the obnoxious Robert Durham. Durham wore tailor-made suits. His hair was slicked-back. They both sat with Connie's brother, Donald King. Angela tolerated Dwayne, a goof who thought he was a gift to all women. Robert Durham was a different matter. He was blatantly crude, often placing his hand on a woman's knee or shoulder inappropriately. Ugh.

Donald King was different. He was just an average-looking guy who always wore jeans. Unlike the two men beside him, he was quiet. It was unusual to see Donald at these meetings, much less sitting with those two. She made a note of it.

One flannel-clad man yelled, "You guys think you can just come into our communities and destroy everything that makes it healthy—all for the almighty dollar. Well, we're not going to let you get away with it. There are rules you have to follow."

"Get away with what, old man?" another man yelled. "And what rules are you talking about? People need homes. Where are we supposed to build them? Why don't you answer that?"

Susan interjected, "That's why we're here today. We can work with city planners to simplify permitting if we cooperate to decide what we need to do. We'll decide where to build and where to protect the landscape." Several people shouted her down. It was difficult to understand what anyone was saying.

"Thoughtfully, my ass. Some of these guys have serious money, and that's what gets you a place on somebody's map!" This outburst from another man created a loud commotion.

Good luck with this meeting, Susan. It was apparent Connie had been the one who controlled these people. She would have shut the hecklers down, led the conversations, and guided them in the direction she wanted them to go. Connie was a con artist, but she was also a mediator—and one tough cookie. For the first time, Angela recognized the extent of Connie's skills.

Angela noted that one person wasn't present, who usually was.

Councilwoman Theresa Bradley, with her stern manner, was conspicuously absent.

A developer Angela didn't know by name sat down next to her. He was fairly new to the area. "Where's Connie? She was supposed to be here today. I had a contract to review with her."

Angela shrugged. "Not sure." He was a friend of Connie's, so she decided to chat him up. "We need her, though. I think this meeting is a bit off track without her."

"No kidding. This whole thing is a waste of time. We won't get anything out of this mess." He looked around. "If she comes in, tell her to call me. I'm outta here."

He handed Angela his card. A few others followed him out.

No developer would have left the meeting early if Connie had been here. Instead, they'd try to get to the head of the line to be the first to strike a deal with her. How many of those had been dirty deals? Angela wanted to think better of Connie, but the woman had been an empty mineshaft. No, not empty, more like a toxic, confined space. The canary never had a chance.

She tucked the man's card into her shirt pocket. She wondered who, aside from the refuge, had the most to gain from Connie's death or, more likely, the least to lose.

But why murder? Any losses could be a tax write-off, at the very least. Most developers always had bigger fish to fry. A lot of familiar faces filled the room, and there were new people in the group today, too. The noise level gradually decreased. Several people had walked out. Susan began to take charge of those remaining.

Another man sat down next to Angela. He was a developer she'd seen at a meeting in Sandusky. She couldn't remember his name. He smiled at her.

Bart Linden, another developer Angela hadn't seen for a while, sat at the front of the room. He'd tried to get Susan's attention without success. He stormed out of the room, slamming the door as he left.

"Well. He's not happy," Angela said.

The man next to her glanced over at her. "Who? Bart Linden? He hasn't been to one of these meetings for over a year. From what I hear, he has a right to be mad at this LECOS group. Connie King dated his brother, who is a friend of mine. She found out about a lucrative business deal Bart Linden created and stole the entire idea out from under him."

"What kind of deal?" This meeting was more interesting by the minute. Angela made a mental note about Linden.

"River Gardens. It's over near Perrysburg. Bart Linden is the developer who created that design." The man leaned toward Angela conspiratorially. "The truth is Linden invested a lot of money into it. When LECOS put out negative information about him, his investors backed out, leaving him high and dry. Then Connie's friend, that fellow up there at the front of the room, Dwayne Palmer, swooped in, picked up the project, and profited from it, big time. I heard something similar happened to Silverman, too. More than once. Understand, you didn't hear any of that from me."

"I had no idea River Gardens wasn't Palmer's project," Angela said.

"Now, you know." He raised his eyebrow at her. "This meeting is a waste of *my* time."

He gave her a gentlemanly nod, standing up to leave.

"Do you have a card?" Angela asked.

The man gave her a card. She saw he was a developer from Sandusky, as she'd remembered. Angela frowned. If what this guy said was correct, her suspicions about Connie making deals with developers were spot on. She'd make sure Det. Lane checked up on Bart Linden and Ray Silverman.

Danny had said Dep. Hill would notify Connie's next of kin. She wondered if her brother, Donald, had heard about her death. Funny he was here. He should have been told by now.

She watched Susan at the front of the room. What would her reaction be when she learned about Connie's death?

The meeting finally fell apart, with only a few people left, surrounding Susan at the front of the room while she tried to calm them down. On her way out, Angela called Danny.

"You ready for some dinner?" she asked.

"Sure. You're early. Det. Lane is still with me."

"That's fine. I'll meet you there in a few minutes."

SEVEN

DANNY WAS WAITING FOR HER WITH DET. LANE when she arrived. She put her backpack and raincoat on a chair before she sat down. They already had menus. Angela knew what she wanted and was ready to order when Det. Lane called the waitress back.

While they waited for their food, Angela introduced herself again.

Det. Lane took her card. "Call me Hugh. Danny says you've been here a while. He says you knew the victim pretty well."

Angela nodded. "She was part of the environmental community before I arrived on the scene. I've had several business dealings with her, but nothing personal."

"Does it surprise you someone killed her?"

"No."

Det. Lane raised his eyebrows.

Angela stopped to craft her words carefully. Not knowing Det. Lane, she decided to speak carefully about her relationship with Connie. She saw no reason to tell him everything she felt.

"I don't know. I'm shocked more than anything else."

Angela filled them in on who was at the meeting she'd just left, including those who had not attended. "One of the developers expected to meet with Connie there. When she didn't show, he was pretty annoyed. Another guy told me Connie was involved with cheating two housing developers, Bart Linden and Ray Silverman, out of lucrative development projects." She told him about Donald King sitting with Dwayne Palmer and Robert Durham. "The absence of Councilwoman Theresa Bradley struck me as odd. She always attends every meeting."

When she'd finished, she asked, "Have you notified next of kin? It surprised me to see Connie's brother at the meeting."

"We notified her parents. He probably hasn't talked with them yet." Det. Lane shrugged. "Anything else?"

She handed him both developers' cards. "The first guy said he had a contract to review with her. The second guy was from Sandusky. He's the one that told me Bart Linden lost all his investors." Angela sipped her water. "Can you tell me what you know?"

Det. Lane finished taking notes as Angela spoke. After a few moments, he flipped to another page before reading from it. He repeated what Danny had told her. "She died instantly. There was no evidence of a struggle. Of course, some of the evidence may have washed away."

The waitress arrived with the food. When she was gone, Det. Lane read from his notebook again. "Ms. King died before the car went into the water. We know this because we found window glass on the road marking where the driver's side window shattered outward from gunshot, and she had no water in her lungs. However, after the shots, the car traveled forward a short distance. Then, someone, the killer, turned the steering wheel sharply to push the car into the ditch. When she entered the water, Ms. King was wearing her seat belt. The ignition was on, with the gearshift in neutral."

He closed his notebook with a snap. "The forensics team searched the side of the ditch and the rest of the roadway for additional evidence. I haven't heard yet what anyone found."

The detective had shared a lot of information with them. The evidence implied passion and anger. Someone had sat in the car beside Connie, brutally killed her, and then pushed the car into the ditch, probably hoping it would take a while for anyone to find it. It was lucky the deputy found Connie when he did before the turtles had a full meal, or they would have less evidence of her condition.

"I still wonder what she was doing on Stange Road. It goes nowhere." Again, Angela was relieved she didn't have to worry about Connie's negotiations anymore. "I guess those are the questions. Why was she out here? Who did she meet?"

Det. Lane leaned forward. "So, other than the guys you just told me about, do you know anyone else who'd want to kill Ms. King?"

There were quite a few people who wouldn't be sorry Connie was dead . . . including herself. Again, careful with her words, she answered. "I don't think I know any murderers if that's what you mean. Some people might have said they wanted to kill her, but doing is different than saying. She could be very unlikeable." Angela looked at Danny. "Shooting someone repeatedly, point-blank, is pretty gruesome, isn't it?"

"Gruesome is putting it lightly," Danny said.

Angela pulled a piece of paper and a map from her backpack. She placed them on the table. "Here's the list you requested of all the boards she was on. The meeting was messy. I had time to jot them down. I hope you can read my writing. Besides serving on the board of LECOS, Connie's official title was Environmental Liaison for the City of Toledo, Ohio. I also brought the map I promised. I marked the roads we traveled last night, both in and out of the refuge. You can see I noted the approximate times we were on them. We had to record the time at every stop, so it was easy to give you a timeline. We didn't see anyone the whole night."

Det. Lane looked at the material as Angela continued, "No, Hugh, I don't have any names to give you. In my view, Connie was not a lovable person, but I can't believe anyone I know murdered her, especially in such a violent way, by shooting her in the face. That's pretty up close and personal. I don't know anyone capable of that."

"Someone had strong feelings toward her," Det. Lane said. "Anger? Jealousy? Greed? It wasn't a robbery. She was dressed in expensive threads. She also wore some expensive jewelry. The real stuff, not fake. She was still wearing it when they pulled her out of the ditch."

Angela remembered water dripping from Connie's red jacket and hair.

"Tell me everything you know about her," Det. Lane said as he took a bite of his sandwich.

"I don't know much." She risked being truthful. "I didn't like her."

He raised an eyebrow slightly. Angela continued. "There's no sense in telling you otherwise. She was supposed to protect the environment. Instead, she was my nemesis. When she became involved with real estate acquisitions, the government was usually stuck cleaning up polluted lands, letting the bastards who polluted them off scot-free. In deals Connie made, the refuge rarely won. She put me through more than one wringer. I stopped trusting her a long time ago, even when she claimed to be helping me."

Det. Lane ate his meal patiently, using silence to allow Angela to talk. She recognized the tactic from law enforcement supervisory training. Other than her argument with Connie, she had nothing to hide. Still, she was thoughtful before she spoke.

Angela continued, "At a minimum, she made everything more difficult. Connie was someone you didn't want against you. She'd slap you down in public with one hand while demanding something with the other. Your worst enemy one day. Your best friend the next."

Det. Lane made a few notes in his notebook between bites.

"She was beautiful, and she used it." Angela paused. "A developer she'd screwed over might kill her, but my best guess is a jealous wife caught up with her. I'm not sure her death had anything to do with her job. I think it has something to do with her personal life."

Neither Danny nor Det. Lane responded to that.

"Now, I have a couple of questions," she said.

"Shoot, um . . ." Danny reddened. "Sorry. Go ahead."

"Are you sure Connie had someone in the car with her? That ditch is pretty far from anywhere. Still, it's possible someone walked away. Neither Jim nor I saw anyone, but I guess we could have easily missed someone walking in the dark. Especially if they didn't want anyone to see them."

Danny answered. "We think someone met her out there and had another car nearby. Dep. Hill found some fresh tracks on the road." He glanced at Det. Lane. Was he holding something back?

"I guess the question is, why would Connie meet someone way out there? She must not have wanted anyone to see her, or she'd have gone to a bar, or Starbucks, or something. Why such a lonely road?" Angela paused. "I suspect it was someone she knew pretty well. My bet is they were up to something they didn't want anyone to know about."

Was Connie in the planning stages of another surprise for the refuge? An offer Angela couldn't refuse? Again, relief flooded through her. She was ashamed she was so heartless.

Det. Lane watched her. She was sure he noticed her discomfort. "Good observations. Do you think she often did things she didn't want anyone to see?" He put his notebook back into his pocket.

Angela raised her eyebrows. "Just my suspicions." Had she said too much?

In spite of everything, hunger won out. The three ate in silence until they were almost finished when Det. Lane hit Angela with another question.

"So," he said after a sip of his drink, "it's pretty clear you didn't like Connie King much, did you?"

A frisson of fear coursed through Angela. "No. There's no point in lying about it. Still, it doesn't mean I wished her dead."

He nodded, his face a blank. "Your worst enemy one day? Your nemesis?"

Angela froze. Her words had come back to bite her already.

Det. Lane's face remained blank when he asked the next question. "Do you know Jack Dumas?"

"Well, yes." Angela was surprised. "Jack is a close friend of mine. He volunteers at the refuge. Why do you ask about him?"

Det. Lane leaned forward. "He volunteers for your refuge and Habitat for Humanity. Am I correct?" He looked up at her. "He's also known to have a bad temper."

"He volunteers for us. Yes, he works at Habitat. As far as his temper, it's all bark and no bite. Why?"

"The gun that killed Connie King belonged to him."

EIGHT

ANGELA NEARLY CHOKED. "JACK?" SHE DROPPED the last bite of her sandwich on her plate. "Jack's gun? I don't get it. Are you saying Jack shot Connie?"

Det. Lane didn't respond.

She exploded. "Bullshit! No way Jack did this. He didn't even know Connie." She wiped her fingers on her napkin, shoving her plate away. Throwing her napkin on the table, she leaned forward, controlling her voice. "Jack and I are pretty close. I've never heard him talk about her."

Det. Lane spoke quietly. "We found the weapon on the floor of the car, passenger side. We ran ballistics on it. It's the gun that killed her. He's the registered owner. According to Dep. Hill, Jack admitted he knew Connie King pretty well. Also, a witness said he argued with her last week. He also physically accosted her." Det. Lane sat back. He motioned the waitress over to ask for the bill.

Last week? "This is crazy. Why would Jack do it?" Angela looked at Danny for support. He shook his head. She bit back her confusion. Det. Lane had already gathered a lot of information on Jack. Why hadn't Jack said anything to her?

"Good question. When we find out what the argument was

about, we might have an answer." He stood up. "I'm sure we'll talk again." He was ready to leave and reached to shake Angela's hand.

Det. Lane had this all wrong. Jack had nothing to do with Connie. She started to say something else until Danny gave her a warning look. Det. Lane paid his bill before excusing himself to go to the bathroom.

"Damn it, Danny. There's no way Jack is involved in this. The detective said Jack owned the gun. Who knows? He might have sold it or gave it away. Are Jack's prints on it? It's bad enough someone chose to commit a murder on the refuge, but I can't believe Jack had anything to do with it."

"Calm down, Angela. He is only doing his job. What do you expect? The police have to ask questions. Jack seems to have a pretty strong connection to Connie right now. It looks like Jack never told you he knew her. Otherwise, how did his gun get there? He's lived here a long time. I would expect he probably knows everybody." Danny put a hand on Angela's shoulder. "He could be a killer. You don't know."

"Like hell." The waitress looked over at them. Angela lowered her voice, shrugging Danny's hand off her shoulder. "I know Jack is not a killer. It's just a coincidence. A mistake."

Danny lowered his voice. "If it is, it'll all work out. I'm more worried about you and your connection."

"What the hell does that mean?" Angela heard ringing in her ears as her blood pressure shot up.

"You admitted how much you disliked Connie and how close you are to Jack. You were conducting surveys when she died, so you have an alibi for the approximate time frame. However, there is the implication Jack might have done it for you."

"Geez Louise! That's the stupidest thing I've ever heard. After Jack killed her, on my refuge, by the way, what, he just threw his gun down on the floor to implicate us both? That's nuts."

Danny put his hand on Angela's arm again. "Look, Angela, you have to be careful. I know you didn't have anything to do with this.

Calm down. Let the detective do his job. I'll do what I can."

She could hear the steel in Danny's voice. Angela might be his immediate supervisor, but he made it clear he had a job to do that went beyond her oversight. As long as he was working with Det. Lane he would remain objective.

Angela looked away. Again, she was losing her temper just like she did with Connie. Danny was right about that. She had no right to jump down his throat. She had to calm down.

Det. Lane returned from the restroom. They walked to the parking lot together. Angela smiled after she apologized for her earlier outburst. She drove away with a wave, not feeling the bonhomie she was trying to convey.

She dropped off the refuge truck at the office and picked up her SUV. Everyone had already gone home. As Angela re-locked the gate on her way out, she looked around. In the deepening shadows of evening, the streetlight over the entry gate came on.

Anger, mixed with a little fear, burned in her gut. She inhaled the sweet, spicy smell of decaying leaves from years of accumulation and damp earth. A cool breeze touched her face. She turned into it, looking at the bright greens of the new leaves around her. As the plant life around her exhaled oxygen, she took it in. As she exhaled carbon, they, in turn, absorbed it. In this way, a connection was made as they gave each other their breaths. Early June would soon give way to the hot, sultry months of July and August. She wanted to savor the season—to let it wash away some of her stress.

This refuge was a sanctuary for her, not just a habitat for wildlife. Her soul rested here. Her friends were the people who worked here. They should feel safe. The struggles of life, along with the reality of death, continually played out in wild places as part of the natural way of things.

Connie's murder was different. Her death was not natural.

She jerked the lock harder than needed to make sure it was secure. A barred owl, disturbed by her noisy actions, hooted in the dusk, *Who cooks for you? Who cooks for you?* The call echoed through the trees.

What was she going to do? She pulled out her cell phone to call Jack. No answer. She called Lilly.

"I know it's late, but have you seen Jack this evening? I have to talk to him."

"Jack's here," Lilly said. Angela heard someone yelling in the background. "He and Ed are having one of their arguments."

"Don't let him leave."

"No worries about that," Lilly assured her. "If you hurry, you'll get a front-row seat."

TWENTY MINUTES LATER, ANGELA PULLED INTO LILLY's driveway just as Ed tumbled out the front door onto the porch. He landed on his rear end. Jack blocked the doorway. He stood over Ed, threatening him with his fist. The screen door hung on one hinge.

"I'll knock you out of your socks if you say another word! Do you understand me?"

Lilly came out of the house, pushed her way past Jack, and stood in front of him. She gave Ed a hand to stand up. "Stop it, Jack. You know he didn't mean that."

"Bullshit! I had nothing to do with killing that woman!" Jack's face was red with anger. "If I can't count on my friends to back me up, they might as well haul my ass to jail."

Ed shouted back at Jack as he brushed off his pants. "Maybe if you worked harder to keep yourself from looking so guilty, your friends wouldn't feel like they had to go out on a limb for you." He stepped up to Jack, clearly not threatened by him at all.

Angela stepped out of her car. "What in the world is going on here?" she called out.

The three of them turned to look at her, realizing for the first time they had an audience.

Lilly came down the stairs to greet her. "Thank goodness you're here. Help me keep these two idiots from killing each other." She turned back toward the men and put her hands on her hips. "Or at least keep them from tearing down my house."

Angela could see the screen door had broken off two of its hinges. It looked as though she was witnessing, for the first time, the full extent of Jack's infamous bad temper.

Jack was seething. "Tell me what the hell that's supposed to mean? How do I make my friends go out on a limb for me? I haven't asked you for a single damned thing."

Ed was calm. "You told the police you were with us when someone murdered Connie King. You expect us to back up your statement. We can't. We won't lie for you. We believe you're innocent, but you'll look guilty as sin if you don't tell the truth now. Why can't you just tell the detective you stayed the night with another woman?"

"When did you talk to the police?" Angela asked.

Jack turned to her. "Today, right after you left. A deputy came while I was still in the greenhouse. He asked me some questions. That's all."

"Yeah. That's when you filled him with a pack of lies," Ed said.

The sheriff's office had been busy. She looked up at Jack. "You lied to the police? Are you crazy? Ed is right. Why didn't you tell them where you were?"

He stepped back from her. "I just can't."

"And why not?" Angela asked. "Geez, Jack. Someone used your gun to kill Connie King. You have to tell them where you were and who you were with."

"Damn it. I can't."

"Why not?" Angela stepped into him. "Are you fooling around with a married woman or something? What kind of woman would put you in this position? This is stupid."

"I am not fooling around with a married woman, damn it. You don't know the situation. She's an old friend of mine, and she's in a really bad marriage. She's separated from the guy and is going through a divorce. The police have jailed him because he won't honor the restraining order she has on him. He came back as soon as he got out of jail the other day. He beat her up. She ran away to escape him. I let her hide at my house for a few nights until she could find somewhere else. She's waiting for a space at a safe house to open up. They have everything she needs for protection and legal help."

Jack put his head back, blowing air out through his lips. "If her husband found out that she went to another man for help, he'd find her and kill her for sure. I'm afraid of what will happen to her until she is somewhere safe. That's why I've kept our relationship quiet. She's a good woman. I gave her my word."

No wonder Jack had been irritable lately. It was just like him to come to the rescue of a friend.

Angela pressed her lips together. After a few moments, she spoke in a low voice. "You are the number one suspect in a murder case. Did you know that? If this relationship costs you your freedom, I don't know what I'll do." Angela looked at Ed. "Do you know this woman?"

Ed shook his head. "No. I don't think so. Jack's been pretty secretive with this one."

She turned back to Jack. "I don't know her either. So, not only are you asking Lilly and Ed to lie for you, you can't even trust any of us to keep your confidences or help you somehow? What are you thinking? We're your friends."

Jack looked from Ed to Lilly before turning to Angela. "It's messy. I didn't want to involve all of you."

"Look, you have to know you're in a lot of trouble. It looks like they might drag me into this, too. They know I didn't like Connie King. They think you might have killed her for me. Did the deputy question our relationship?"

Jack looked alarmed. "No. He just asked me some questions about whether or not I knew Connie. That's all."

"You told him you knew her? Right? Did he ask you when you saw her last? Someone saw you arguing with her last week. They said you accosted her." Angela was beside herself. She threw her arms into the air. "Geez Louise, Jack. How did someone get your gun to kill her?"

"I don't know," he yelled back. "I gave it to Connie a long time ago."

The screen door creaked and fell off the hinges, making everyone jump.

"So, the gun is yours. You gave it to Connie?" Angela said quietly. She didn't know what to think anymore. Danny had it right, after all. Who was this man standing in front of her?

"I'm exhausted. It has been a long day. I have many more things to say to you, Jack Dumas." She turned her head toward the broken door. "But right now, you should fix Lilly's screen door. You should also tell your friends you're sorry."

Angela crossed her arms across her chest. "Talk to Danny or Det. Lane. This time, tell them the truth. You need to give them your alibi to clear yourself."

If Jack told the truth, everything would be okay.

Jack deflated. The fight left him. He turned to look at Lilly's screen door. "I'll fix this for you, Lilly." Turning to look at both of them, he said, "Sorry."

Angela turned to go. As she stepped off the porch, Jack called her back. "Sis, I'll talk to the police tomorrow. I'll figure out something."

"Good. If the woman cares about you, she'll understand why you had to speak up. If you explain yourself to the police, they'll probably keep your confidence." Angela stood in front of Jack, toe to toe.

Jack looked at Angela. He didn't say anything. His eyes welled up with pain. He must care a lot about the woman he was shielding as much as he loved his friends. Angela wasn't entirely sure she understood that kind of devotion. Of course, she wanted to protect Jack, didn't she? Or was she more worried about herself?

Angela shrugged. "I better go. Who knew I'd find Lilly refereeing a fight?"

Lilly walked Angela to her car. "Is Jack really a murder suspect?"

"I heard it today. I'm surprised the police haven't already arrested him."

Jack had argued with Angela before, so she had seen his temper. She'd never witnessed this palpable anger. This display was probably not the first time Jack had gotten into a physical altercation with Ed. They were old friends who understood each other well. All at once, she felt isolated from them. Shut out.

As if she sensed it, Lilly took Angela's arm. "You were just the magic Jack needed to get him to cool off quickly. I usually end up with two or three things broken before those two settle their differences. This is a first for the screen door."

"They do this often?"

Lilly nodded. "They've done three or four times since I've known them. Too much like brothers, I think. He calmed down pretty quickly tonight. It usually takes longer."

"Hearing that he was making us suspects for Connie's murder might have subdued him a bit." Angela hugged Lilly. She stepped back to look into her face. "You've been through a lot this past year. It's good you all have each other."

"We're peas in a pod, I guess." Lilly sighed.

Jack had already pulled a toolbox from his truck and started to remove the hinges from the screen door while Ed held it. She heard both men laugh about something. The fight was over. They were friends again.

Yeah, peas in a pod. That's who they were.

NINE

LJ WASN'T HOME. THE CATS GREETED HER IN the dark as she came through the back door. The house didn't feel empty or lonely with the cats.

Angela dropped her backpack onto a chair and checked the house phone for messages. She was glad to hear LJ's voice. They used an old-school landline to leave messages because they'd found a vintage push-button telephone and tape recorder answering machine on one of their road trips. The old-fashioned quality appealed to LJ because of his high-tech job.

The job required him to stay overnight to meet with the rest of the company executives. He would be home sometime tomorrow. Angela played the message twice, only to hear his voice. He left no number for her to call back. When she tried his cell, she got his voicemail. It would be nice to talk to him.

After giving the cats attention, Angela ate a piece of cold chicken from the refrigerator, turned off the lights, and went upstairs to run a bath.

Cold to the bone, she eased her body into the steaming water, letting the heat soak into every pore. She tried to shut out the day's events as she closed her eyes. She imagined vacationing with LJ. Taking a road trip to Arizona would be nice. She'd like to see the Sonoran Desert again.

Climbing into bed, Angela tried to fill her mind with thoughts of LJ. Instead, Connie's murder kept her awake. Who was the woman Jack was protecting now? When sleep finally found her, it came with weird snatches of dreams. Something lay across her chest, trapping her under muddy water. She struggled to get to the surface for air.

Angela woke with a start. Pete was lying on her stomach, kneading her with his front paws, staring into her face. He studied her with partially closed eyes. She reached over to shut off the alarm before it went off, stroked Pete's head for a few minutes, then jumped out of bed and hit the ground running.

She arrived at work early.

To her surprise, Jack, Ed, and Lilly were already there, working in the greenhouse. She popped in to say good morning. They were their usual easy-going selves as if nothing had happened the night before.

"Jack. Why don't you join me in my office for some coffee?" Without a word, Jack took off his gloves. He followed her inside to Angela's office. She closed her door before taking her place at the desk. Jack walked to the window.

"I'm really worried, Jack. Det. Lane told me your gun killed Connie. He implied you were his chief suspect. There's also the implication I pushed you into doing it."

Jack sat down in front of her desk. "I wondered why they came here to question me. As soon as we finish planting those acorns, I'll have Lilly take me to the Sheriff's office this morning to get this cleared up." He leaned toward her. "My way."

"What does that mean?"

"It means I'll take care of this."

Angela pressed her lips together. "Det. Lane also told me you argued with Connie last week. I don't understand. How did you know Connie? Tell me, why did you give her a gun?"

"I'll tell you everything I told them." Jack sat in a chair. "I knew Connie from Leno's Construction Company just before I retired.

I was a truck driver there. She'd been dating the boss. Sometimes, she'd bring me coffee while waiting for him, or the boss would have me drive her somewhere to meet him. He was a real lady's man, so I was sorry for her at first. She seemed like a mixed-up kid, another of his short-term bimbo girlfriends. It wasn't until later that I learned more about her. That's when I realized she wasn't stupid or innocent."

He stopped and looked down at his hands, remembering. "After Connie broke up with my boss, she came to see him a few months later when he wasn't there. She was upset. The stupid bimbo act was gone. I sat her down to talk. The woman was scared, really scared. She told me she was involved with someone dangerous. She wanted my boss to help her. Then she started coming on to me a little. I figured she trusted me and didn't know how to act any other way. I don't think she had anyone else to turn to. I mean, if she was coming back to get help from my boss, who was a real jerk, I figured she had to be desperate."

He glanced up at Angela before continuing. "She said someone had threatened to kill her. I thought she might feel better if she had a gun. It was a spur-of-the-moment decision. I realize now she lied. I must have given her some piece of information she wanted without ever knowing it, maybe something about my boss because I didn't see her again. She never returned the gun. It was a cheap nine-millimeter. I forgot all about it."

"Did she give you any details about the person threatening her? Was it someone else she had dated? Or the wife or girlfriend of one of them?" The interaction had occurred long ago. The person might have still wanted to hurt Connie. Hell, there was probably a string of people lined up to do it.

The strain on Jack's face was evident. "Connie told me no one would ever suspect this person was having an affair with her. It wasn't one of her usual lovers—most of them were flings, even my old boss, so I guess that clears him. She said she was sick of going nowhere having to hide their relationship all the time. She said she was ready to move on, but the person wouldn't let go. The guy must have been married, a politician, or someone in an important position. He didn't want to leave his life to start one with her. Who knows? Maybe he was important enough to hurt her if she talked."

Angela watched Jack's face.

"It all happened some time ago." He continued. "I know I shouldn't have given her the pistol. I should have asked her to give it back. All of this happened right after my wife died. I was struggling emotionally. I was a mess."

He shrugged. "I guess I felt helpless after losing my wife. I thought I could help or fix something for someone else." His voice trailed off. They sat in silence for a few moments.

The rescuer of women. That was Jack's pattern. Angela knew the compassion this man could have. She'd experienced his care. She saw him bracing himself as determination showed on his face. He hit her desk with his fist, but she wasn't startled. She wasn't afraid of Jack.

"Believe me, Connie and I were not lovers. We weren't even friends. I was just a ready-made sucker."

"What about the argument you had with her last week?"

Jack shook his head. "That? She came to my Habitat for Humanity construction site. She said she wanted information about one of our other volunteers. I don't think she recognized me. At least, she didn't acknowledge it. I told her we couldn't give her that information. Boy, she sure got mad." Jack smiled. "I guess she was used to getting what she wanted. She started yelling. When she poked me in the chest with one of her fancy painted fingernails, I took her by the arm to escort her off the site. I might have done it a little roughly, but she was a pain. She was making the other volunteers nervous."

"Who was the volunteer she asked about?" Angela asked.

"I don't have any idea. I didn't know the name, and I don't remember it now. She was loud and abusive. I wasn't going to let her keep interrupting our work. I had to make her leave."

Angela sat back in her chair. "Tell me how your gun ended up in Connie's car?"

"How should I know?"

"Jack. You have to talk to the police. Right away. Do you understand?"

Jack stood up. He walked around the desk to hug Angela. "I'm really sorry, Little Sis. Don't worry about me, okay? I'll talk to the police again. I'll have my lawyer fix this."

WITH JACK GONE, SHE TURNED ON THE COMPUTER. Once again, the screen lit up with a cascade of emails. She'd been at her desk for less than an hour when Det. Lane knocked on her door, asking for Gilbert.

"Gilbert is in the field. I'll contact him." Angela sent a hurried text to Gilbert on her cell phone. She approached Det. Lane as she spoke. "Why do you want to talk to Gilbert?"

Ignoring her question, Det. Lane stood near the wall where she had framed photos of wildlife on other refuges where she had worked.

"What's this?" He looked at a print of a pair of gemsbok with doleful expressions, staring back into the camera lens.

"African antelope on White Sands Missile Range, New Mexico. I studied them during college."

Gilbert called her on the cell. "Yeah, Angela? Whatcha' need?"

"You need to come back to the office. Det. Lane is here to speak to you."

Gilbert took a second to respond. He didn't sound concerned. "Sure, I'll be there in about five minutes."

She informed Det. Lane, "Does this mean you're redirecting your efforts? You know Jack is innocent?" Despite his mild-mannered appearance, she could sense the immense strength in the man, making her step back involuntarily.

"You don't suspect Gilbert, now, do you?" She heard the anxiety in her voice and covered it with a smile. "Are you going to start questioning everyone on my staff?"

"We're just gathering information. Gilbert Chavez is not a suspect at this time."

At this time? She didn't like the sound of that news. It concerned her that the sheriff's office thought she or anyone on her staff was involved. It bothered her enough that Jack had been a part of Connie's weird life.

Det. Lane looked her in the eye. "You argued with Connie King the day she died."

It was a statement, not a question. Angela stiffened. "Yes, I did."

He nodded. "You didn't mention it. I understand it was pretty contentious."

Don't get excited. Angela took a deep breath. "I lost my cool. Connie could push buttons like that. It doesn't mean I killed her or wanted her dead if that's what you're insinuating."

"It confirms you didn't like her. It also confirms you were very angry with her. Tell me, what buttons did Ms. King push?"

Angela waited a moment to answer. "I told you I didn't like her." What should she say? She didn't have to answer his question. "I was honest with you."

"You didn't answer my question." He tilted his head. "How did she get under your skin? If she could get to you, I'd like to know how."

She was a little relieved. "She just had her ways. I don't know. She always had ulterior motives for everything. Am I a suspect?" she asked.

When Det. Lane didn't answer, Angela's anxiety returned. Gilbert came in, pulling off his leather gloves to shake hands with Lane. They went outside to the porch in front of the office. Gilbert was a little taller than Angela and athletically built, like LJ. His black hair just topped his ears, and he had dark brown eyes that many women said they could drown in.

Det. Lane took out his notebook to read something aloud. Gilbert responded while the detective took notes before flipping the notebook closed again. Angela couldn't hear them, but she positioned herself at the front counter to watch them through the window.

Gilbert looked calm, as always. It wasn't easy to get a rise out of him. Det. Lane was relaxed, too, as he leaned against the rail, looking out across the pond.

Pearl came to the counter to tell her she had scheduled a meeting with the muskrat trappers. "And a newspaper article about the refuge is on its way to your email. The reporter just called."

Angela nodded, and Pearl walked back to her office. Pulling out her cell phone, Angela checked her emails quickly. Sure enough, an email from the local paper was on the list. She opened it, quickly scanning the story. It was to the point—*Murder at the Ottawa National Wildlife Refuge*. The story had few details other than the car was found in a ditch. Nothing to worry about with that piece.

Angela refocused her attention outside. Det. Lane said something to Gilbert, and they both laughed. Det. Lane stepped off the porch. He walked toward the shop area. Angela waited a few seconds for Gilbert to come in. When he didn't, she joined him.

Gilbert continued to look out over the marsh. "I talked to Det. Lane yesterday about how well I knew Connie. He had a few follow-up questions this morning. I told him everything."

"You knew Connie?" What the hell was going on? Was Connie involved with everyone on her staff?

Gilbert shrugged before turning to face her. "Yeah, For a while. Det. Lane is going to the greenhouse to arrest Jack. Looks like they have some evidence against him."

"Good Lord. Is he going to arrest him here? I hope there aren't any other volunteers or visitors present." Why hadn't Gilbert told her right away? Angela was already running off the porch toward the shop yard, passing Dep. Hill, standing next to his SUV. She yanked the greenhouse door open to see Jack putting down his tools and preparing to leave with Det. Lane.

"You've got to be kidding me," she said.

"No, Ma'am."

Jack shook his head slowly. "It'll be all right, Angela. I'll talk to them. My lawyer will straighten these guys out."

Dep. Hill opened the rear door of his SUV as they walked out into the parking lot. The maintenance crew stood by with a couple of volunteers to see what was happening.

Angela pulled Det. Lane aside and spoke quietly. "Look, I want you to find whoever killed Connie as bad as anyone. All I can tell you is that Jack is innocent. We don't harbor fugitives out here." Angela ran her fingers through her hair. "Believe me, Jack is not guilty."

"More evidence has come to light," Lane said. "Mr. Dumas has no alibi for his whereabouts that night. Right now, we have a lot of questions. We'll see where it goes from there as far as charges."

They were arresting him but not charging him. Not yet anyway. "More evidence? Like what?" Det. Lane didn't respond. "Do you think Jack is really guilty?"

He shrugged. Angela continued. She didn't want a repeat of her unprofessional outburst with Connie. With difficulty, she stated her concerns calmly.

"Okay, I understand. I know you have to do your job." She looked around. It wouldn't do her any good to defend Jack right now. Still, she had to protect the refuge. She fixed her gaze on the detective.

"You're single-handedly destroying our visitor service and volunteer program. When you show up out here with the deputy to haul people in, it frightens everyone. It makes them nervous. We struggle to maintain a decent number of visitors to the refuge, not to mention volunteer recruitment. No one wants to visit a refuge with their children or volunteer to work out here if they believe there's a murderer among us. The newspaper is already on this story. The negative publicity will take years to repair." She didn't want to think what the paper would write after today. She'd have to call them right away. Otherwise, they might exploit the situation.

Det. Lane nodded. He looked around, noting the people staring at them. "I understand."

"That's it?" Angela bit her tongue.

He walked away to his car.

Dep. Hill put Jack into the back seat of his vehicle, shutting the door. "Danny can brief you." Dep. Hill tipped his hat at her as they pulled out of the parking lot.

Angela ran back into her office, meeting Kate at the back door. They were only picking him up for questioning now. Sooner or later, they'd charge him if something didn't happen to help. It didn't look good for Jack.

"Gilbert told me they're taking our Jack. Incompetence," Kate said. "The idea that Jack would be involved with this in any way or be capable of doing such a thing is crazy. They don't know our Jack. He may be a bit of an ass, what with his bad jokes and gruff manner, but he's no murderer."

Kate lifted her chin. "He'll clear this up. They'll see they're barking up the wrong tree."

Angela pushed past her, leaving her steaming. She closed the door to her office to call Danny. She let Danny know about her conversation with Det. Lane.

"They have to do their job, Angela." He paused. "If they need to question anyone else, I can try to make it happen quietly. Hopefully, away from the refuge. Det. Lane has a good reason to pick Jack up right now. As you know, they have Jack's gun. A witness saw Jack in a physical altercation with Connie not too long ago. Jack won't tell Detective Lane where he was the night Connie died, leaving him without an alibi. The latest nail in his coffin is that they found one of Connie's earrings in his car. Det. Lane is pretty sure Jack is hiding something and thinks a few hours of questioning will wear him down. If he doesn't come up with an alibi, they'll formally charge him. Jack is their best bet until they finish forensics on Connie's car."

An earring? When did they search Jack's car? Jack didn't mention that. "Jack used to work for a guy she dated. He said he used to drive her to meet him sometimes. Connie has been in Jack's car many times. She probably lost it then."

"I'll make sure Det. Lane is aware of that."

Angela hung up. Gilbert tapped on her door before stepping in. "Are you okay?"

She shook her head. "No. I don't know what to do." Angela bit her lip, holding back tears of frustration.

He sat in the chair in front of her desk, leaning forward. "Don't let this upset you too much." He lowered his voice. "I know you're upset because he's your friend. I'm sure Det. Lane will figure it out. If Jack is guilty, they have him. If he isn't, well . . ."

Angela stood up, placed her hands on her desk, and leaned toward Gilbert. "This. Is. Crap." She lowered her voice. "What do you mean if Jack is guilty? He's innocent, Gilbert. I don't doubt it. I hope no one else here doubts it."

Although she hadn't raised her voice, the tone was unmistakable. Gilbert sat back. "You may be right," Gilbert said. "You know Jack pretty well. Did you know Connie? At all?"

"What does that mean? I think I knew her pretty well."

"I mean, you didn't know how she was with men."

"Oh, please. Don't patronize me. I've seen Connie turn men into mush with a touch of her finger. I am a woman. I know the way those things work." Angela stood up straight, a red blush running up her neck.

What Angela didn't understand was how stupid some men could be, though she did know Connie used her charms effectively. She'd witnessed it at several meetings. "Okay, I know that Connie could get to a man. After they figured out how she used them, they'd get mad at her. A lot of people I knew were mad at Connie. Maybe Jack was one of them, for some reason or other. Did he get mad enough to murder her? Mad enough to blast her face to oblivion? If it was Jack, as you say, I know him very well. I think I would have noticed something going on between them."

"Okay. I'll give you that. If Jack was seeing her, you might have known it. Maybe." Gilbert stood up. He was one of the few people who was never afraid of disagreeing with Angela. It usually pleased her.

"How well did you know Jack?" Gilbert continued. "You didn't even know about his old relationship with Connie in the first place. Do you know why he gave her his gun? We'll know they have something pretty solid if they charge him. That's when it will all come out."

Gilbert looked at her for a few minutes. "Try to stay out of it, Angela. Because if you're right, and Jack didn't do this, there's a murderer somewhere. It might not be a coincidence it happened here."

She stared at him. What the hell did he mean?

He started to leave when he turned back. "Don't forget you were going to help me with property inventory after lunch." He closed the door softly behind him.

Angela turned her face toward the window, shaking with anger at Gilbert's words. It wasn't Jack. It couldn't be. What did Gilbert mean? It might not have been a coincidence that it happened on the refuge.

Angela knew all too well what Gilbert was implying. The killer might be one of them or someone who wanted to harm the refuge. It worried her, too. She slammed her fist onto her desk.

One thing was certain. There was something personal in the attack on Connie. It was too violent to be only business. She understood Lane had good reason to talk to past lovers, to people who traveled in Connie's circles. People that Angela knew. Like Jack and Gilbert. Who else?

Angela plopped into her chair. The meaning behind Gilbert's words rang in her ears. She didn't believe it could be anyone on her staff, but the killer might be connected to the refuge. Who? She knew the investigation wouldn't stop with Jack. If they cleared Jack, they would look at her. Or Gilbert. She caught her breath. She couldn't allow that.

Angela had crossed swords with Connie often enough in public. She'd given Lane enough information to make him think she had a motive. In a sense, she did. With Connie gone, Angela wouldn't have to accept a land deal she didn't want. It was good that her alibi was conducting frog surveys with Jim. The police knew Connie had died during that time. She was nowhere near the crime scene when it occurred. Still, they could claim she had an accomplice, just as Danny suggested. What a mess.

Who else on Angela's staff knew Connie? The woman had a corrosive effect on people. Anyone could become a suspect in her murder. The sheriff's office would do their job. The problem was they didn't know these people like Angela did or care about them. Whoever killed Connie put Angela, her staff, her refuge, and its reputation in the middle of it.

Angela called the sheriff's office to find out when she could see Jack. The deputy who answered the phone told her she'd have to talk to Jack's attorney. Angela jotted down the number and called his office. She left a message with his secretary asking him to call her.

Her next call was to the local paper. She stated that a volunteer was a person of interest and was undergoing questions. She didn't mention anything about an arrest or imminent charges.

The last thing she had to do, she deeply dreaded. It was time to call the Refuge Supervisor again to tell him about the arrest. She dialed the number with trepidation. He was supportive of her efforts, which was a relief. There wasn't much she could say to him except that she believed her volunteer was innocent. Her supervisor hoped she was right. Angela hung up, knowing her boss wouldn't throw her under the bus.

Two days ago, someone murdered a woman on the refuge. How did it evolve so quickly to engulf the refuge completely?

PEARL POKED HER HEAD INTO HER OFFICE later that morning. "Wow. I just heard it was Connie King they found out there. I don't know what to say. I feel bad after everything I said about her."

Angela had completely forgotten she was supposed to meet with Pearl first thing this morning. Well, she'd remedy that right away.

"You didn't feel any different than many others. How were you to know you were watching Connie's last show?" Angela motioned to a chair. "Come on in."

"Yeah, I feel bad anyway." Pearl sat down. "Are you ready to go over my trapping plan changes?" As the refuge biologist, Pearl managed the trapping program that controlled the burgeoning population of muskrats responsible for eating the habitat the staff worked so hard to create for waterfowl. If there were too many muskrats, the marshes lost all their cattails and tules. Without muskrats, the wetlands would become choked with vegetation. Without natural predators in the marsh, management of wetlands depended on trappers to balance the numbers.

Angela wished she could brush off Connie's murder as quickly as Pearl. Shoving away thoughts of Jack, Angela pulled a file in front of her. "I'm sorry. With everything going on, I forgot about our meeting. I haven't had a chance to review your changes."

"I totally understand. Why don't we go to the field now? Jim is here. He can go with us." Pearl suggested. "Instead of reading the changes, we can review the units together. That way, I can explain the changes to both of you. Jim will learn from it."

Getting outside was precisely what Angela needed right then.

"That sounds great. I have to be back by lunch. I'm meeting with Gilbert." Angela grabbed her field bag.

Jim followed them to Pearl's SUV.

"Are you doing okay, Jim?" Angela asked. She put her hand on his shoulder. "I'm glad to see you back."

"I love this place. I won't let a little thing like murder keep me from hanging out with you guys." He smiled. "No, really. It was awful, but that lady wasn't anyone I knew. I'm fine."

Just as they were pulling away from the office, Angela spotted one of the trappers walking toward them on a levee trail.

"There's Tony now. He'll be happy to see you," Pearl teased as she stopped the truck.

Ten

EVERYONE ON STAFF THOUGHT TONY LaROCHE was fond of Angela. She knew it wasn't romantic, only respect for her position. Her staff told her that no other manager paid much attention to Tony before she arrived. She didn't understand why since Tony carried with him valuable expertise for the management of Ottawa. Angela learned long ago to listen to experts.

He always asked about her when she wasn't around. Every Christmas, he left her a package of deer sausage he made himself. Tony had worked the swamplands of Lake Erie his entire life, doing anything from trapping to selling firewood. He was a disheveled-looking man, a descendant of French fur trappers and the Native Algonquins who inhabited or first settled this part of the country in the late 1700s.

Everyone knew that Tony's ancestry included French royalty. Small, built like a jockey, his age was an enigma, between thirty and sixty. As he walked, his loose clothes hung from his wiry, weathered frame. Tony smiled at Angela. One of his eyes was slightly askew, as if his optic nerve were damaged.

Angela had to admit he was charismatic in a rough, strange sort of way. He was also a little slow. Or a bit cunning, Angela wasn't sure which.

"Hello, ladies." He tipped his worn ball cap at them, giving Angela a boyish smile. "How is Miss Angela today?"

"I'm doing fine, Tony. How are you?" She couldn't help but smile in return.

"I'm walking on my own, aren't I? Can't get better than that." He turned to look out over the water and lifted his chin. The image of an animal sniffing the air struck Angela. "There's likely to be 'nother storm coming in, I think." He turned back to them. "Fairly soon." The sky looked clear at the moment. That meant nothing on the south shore of Lake Erie. Still, there were no predictions of rain in the weather forecast.

"Have you looked at the muskrat trap units I told you about, Tony? I want your opinion." Pearl asked. "I still might make some changes, but I'll let everyone know if I do." Pearl stepped out of the truck with a map in her hand. Jim followed Pearl. Angela stayed put.

While Pearl spoke, she listened as the trio looked over Pearl's maps. Tony nodded from time to time. His demeanor changed as he shared his knowledge with them. His stature seemed to grow. "You might want to take a look at the northern unit out by Metzger. It's starting to dry up. The willows are coming back into it real strong like. Needs more water to flood them out. There aren't enough 'rats in the inner pool to make much headway. I think the water is too shallow. Might want to deepen it, too."

He smiled and held Angela's gaze for a few moments. Angela nodded at him. His advice was important. Listening to this man meant that the other trappers might have more trust in Pearl's decisions. Pearl was smart enough to draw from his expertise.

"No," Tony continued, looking back at Pearl, "you don't want to trap those units, not this year, anyway. Give the 'rats a chance to clear things out."

Pearl and Jim rejoined Angela in the truck as Tony walked to the parking lot.

Jim pulled out a tablet. He began to sketch a drawing of Tony looking across the marsh. "That guy is authentic, man."

Angela smiled. Yes. Authentic was a good word to describe Tony.

They drove to the Darby unit of the refuge. Located fifteen minutes east of the central Ottawa unit on the lakefront, it was a series of wetlands separated by levees. Three black-crowned night herons were feeding across the water from them. Several snowy egrets were in the same area, which was a good indication of fish presence. Jim put away his sketch of Tony and followed them around as they inspected the vegetation in each pool. A bald eagle perched in a tree above them, watching their movements as rays of sunlight fanned out through the leaves, looking like tire spokes through the canopy.

Angela could smell the lake on the breeze as Pearl discussed the condition of the pools. The short trip made Angela relax from the stress of the day. "I'm ready to sign off on your plans, Pearl. They make sense. It's a smart idea to have Tony working with you. You'll get buy-in from the other trappers."

Back at the refuge, Kate informed Angela the press had called. They left her several messages. Angela read through them. The other reporters heard about Jack's arrest. She'd discussed the situation with her supervisor. There was no sense delaying the inevitable, so she returned their calls. Angela was relieved the reporters were not looking for a sensational take on the situation. By the time she hung up from the last call, she knew she'd done her best to answer questions without ramping up the tension.

After a hurried lunch, Angela went to the field with Gilbert.

Clouds filled the sky as he drove to Cedar Point, a refuge in the opposite direction from the Darby Unit she'd just visited, to review work on levee repair. Gilbert's primary job was to supervise the maintenance crew and organize their work schedule. He also maintained the refuge website. When he had time, he helped Angela write grants for restoration project funds. Some volunteers, including Jack, worked for him occasionally.

"Looks like the guys finished the work on the levees just in time," he said as rain splashed across the windshield.

Tony had called it correctly. The sky darkened quickly. A new storm was moving in fast. "It's great to have you back, Gilbert." Getting out of the office twice in one day, even if it was beginning to pour, made Angela feel expansive.

After the rough start to the day, she allowed herself to calm down. "I'm sorry I was cross with you this morning. Connie's murder has really thrown me for a loop. Mostly because I had no idea that so many people here knew her."

Gilbert didn't respond. Angela wasn't in the mood to pry further into his relationship with Connie.

Angela changed the subject. "So how did the training go?"

For part of the past week, Gilbert had trained in West Virginia at the National Conservation Training Center. He learned the latest version of the Geographic Information System program the refuge staff used. Gilbert had several global positioning, or GPS, units to loan to staff as needed and had received training he could share with them. Although he was gone for four short days, Angela had missed him.

"It was good. I learned some new things, which means I want an upgrade on my computer software." He glanced over at her with a grin.

"Of course. I happen to know a lot about software updates." She wondered if LJ had made it back from his client meeting in Chicago yet. She quickly checked the messages on her cell phone but found none. She wished he would call.

They drove on for a few minutes without speaking. Angela broke the silence to fill Gilbert in with as much as she could about Connie's death as he drove across the refuge to go out the back way to the dirt road where Connie had died. "Stop on the other side of the gate. I want to get another look at the area in daylight before the rain washes too much away."

They walked down the ditch, careful not to disturb the plastic tape still in place to keep people out of the crime scene. They also checked the spill rolls, but there wasn't any trash from the car caught on them. Detective Lane's forensic team must have taken it all. As soon as the police released the site, Angela would dispose of the absorbent rolls.

Angela looked down the ditch. The forensics folks had scoured the area. She hoped they'd find something to tell the story. A story that didn't include Jack.

Despite not wanting to delve into Gilbert's personal life, curiosity overcame Angela. "Aren't you surprised Connie was murdered?" she asked, watching muddy runoff from the road enter the ditch.

"Nope. Knowing Connie like I do, I'm not surprised at all."

"I didn't know you knew her at all. I've never heard you talk about her."

Gilbert shrugged.

"Do you have any idea who might have killed her?"

"The problem is I know too many people who might have wanted to do it, myself included. Connie and I had been an item a couple of years back."

Angela's eyebrows shot up. Calm, levelheaded Gilbert in a love relationship with a hot-blooded politico like Connie? She couldn't imagine it.

"Don't look so shocked. We spent the better half of a year together. I was crazy about her. The problem was that she wasn't crazy for me." He paused. "I sometimes wonder if she even liked me. I still don't know what happened. She dumped me one day for no reason, without warning. At first, I was mad. After that, I moped around like a puppy dog for weeks."

He grinned at Angela and shook his head. "Right after Connie dumped me, she started dating one of the councilmen out of Toledo. It wasn't a bitter breakup for us. She just told me to go away. It made me mad. I left. Anyway, I didn't talk to her anymore. She didn't act as if she cared. I think her lack of interest tore me up more than anything. It took a while for me to get over it."

Angela had never heard Gilbert say so much at one time. She was trying to imagine Gilbert being in love with Connie. In love.

Did Jack know about the two of them? Had Jack also been in love with Connie? One thing was clear now. Gilbert had a motive.

Gilbert continued. "I guess she left the councilman a few months later. The difference was that the councilman didn't take it calmly. Photographers caught him arguing with her frequently. He'd left his wife for her, putting him in a bad jam at home. It didn't help him on the political scene either."

He looked at Angela. "It must have been a pattern for her. I met her ex-husband once. According to him, it was pretty much the same story. She was a damsel in distress type. She made you believe you were the only one who could take care of her. I thought I was different. It turned out I was exactly like all of the rest of them."

Connie had an ex-husband? That was news. Jack had said almost the same thing about Connie's behavior. Damsel in distress syndrome? "Did you date Connie before or after Jack met her?" she asked. "Who else on the staff knew Connie well?"

He looked back at her. "I didn't even know Jack knew her. As far as I know, no one else on the staff dated Connie. I guess there are things I don't know either." He looked away. "Connie was secretive like that."

"You met her ex-husband? I had no idea she was married. What was he like?"

Gilbert shrugged. "Just another schmoe like me."

Angela watched an egret land a few hundred yards away begin its fish vigil. Angela would never consider Gilbert another schmoe. Why did she feel like she was in an episode of *Twilight Zone*? She thought she knew the people around her. Evidently, she didn't.

"They found Jack's gun on the floorboard of the car. I think that in itself is very odd, don't you? If you shot someone with your gun, would you leave it behind? I'd dump it in Lake Erie as far from here as I could get. I don't think Jack would be stupid enough to leave it behind. Which proves he didn't do it."

Gilbert didn't respond. Angela continued. "I think whoever used it left it there on purpose. Probably to frame Jack. The question is, why? To hurt the refuge? I hope once they get the forensic work done, they'll know something new, taking Jack out of the picture."

Angela looked over at Gilbert, who was facing the other direction, as if he saw something down in the ditch. "When they clear him, the police will look for someone else. They may want to question you again if they know about your history with Connie."

It bugged her to learn Gilbert knew Connie so well. She softened her tone when she realized she'd sounded almost accusatory. "It's good that you were training in West Virginia when it happened."

Gilbert continued staring at the ditch. He turned back to the truck and spoke without acknowledging a word she'd said. "We'd better get going so you can get back to your computer to do your reports. It's time to put some of my newfound training to work."

Stopping at every water control structure along the road, Gilbert marked them on the GPS unit with annotations about measurements to help identify each one later. Each consisted of a pipe that ran under the road into a ditch. A screw gate was attached to each pipe. Angela took photos of the structures for him. Gilbert would enter the data accompanied by pictures into a property inventory program. If anything required maintenance, replacement, or repair, they'd know what was already there. Gilbert's job included preparing property forms for each new structure and entering them into the Service's computerized system. Funding for refuge work was dependent on accurate records, and if there was one thing every refuge needed, it was more money. Partnerships, like the one she had with Connie, focused on finding new funding. Was that a motive to kill Connie?

ELEVEN

THE DAY WAS OVER AT LAST. ANGELA STOPPED at the grocery store before it closed for a few groceries. She also picked up the evening newspaper. The paper had a full front-page story about the murder, mentioning the sheriff's office had arrested Jack with charges pending. It also suggested Jack was the only suspect. There were a few details in the report like Connie was found dead in the car, the ignition was on, and the vehicle was left in neutral when it went into the water. They didn't mention how Connie died or anything about a gun or where the police found it. The paper made it sound like Connie had drowned. The reporter had tried to interview Jack, but his attorney didn't allow him to give an interview. From the pictures, it looked like the paper decided to improvise. The image on the front page was of the refuge entrance sign, with a headline above it that read "Remote Refuge Slaying."

She pulled a copy out to read the article. Since Jack didn't give the paper an interview, they filled the space with his volunteer efforts at the refuge. She wondered who had given them all the additional information about Jack. It certainly wasn't included in the information she gave the reporters. Angela decided to chat with Kate in the morning. Apparently, Kate had done more than just take names and numbers.

It was a heck of a way for the refuge to get publicity. Angela was sure it would impact volunteer recruitment. She doubted it would do much to attract visitors or for their children's education programs, even though Jack wasn't involved with kids. Who wanted to work with people who were murder suspects? She wasn't happy about the press coverage. She would have to arrange another interview in the morning.

Susan Worth tapped on her shoulder in the checkout lane. She nodded at the newspaper in Angela's basket. "Did you know about Connie when you came to the meeting yesterday?"

Angela was surprised to see her. "I did. Couldn't say anything. You're a little far from home, aren't you?"

Susan sniffed. "Excuse me. My allergies are acting up. I just drove to this pharmacy to see if they had something different. They didn't." She held up her hand. "More of the same."

Angela studied Susan's face as she spoke. Her face was puffy. She looked like she'd been crying, not suffering from allergies. "Do you have any idea why Connie might have been out there? Was she looking at land? Is there a development planned somewhere nearby?"

"I have no idea why she was out there." Susan wiped her nose with a ubiquitous pink tissue. Since Connie's death, Angela noticed pink tissue everywhere.

"There aren't any projects planned near the refuge I know about," Susan continued. "At least Connie didn't mention any to me. I certainly would have discussed it with you if there were. I just hope they find the killer. The paper says your volunteer is their number one suspect."

"The paper is dramatizing."

Susan ignored her comment. "I can't believe this happened. Connie was so vital to the LECOS. Without her, we'll have a tough time getting people to cooperate. Connie wanted to meet with me that night. Now I wish I'd agreed to do it. Unfortunately, I couldn't miss a family event in Ann Arbor, Michigan. It was too late to reach her when I returned to town."

Angela bit her tongue. The meeting she'd witnessed indicated Susan would indeed have her hands full. Connie could have been many things, but Angela would never have said she was vital to cooperation among developers and environmentalists before her death. Now she understood she had grossly underestimated her.

How did you describe what Connie really did? It made Angela tired thinking about it. It was time to relax with her cats, a glass of wine, and a handsome boyfriend.

If he was home.

She checked her phone again—no messages from him.

Tomorrow, she'd get busy with her plan to clear Jack. Tonight, she had to stop worrying about it.

LJ WAS HOME. HE MUST HAVE BEEN READING her mind because he met her at the door with a smile. His mood indicated Angela wouldn't spend the night with just the cats. He'd arrived back from his trip an hour earlier.

"Everything worked out well, Angie." He only called her Angie when he was in a great mood. "We're already putting some new projects together. That'll mean more work for the company. We're building a strong relationship with this firm."

He put his arms around her. "We're even expanding to an international level with this account."

Angela looked into his eyes. "You're brilliant," she said with admiration. She wasn't going to fuss at him for not calling. He must have been too busy. "No other man could be as handsome, charming, or convincing as you. Did I say smart, too?"

"Ah, woman. You know what a man likes to hear." Laughing, he released her, taking a bottle of champagne from the refrigerator. Angela took a deep breath, pushing the last two days' events out of her mind. The cork popped, they sipped the refreshment, and she allowed herself to be swept up into his bliss, making his mood her own.

Later, LJ was in a euphoric mood. He cuddled with her in the dark. "Angie, I made some great connections on this trip. I'm creating a new contract with this company that will elevate us to international status. Our work will be global."

She didn't talk about the murder. Angela was glad she wasn't spending another night alone. LJ was riding a high she could only imagine.

TWELVE

FRIDAY ARRIVED BRIGHT AND SUNNY. Even though she was worried about Jack, Angela had several tasks to deal with before she could look forward to spending time with Lilly.

Her first task was to chat with Kate. After that, she spent another hour calling the newspaper reporters on her list. When she finished her discussion, Angela went to the kitchen for coffee. "I'm going to make a few more phone calls. Please make sure no one disturbs me." She didn't wait for an answer.

Kate looked a little peeved about having to redirect people. Kate was an Administrative Officer, not a secretary. She respected Angela's request to take messages when she was out rather than having them go to voicemail. Being a gatekeeper in the office didn't fit her idea of her job description. She was also annoyed that Angela had lectured her for gossiping about the murder, denying that she had said much. However, the paper had information they could not have gained from the refuge website.

Angela ignored the look on Kate's face and stopped in Pearl's office. "Throw together a couple of upbeat stories for the paper, will you? Make them about the migration of birds coming to the refuge. We need to be a little more proactive. Get some positive information out there. The more, the better."

The papers each gave her a second interview earlier that morning when she called. Angela cleared up some misinformation while saying positive things about the refuge. Angela wanted to see more fun news about the refuge filling their pages.

Pearl nodded. She'd have something out before the end of the day. With a cup of coffee in hand, Angela closed the door to her office.

Canada geese glided through the bulrushes in the pond outside Angela's window. Located in an old duck club built in the 1950s, the refuge headquarters office was about two hundred yards off Route 2. A wet meadow with a row of trees blocked the view of the roadway to the south. To the north, a deep water pond with trees and marshes beyond it blocked any possible view of Lake Erie. The wetlands on the north also buffered the office from the occasional nor-easter that blasted the lake's shoreline.

She took a deep breath, enjoying the view. The sun reflected with sparkles off the water.

Enough dawdling, Angela had work to do. Jack's goose was cooked unless she did something for him. She had to give Det. Lane other suspects to consider seriously. It was time for Angela to do some investigating of her own.

Some people on the committee list she gave to Detective Lane were developing properties near the Cedar Point Refuge, including Bart Linden.

For political reasons, if Angela had questions about projects, she usually didn't openly ask them at the meetings. As a federal employee, her queries often created too much interest. If misconstrued, her questions could require a lot of explaining or back-pedaling. She'd call each one to find out how well they knew Connie somewhere in the conversation.

Angela jotted down a few names of people who were at Connie's meetings on a regular basis. They were primarily men. Looking through her cell phone, she realized she didn't have their numbers. They weren't in her Rolodex either.

Angela flipped through her meeting notes, wondering how many of those men were married to a jealous wife. Jealousy would explain the vicious nature of Connie's murder. She might be able to get information from the guys involved with the Cedar Point area development and, while she was at it, learn a little more about Connie's relationships on the side. It was time she knew more about Connie King and all the people associated with her. Especially the people who were on Angela's staff or volunteer crew.

Exasperated when her files didn't produce the expected results, Angela called Susan Worth.

Susan answered in an upbeat way. "I was about to send an update on our meeting with the developers. I have some exciting news to share. This morning, a major developer in the area, Mr. Bart Linden, informed me that his company would purchase some industrial riverfront land on the Ottawa River to include it in one of their developments. Thanks to our input, they will clean it up. Once they finish cleanup, they'll manage it as a parkway or wetland open to the public. Isn't that wonderful? It's a great start for us. I'm putting all the details into an email for everyone on the committee. Other developers might rethink their attitudes about mitigation within the Ottawa River Watershed." She came to a stop. "I'm sorry, I'm talking too much. What's up?"

Angela wasn't sure how to change the direction of the conversation. She was surprised that Susan was so upbeat, considering Connie's demise. It was also interesting that Bart Linden had returned to the table after getting cheated by Connie and leaving Susan's meeting abruptly.

"That's wonderful, Susan. Especially the part about developers cleaning up contaminants. I guess I didn't have much faith in the outcome after yesterday's meeting." It was good news, even though the eventual home buyers in the area would pay for the cleanup, not the polluter. It still wasn't fair, but at least it didn't come out of taxpayer dollars.

Susan laughed. "I know it did seem like a daunting task. What a fiasco. In this case, Linden approached me because of some prior urban development work that Connie had done. Connie had quite a bit to do with the success of LECOS. You know she had a special way with all these people. It's terrible what happened to her. On your refuge," she paused. "I read about her death in the paper this morning. If that volunteer of yours is the killer, I hope the man gets what he deserves for what he did to her."

Angela took a breath before responding calmly. "As a matter of fact, Susan, I don't think Jack did it. Jack is my friend."

Susan was silent on the other end of the line.

"Jack has done so much for us here at the refuge," Angela continued, "and since his wife died, the refuge is his family. We're all very close. He must have known Connie. I don't think he dated her. At least not since I've been here."

"Connie was much more than just my friend. How can you be sure your friend is innocent?"

"I just am. I've known Jack for a couple of years. We've spent a lot of time together both on and off the refuge. There may be a lot of details I don't know about him. The one thing I know is he's not a murderer."

"Hmm, well, you may be right. I don't remember Connie dating or knowing anyone named Jack at any time. I would have known if she was seeing a refuge volunteer. She did have plenty of boyfriends, though. It was hard to keep up."

Susan paused. Angela could hear something tapping in the background. "I do seem to remember her seeing someone from the refuge, but I think that was a long time ago." Her tone was terse. "In any case, there isn't anything you can do. Someone murdered Connie. If it wasn't your volunteer, how did the person get his gun?"

"I don't know."

"So, why did you call?"

"I'm reviewing some environmental assessments. I want to follow up with a couple of folks who have attended your LECOS meetings. Unfortunately, I don't have their contact info. Rather than ask you for each one, could you send me copies of the sign-up sheets for the last two or three meetings that we've had? I can get what I need from those."

Susan always saw the good in people. Angela didn't want to put her off by sullying her memory of Connie. She needed her help to take care of refuge business, but she didn't want Susan to know that she was also trying to figure out Connie's schemes. Seeing other names on a sign-in sheet might jog Angela's memory so she could give Det. Lane some other leads to investigate.

"Hold on a minute. Let me check my files. I always keep original copies for reference." She came back to the phone a few minutes later. "I have the sign-up sheets from three different meetings. I can scan and email them to you immediately. Most of these names are repeats. You know how that goes. The same folks are involved with everything. Your name is on all of them, too."

Before Angela hung up, Susan warned her. "Angela, please, be careful. If Jack is innocent, the murderer is still out there, someone who knew Jack well enough to get his gun. Or, it could be Jack. You might find yourself defending a murderer. I'm sure the detectives know how to do their job. Where there's smoke, there's usually fire. The police don't act on flimsy evidence."

At this moment, Susan had more faith in the justice system than Angela did. "Don't worry, Susan. Jack didn't do this. I'm sure the detectives will figure it out. Thanks for the sheets."

Angela couldn't wait to get those lists. Someone might know something helpful. She began to feel excited about the prospect of clearing Jack. Even though getting the attendee lists of the meetings was a small thing, it made her feel useful. Angela told Kate she was back in business and left her door open. It didn't erase Kate's scowl.

True to her word, Susan sent the lists within the hour. Angela printed them off before setting them aside. At last, she concentrated on an environmental assessment forwarded to her by the

Army Corps of Engineers about a project that involved ditching next to the refuge to improve water drainage on nearby farms. Any drainage or ditching projects in the area could affect the hydrology of refuge habitat, which was critical to the growth of vegetation or other food for wildlife.

Angela looked out the window. She saw Tony walking past. He was here for Pearl's trapper meeting. With him was Sean Rousseau, another trapper who consistently managed to win bids to trap refuge sites each year. Sean had inherited the looks of a brooding Tarzan. His muscular physique, long hair, and dark skin completed the package. He was always polite but never smiled or spoke much. Tony and Sean helped each other when weather or other issues put them behind.

The last thing Angela wanted now was to get caught up in a conversation about trapping. She had to focus on the document before her. Angela closed her door before they came into the building. Pearl had managed to get quite a few trappers in for her meeting on short notice. Of course, when you announce you will make changes that might affect someone's livelihood, it gets their attention.

Several hours later, Angela had just finished making the last comments on the EA when Jack's attorney called. "You can see Jack anytime you like."

"How solid do you think the case is against Jack?"

"I'm still reviewing the evidence. The DA will charge him later today. They have evidence he had a relationship of some kind with Ms. King. With the gun and witnesses who said he argued with the woman, they certainly have probable cause to build a case."

"You should know there are a lot of people in Connie's life who could have wanted to do her harm. I'd be happy to give you a list."

THIRTEEN

NO MATTER WHAT HAPPENED ON A REFUGE, life continued. Jack was in jail without bail. The DA believed Jack could harm someone else in Connie's circle. Whether or not Jack returned, his friends would pick up the workload, convinced he'd return eventually. It was up to Angela to do all she could to make sure Jack did return.

Now that Jack had charges against him, she'd had to respond to several news reporters. There wasn't much to say except that they believed Jack would be proven innocent.

It was time to recruit Lilly to see if she could help. Lilly had experience with research on criminal cases. Maybe she could find more information.

After hanging up with Jack's attorney, she called Lilly to fill her in on her investigation. Lilly was sad to hear about Jack but thrilled to help clear him. Angela sent the email with the sign-in sheets to her. They agreed to compare notes later when they met for the weekend. Lilly would dig up as much information on each person as possible.

Angela picked up the lists. One of the first names on the list was Bart Linden. Susan said he was interested in a piece of land on the Ottawa River. Since he served on the Perrysburg city council, it fit. Since he was already working near the Cedar Point Refuge, Angela had an excellent reason to call him. Looking over the sign-in sheets, Angela remembered Linden's brother had stormed out of a previous meeting when Dwayne Palmer presented his new River Gardens development. Now she understood why. Bart Linden was involved in a large number of property development projects, making him the best place to start.

A call to Linden could kill two birds with one stone. First, she could get the information she needed from him about the project near the refuge. Second, if she were lucky, she'd learn more about his interests on the Ottawa River as well as his involvement with River Gardens. Since Mr. Linden was involved with politics, Angela wondered if he was the guy Gilbert had told her about that Connie had dumped.

The phone rang twice before Linden answered. The voice on the other end had a pleasant tone. After Angela introduced herself, he had no problem remembering her. "Yes, you were at the last LECOS meeting. What can I do for you today?"

"I've read your proposal on the Cedar Point area project. I have a couple of questions."

Bart Linden satisfactorily answered Angela's inquiries about hydrology, the number of acres involved, and where discharge would occur. Everything was in order. After he agreed to send Angela a few drawings electronically, the conversation ended.

"Thanks for helping me out," she said. "I know you're preparing an environmental assessment. Eventually, I'll have a chance to review and comment. I like to get ahead of the game to address potential problems for the refuge before they hit."

"Well, I appreciate it," he said. "Our discussion may result in changes in how my company, Linden Homes, addresses the water discharge situation, as well. Better to know now than later."

"I was going to try to catch you at the last LECOS meeting, but you left early. The meeting was a mess." Angela leaned back in her chair.

"It was a mess. I didn't have time to wait around for it to get settled. I'm interested in a property along the Ottawa River. There's potential to do some great work there."

"I heard about that. Susan is excited. I think any developer interested in cleaning up industrial waste is good in my book." Angela paused. "It's too bad the meeting didn't go well. I'd like to hear your ideas. I don't know if you heard the news that Connie King was murdered. It will take Susan a while to get the hang of running the meetings without her."

"What?" His surprise sounded genuine. "Connie was murdered? When?"

"It happened Tuesday night here on the refuge. Haven't you seen the news? A deputy sheriff found her in a car in a drainage ditch." Angela waited to see if he would respond. *Nothing. Time to improvise.* "Come to think of it, you might be able to help me with a small issue. Connie kept a field bag at the refuge that she used when she hiked the trails. The police looked through it, but it's still here in my office, they didn't take it. It contains a few personal effects, with one strange item. I wonder if it might belong to you?" There was no field bag. Angela fought to think of a plausible story.

"Something belonging to me?" he asked. "Why would Connie have something of mine?"

She was making it up as she went and had to think fast. "It's a jeweled tie clip. It looks expensive. You're one of the few people I know who wears a tie. Connie must have picked it up at one of the meetings and, for whatever reason, never returned it. I doubt it's a gift. It isn't new."

Hopefully, Mr. Linden was not missing a tie clip, or Angela would have to make a trip to a jeweler to conjure up a fake one.

"Well, I haven't lost a tie clip, much less one with jewels on it," he laughed. "And I'd be the last person Connie would send a gift to. You have the wrong guy. Sorry, I can't help you. Well, I'll see you at the next meeting."

He was about to hang up, so Angela jumped to the point. "Why would you be the last guy she'd give a gift? I thought you knew each other well."

Silence.

"Mr. Linden?"

"I was just a business acquaintance to her."

"I see. Well, would you have any idea who might have lost it?" It was weak, but all she had. Angela was afraid to ask more personal questions. "It looks expensive. Someone might like to have it back."

"Oh." She heard relief in his voice. "No, I don't know anyone who might have lost a tie clip. Connie had a lot of friends I didn't know. Sometimes, she had information about other offers, land deals, or conservation easement issues. We went out to dinner a couple of times to discuss some issues. That was the extent of my dealings with her."

"What a shame I can't find the owner. Well, thanks for your help. If you think of anyone who might own the clip, could you give me a call? You have my office number?"

"Sure, I'll call you if I think of anyone." He hung up quickly.

Screwing up more courage, Angela picked up the phone and started again.

Her next call was to Robert Durham, another property developer. She generally avoided him because he was crude. He liked flirting with women, whether they wanted his attention or not. Angela didn't have anything to discuss with him, so she decided to ask whether or not he was involved with the Cedar Point project. If that didn't work, she'd try plain gossip. His secretary put Angela through immediately.

"Hi, Hon. What d'ya need?"

Hon? "I'm reviewing information about the Cedar Point area project involving Bart Linden. I didn't see your name in any of the material, but I thought you might have a part in it."

"Nope, not me."

Short and sweet. It was time to dive in again. Angela told him about Connie's murder, then repeated the tie clip story.

He laughed out loud over the phone. "You gotta be kiddin' me. Do I look like the kind of guy who wears a diamond tie clip? Besides, what Connie and I had together didn't involve our clothes." He laughed again.

Angela cringed.

"No, Honey. She was a good source of information. She'd let me know what you *en-vi-roes* were up to and how I could get around all your regulations. She'd tell me what to do if I found an endangered species on one of my properties. I always made it worth her while so she could buy some of that pretty jewelry she loved to wear. Of course, she always made it worth my while by showing me how she looked in it with nothing else on." He was enjoying himself at Angela's expense. She bit her tongue.

He continued. "No, I'm sorry to hear this happened to the pretty little thing. I guess it's like they say, all good things must end. Hope you find your tie clip guy." He hung up, laughing.

Angela held the phone away from her ear, looking at it. She shuddered at the mental images he evoked.

Half an hour later, Angela had a suspect list of three men and one woman, including Ray Silverman, who called Connie a swindling whore. Angela figured he had enough passion to murder her.

Then there was the obnoxious Robert Durham. She was more than a little offended that he was skirting environmental regulations with Connie's help. The world was full of guys like him.

The woman on the list was Mrs. Theresa Bradley, on the Toledo Council of Governments board. Angela couldn't remember her position on the council. Instead of a tie clip, she described an earring.

Mrs. Bradley had responded with acid in her tone. "Not mine. I want you to know I never had a very high opinion of Ms. King. Her lack of professionalism excluded her from any social circles I am acquainted with."

Along with the snobbery, there was heat behind those words. Angela had to believe Mrs. Bradley's opinion was more personal than professional. Did the woman have a philandering husband?

The real question was, did she have an alibi? Did any of them have alibis?

FOURTEEN

After talking with Mrs. Bradley, Angela called Danny. Angela enjoyed the thought of pointing the finger at Robert Durham, especially if he couldn't clear himself. Connie sure worked her way through the political process.

Danny answered immediately. She told him about Bart Linden, Councilwoman Theresa Bradley, Robert Durham, and Ray Silverman.

"They were all pretty passionate about Connie, one way or another. When I spoke with Linden, he mentioned having dinner with Connie occasionally to discuss deals. He's also involved with a new project on the Ottawa River, which is interesting to me because he was the guy who lost out on a project in the same area, thanks to Connie. He had stopped attending our meetings. It's odd he's back right after Connie dies."

"Thanks, Angela. It didn't seem weird to anyone you were bringing up the subject?" asked Danny.

"The calls started with a legitimate topic, Danny. I only mentioned Connie. After that, I only listened to what they had to say. The paper has printed so much about the refuge the subject is hard to avoid."

"Okay. That's good. My supervisor told me to continue working with the Sheriff's office to get this cleared up as soon as possible.

That will curtail some patrols on the refuge, but I'll get out often enough. Why don't you send me the email with the signup sheets? We can follow up on those names."

"Thanks, Danny." Angela sent the lists right away. She made one last call to Lilly to share the information she'd gathered. Lilly had already started doing background checks on the names on the list.

"I'm on my way to Port Clinton to visit Jack at the jail," Angela said. "I had to register online to get in for a 5:30 appointment. They have pretty rigorous security."

"Let me know how he's doing. Ed and I owe him a visit, too," Lilly said.

Angela had just hung up the phone when Pearl came in. "I'm heading out."

"How did your meeting go?"

"It was great. At first, the trappers were all worried I would make more rules for them to follow. They relaxed once they realized I was rotating the trapping areas to the most heavily populated ones each year. Of course, they'd rather trap everything, but they'll go along with the new plan." She smiled slyly. "Tony was helpful. He asked about you."

"Oh?" Angela wiggled her eyebrows. "I think he's becoming more used to me. I kind of wear on people after a while. Anything special planned for your weekend?"

"I'm working on a new house project. We're building a couple of houses on the edge of Toledo." Pearl stopped. "Did you know Jack talked me into volunteering to work for Habitat for Humanity? I love it. We often worked together."

Angela knew Jack worked for Habitat. Learning Pearl worked there was a surprise. Most biologists went birding or joined other nature clubs to fill their weekends. "I didn't know you volunteered for Habitat. That's exciting." Angela paused. "So, you're involved because of Jack?"

Pearl slung her field bag over to her other shoulder to reposition it. "Yeah, it's a lot of fun working alongside him. He's good at carpentry. He's taught us a lot of skills. I've been able to repair a lot of things in my house because of him." She paused. "He can cuss like a sailor when he gets mad, but he never takes it out on anyone. Everyone loves working with Jack. He's not a murderer. I know you're worried about what the volunteers think. All my volunteers, including Jim, think Jack is innocent, too. Everyone is worried about him."

Angela was glad to hear about the other volunteers. She knew Jack had a bit of a temper. He didn't show it much around her, probably because what he dished out, Angela gave right back. It rarely escalated until she witnessed his behavior at Lilly's house. The stories about his temper didn't put him in a good light with the police.

Angela went out to see if Kate had anything left to go into Angela's inbox. The scowl was gone, and she was in a better mood. Everyone must have completed their timesheets without causing Kate too much trouble.

Her routine was to let Angela know if something would be pressing on Monday so she'd come to work prepared or put in the extra time on Friday night to be ready. Her efficiency always allowed Angela to have a relaxing weekend. Despite Kate's frequent bad moods, she always displayed professional respect for Angela's time.

Kate had worked as an Administrative Officer for Ottawa Refuge for over twenty-five years, which wasn't unusual in the U.S. Fish and Wildlife Service Refuge System. Most of the administrative or maintenance staff were locals whose families were involved with farming or other local businesses. They liked having a federal job for health or retirement benefits.

Kate had seen more staff turnover through the years than Angela could imagine, making her sometimes act like she was in charge. Unlike administrative or maintenance workers, most managers, biologists, or visitor services staff moved every three years. If you didn't move, you didn't get a promotion.

"How was your day, Kate?"

"Oh, lovely," she said with sarcasm. "This has been one heck of a week with that woman getting killed in her car. Then Jack gets arrested right here." She picked up her purse and pushed her chair into her computer desk. "We've had reporters calling all day long. I did what you told me to do. I just read the damn statement telling them to talk to the sheriff's office."

Angela softened her tone. "It's good you stuck to the statement. I'm trying to stay on top of what the reporters are saying. We don't want to interfere with the investigation or tick off the regional office. Mostly, the regional office wants us not to comment since it's an ongoing investigation."

She also didn't want another article in the paper that sounded like someone had been talking out of turn. Angela's boss in the regional office expected her to communicate yet at the same time distance the refuge from the murder to ensure the refuge didn't become the story. Not an easy thing to do since the murder happened on the refuge.

Kate nodded. "I was about to put this in your signing box. You don't have anything pressing. I just need your signature for some credit card statements. Then you can go home, too." She handed Angela a stack of papers. "I can't believe the police think Jack did this. He's one of us, for Pete's sake."

She continued. "The maintenance guys wonder if the police will figure out they made a mistake or if this will be one of those cases where an innocent man goes to prison for something he didn't do. I told them not to worry. Jack has never done anything before. The whole thing happening right here on the refuge makes everyone nervous. Why did the stupid woman have to come out here to get killed?" she demanded.

Angela choked back a like response. "I don't think anyone plans to get killed. Like you, I do wonder what she was doing out here. The detectives working on the case will figure it out. Try to take it easy this weekend."

Angela walked Kate to the front door.

"Isn't there anything you can do to make them stop coming out here? You should have some say about whether they can harass people or not," Kate said.

"I spoke to Detective Lane. The crime happened on the refuge, so we're on the hot seat. I'd like them to be more discreet. They agreed to try," Angela answered.

"Well, I think it's awful. Goodnight. Don't stay out here too late by yourself. God knows who might be hanging around."

Thanks for the cheery thought. "I won't. I'm ready for a weekend, too." She locked the front door behind Kate.

Dave Bennett, the Outdoor Recreation Planner supervised by Sally Griffin, the refuge Chief of Visitor Services, was going out the back door when Angela stopped him. "Dave, is everything going okay for you this week? I haven't had a chance to check in with you. I know you've been busy with Sally gone."

Dave ran the recreation programs or worked on interpretive materials for Sally Griffin, who was on vacation. Normally, his main responsibilities were to oversee the maintenance of trails and interpretive signs, as well as provide educational activities for adult visitors. With Sally gone, he had to take care of her duties, giving field trips and educational programs to school children, making sure the volunteers had training and equipment to do the jobs they were assigned, conducting safety briefings, and logging volunteer hours so they could earn recognition awards.

Several months back, he'd done a great deal of work on a grant to get funds to rebuild some of the kiosks on the refuge trails. Connie had helped him with this one by finding additional funds.

Okay. One for Connie.

"Everything's been great. Doing Sally's work makes me appreciate not having her job. I never knew she had so much to do, especially mediating issues between volunteers. You'd think everyone would get along, but they don't."

"Sally's job isn't always fun." She thought about the relationship between Jack and Ed. At least Jack got along well with the other volunteers.

"Have you heard anything about the grant?"

"Not yet. We should hear something within the next week. If you don't need anything else, Angela, I have to run. I'm meeting some friends at the gym. We're going out for pizza. It's our pool night. I'm already late."

"Go. Have a good weekend!" At least he wasn't dwelling on Jack.

She locked the door behind him and walked through the office to secure the building. She was alone. For just a moment, she felt a frisson of fear.

After reviewing the credit card statements, she signed off on them. Grabbing her things, she turned off the lights, set the alarm, locked the door behind her, and ran to her SUV. She had to hurry. Visiting hours at the jail were limited.

FIFTEEN

When Angela finally made it through security to see Jack, she found him defensive, acting like a martyr again. He quickly learned Angela was in no mood to indulge him.

"Knock off the crap, Jack. You're here because you refuse to cooperate. This murder was very personal. Someone hated Connie enough to shoot her several times. In the face. They were pretty mad about something. We have to find a way out to get you out of this mess."

Jack stayed quiet. Angela understood his reaction. Leaning forward she spoke softly to calm him. "I'm on your side. Okay? Your life is on the line here. Mine too, if they think you did this for me."

Jack blew out his breath. "I'm sorry if I'm acting like a jackass. I don't know if anyone can do anything."

"You're not acting like a jackass. You're acting like a loyal friend. The problem is, no one can help you if you don't help yourself," Angela said. "You were supposed to tell Det. Lane about the woman you're helping. As long as you continue to shield her, you're the only suspect they have. You have an alibi—use it."

"I won't put her in that position. If anyone leaked anything, that creep of a husband might kill her. I don't trust the police to keep it quiet. On top of that, I know that newspaper reporters are all over the place. You know how good they are at getting hold of stories like this. You don't understand the abusive relationship she's trying to escape. She's safe if she stays where I put her. Look, Angela. You might be better off staying out of it. There's a killer out there. I don't want you to get hurt." He shook his head. "You do believe I'm innocent, don't you?"

"What? Of course, I believe you." Angela took a breath. "The person who shot Connie left your gun in her car to set you up. How did they get hold of it? Why did they leave it? Is someone framing you? Or trying to implicate me?"

The frown on his brow told Angela her comment annoyed him. To his credit, he controlled his emotions. "Maybe Connie put the gun in her car when I gave it to her. She probably left it there. Forgot about it. The killer found it."

Angela sat back in her chair. Of course. Why hadn't she realized this sooner? She'd made everything way too complicated. What Jack said made perfect sense. He was an innocent bystander, more or less in the wrong place at the wrong time. The gun, forgotten in a glove box, worked to the advantage for someone in more ways than one. Someone who knew it was there.

"Look, I understand what you're doing. If you tell me the woman's name, Lilly and I might be able to help her hide somewhere her husband would never find her. That way, you have an alibi, and you've protected her."

"I don't know. Let me think about it. It's not that I don't trust you. I'm just not sure I want to have you or Lilly involved at that level. What if my friend's husband found out somehow? I'm telling you, he's sneaky. He's lived in the area all his life and knows everyone. I don't doubt he'd kill you or Lilly, too. He's crazy. I couldn't bear it if something happened to you or Lilly."

ANGELA MADE IT HOME LATE TO FIND LJ AT the barbecue. Longer summer days meant several other families could be seen out in their backyards, enjoying the start of the weekend. She poured a cola over ice, and after changing out of her uniform into sweats, she joined him on the deck.

LJ was a tall blond with an athletic frame. While his striking blue eyes, sharp jawline, and shy demeanor caught her attention, his smile floored her. His teeth were perfectly even pearly whites. The first time she met him, she thought he looked like a Danish superhero in a polo shirt. Angela's Mediterranean genealogy was a sharp contrast to his, with her olive skin and black hair. She stood five-six but barely reached his chin. They were both considered too thin.

Angela made herself comfortable in a deck chair. So many people had lives they hid from each other. LJ traveled a lot for business. Did he have a secret life in another town? Did she know this man? Lately, she knew so little about people. Did her ignorance extend to the man she lived with as well?

She recalled stories Lilly had told her over the last three years about her husband, Harry. They were best friends who knew everything about each other. Their marriage wasn't always easy. They went through some tough times financially for a while. They both wanted desperately to have children, but after several miscarriages, her doctor said it was too risky. Lilly said she and Harry were hard-wired to each other. They overcame all their problems by working together. Sure, they argued from time to time. But nothing came between them. Lilly's husband made her swoon even after more than thirty years together. Angela had laughed over the word swoon.

They were committed to each other completely, yet they still managed their independence. Angela never thought the two could go hand in hand. She had independence with LJ. There was no deep love in the way Lilly described. Could she and LJ survive half the things Lilly and Harry went through? She wasn't sure.

An emptiness began to open inside Angela. In her thirty-six years, she'd never allowed herself to think much about her love life. Love was always something she thought was foolish or, like in her parent's case, destructive. It was absurd to consider committing yourself to someone until death. It was enough work to have a relationship with no demands. If it was fun, that was good enough. Wasn't it? She knew she was missing something. Was she willing to change after all this time?

A fly buzzed past her head. She waved it off. "Did I tell you they arrested Jack for Connie's murder?"

LJ raised his eyebrows in surprise, his lips pressed together.

"Connie's murder is on my mind. I can't think of much else these days."

LJ shook his head at her. "I know how you like to fix things. I wish you'd let this go."

She pulled her knees up to her chest, wiping the sweat off her glass before putting it down. "Jack is my friend. How can I let it go? After someone used Jack's gun to kill Connie, they left it in the car. Det. Lane withheld the information about someone shooting Connie or finding the gun in the car from the public, so I hope he thinks Jack is innocent. My assistant manager, Gilbert, said Det. Lane asked him questions about Jack. He also asked about his other friends. Me included."

Her cats, Pete and Poe, had stationed themselves on the windowsill, watching them through the screen.

"You might find out all sorts of things you don't know during a murder investigation like this," LJ said as he turned the hamburgers.

Angela made meow faces at the cats while LJ talked to her.

"I know Jack is your friend," LJ continued. "Listen to me. You should be careful, Angela. You don't know who's involved in this. It already sounds like the police think you're involved."

"Well, I don't think Jack, or anyone else on the refuge, did it. I won't sit by watching him get railroaded without doing something. He wouldn't let me rot in jail if the shoe were on the other foot. I know most of the people who were involved with Connie. She made a lot of those people angry. The least I can do is find other leads for Det. Lane to follow."

"Are you so sure Jack is innocent? You said you didn't know about him and Connie. What else don't you know? You say you know people, but I don't think you know them like you think you do. Your friend could be guilty as hell. If you stick your nose into it, you could get hurt." LJ picked up a platter to place the burgers on.

Angela couldn't bite back her irritation. "Please don't tell me you think Jack is guilty."

"I don't think they would detain him for no reason. Where there's smoke, there's usually fire."

She'd heard this comment before. It was getting on her nerves. "Jack had a good explanation for why Connie had his gun. I believe what he says."

LJ plopped the last burger onto the platter and set it on the table. "If it's a good explanation, why don't the police believe it? Do you really believe he has a friend stashed away somewhere? Why is he afraid to name her? He says it's because he's afraid the woman's husband will find out. Sure. You should be careful. I don't want you to get hurt."

Pete let out a loud meow. Poe hissed at him. Copycats.

They sat in silence while they ate their food. There was no sense arguing with LJ. He was right. Jack could be lying. There must be something else Det. Lane knew that he hadn't shared with her. Otherwise, Jack wouldn't be in the spotlight.

Angela shook her head. LJ was also wrong. There might be things she didn't know about Jack, but Angela knew he wasn't a murderer.

LJ had a faraway look as if he were in another world. Was he puzzling over a computer program? Probably. In any case, he wasn't too concerned about Jack.

"What are you thinking?"

He spoke absently. "Work."

She nodded, not wanting to pursue it. Her mind wandered back over her day. She wanted to clear Jack's name, give Det. Lane other leads and get the refuge out of the limelight.

Angela did not intend to find a killer, only move suspicion away from Jack.

The phone rang, but the caller hung up by the time Angela reached it. The light began to flash, indicating a message on their answering machine. The voice was muffled. She couldn't tell if it was a man or a woman.

"Angela Martin? Want information about Connie King? Call me at 11:00 a.m. sharp. Tomorrow."

The caller left a number and hung up.

SIXTEEN

BREAKFAST THE NEXT MORNING WAS A QUIET AFFAIR. LJ no sooner finished his when he went to his office to work on a program. Angela had a third cup of coffee while reading the newspaper. She checked her watch for the hundredth time.

She didn't tell LJ about the call the night before. She'd jotted down the number, cleared it from the machine, then tucked the note into her purse.

This morning, she saw an open house advertisement for Dwayne Palmer's development in the paper.

Angela planned to spend Sunday with Lilly shopping. She gave Lilly a call. "Instead of shopping, how would you like to look at new houses with me tomorrow? A developer who worked with Connie King has an open house in the morning. While you are pretending to look for a new home, I can get some information from him."

"If this is to help Jack, I'm in. Pick you up about nine o'clock tomorrow?" Lilly suggested.

"Perfect." Angela hung up. She ran upstairs to get dressed, popping into LJ's office on her way back down the stairs.

She kissed his cheek. "I'm on my way to the store. I'll be back in a while."

"Whoa, wait a minute. I need your opinion. What color do you think I should paint these walls?" LJ was testing another piece of software for a home improvement product line. This client was a lot of fun. LJ created layouts for several dream houses. Angela had helped him furnish them in various styles, adding new palettes of paint color and drywall plaster textures.

"I think a palette of light greys is nice. It's not too dark but adds richness. If you make all the trim white, it's cool and classy." She kissed his cheek again before she dashed out.

Angela drove until she was out of sight of her home. Then she parked on a side road to make the call. A woman answered.

"This is Angela Martin. You left a message for me last night?"

"Yes." The woman answered. "Yes, I did. I want to tell you about Connie."

"I'm going to the grocery store in Fremont right now. Do you want to meet me there in, say, thirty minutes?"

"No, I can tell you what I want you to know over the phone."

Angela frowned. It was one thing to ask innocent questions, gossip, and dig up information from people she knew. It was scary to have a stranger call her at her home, someone who had figured out what she was doing.

"I don't know you, do I? How did you get my number? What makes you think I want information about Connie King?"

"I know you. You don't need to know me. You made a call asking about Connie yesterday. I figured you must be looking for something."

Who was this woman? Angela didn't recognize her voice. Was she someone's secretary? She must be someone in one of the offices she called. Everyone except Robert Durham answered their own phone. "I was only trying to find out who owned something in Connie's effects."

"Yeah, right. I won't waste a lot of your time, but I knew Connie very well. We were lovers."

Angela wasn't sure she'd heard right. It surprised her that

Connie was bisexual. Angela had never seen her with any other woman except Susan.

"I guess you're surprised. You have a problem with that?"

"No, I don't have any issues with someone's sexuality. It does surprise me about Connie. I mean, she had a lot of boyfriends. I never saw her with other women."

"She kept it quiet. We met when she was going out with my boss. He paid her for information to evade some environmental laws, making out like a bandit on some of his land deals because of her. I knew Connie was calling the shots. He's too stupid to have come up with the stuff he knew."

Angela was certain the woman was Robert Durham's secretary.

She heard the other woman sigh over the phone. "The first time I saw Connie, I caught her watching me, so I asked her out one day while she was waiting for the boss to finish up some work. They were going away for the weekend. If I'd made a mistake about her, misread her, she'd say so. She said yes right away, and we met the same night she came back from her trip with him. We went out several times after that."

Angela's mind was still stuck on Connie being bisexual. Another side to Connie she would never have guessed. "Why are you telling me this?"

"Because I'm scared. I think I was the last person to see her alive. Connie had a lot on her mind and was nervous, too. She said she had problems with someone a long time ago. This time, it was different. It had nothing to do with the old guy they have in jail right now. She never mentioned him. I don't think he had anything she needed."

"You were the last person to see her alive?" Angela couldn't believe her ears. "Have you talked to the police? You should be talking to the police, not to me. If you know Jack didn't do this. You need to come forward."

The woman went on as if she hadn't heard Angela. "We always met on the north end of Stange Road. She parked her car in one of the abandoned driveways where an old house used to be. There are a lot of bushes along the road there. You can't see a car parked between them unless you're right in front of it. She was in a strange mood that night. She kept talking about how you just never knew who you could trust. She sometimes liked to vent, so I let her talk. I brought her back from my house around midnight and dropped her off. I didn't see any other cars or anyone else around, but I wasn't expecting to see anyone. We'd done this so many times before. It was no big deal." She paused. "I pulled into the driveway next to her car. After she got out, I left. No one drove in while I was going out. There must have been another driveway or pullout farther down. I'm convinced someone was out there, waiting."

Angela pictured the scene. There sure was a high level of activity at the refuge that night, which surprised her.

The woman continued. "Connie and I were afraid my headlights stopping out there might draw attention to us. I always made it look like someone took the wrong road and turned around. That's why I didn't wait to see her get into her car. I didn't think anyone else knew about us. There was no reason to be overly cautious or worried."

The woman's voice broke. "I wish I had stayed. Maybe she'd be okay. The paper said someone killed her about the same time I dropped her off." Angela heard a sniff, and the woman blew her nose. "Whoever was out there must have seen me, too."

"I don't understand."

Her speech slowed as if she was thinking out loud. "Someone saw us together. It's the only way anyone would know about me. Now, I'm pretty sure the person who killed her is coming after me. They must think I saw something that night. Do you understand?"

"What do you mean, they're coming after you? How? You need to go to the cops, not me."

"I'd go to the cops, but they might think I killed her. Besides, she used to have something going on with one of those guys. I don't trust any of them. One of them could have done this. I hoped if you knew my story, you could convince them to keep looking." Her voice faltered.

"What makes you think someone is after you?"

"Connie bought a new perfume to wear just for me. She wore it every time we met. I found one of her blouses on the gate next to my garbage can yesterday morning when I put the trash out. The blouse was just lying there. I could smell the perfume on it. I didn't know what to think or do, so I took it back into the house, stuffed it into a plastic bag, and hid it in the garage."

The woman stopped talking again. Someone who had access to Connie's belongings left the blouse for a reason. It had to be someone who knew intimate details of Connie's life. The police already had a suspect. The woman was probably right. Whoever murdered Connie must think the woman saw something to incriminate them. Could it be a cop? They had access to Connie's belongings.

"Your garbage can is an odd place to put the blouse. What if you hadn't seen it? It might have blown away or been picked up by the garbage service before you found it. Do you usually take your trash out every day?"

"Yeah, so what?"

"Never skip a day?"

"No."

"It explains someone knowing you'd find the blouse when you did. You may be under surveillance. Be careful. Please. Your best chance is to go to the police right away. Even if you don't trust them."

The line was quiet for a few moments. Was Connie's killer a serial murderer, and was this woman the next target? This was crazy.

Most likely, the killer was a jealous lover. It made sense. Catching your lover with someone could send you over the edge. This woman might not care if Connie was faithful, but someone else might. Gilbert said Connie could really mess with a person's mind. It wouldn't matter if you were a man or a woman. Emptying an entire clip into someone at close range was a brutal way to commit murder. It spoke of passion and jealousy. It could explain why the murderer turned his or her attention to the other woman.

"Connie's blouse might provide some evidence to catch the killer," Angela continued. "Get it to the police. Today."

"I told you I don't want to go to the police. I need your help."

"I don't have any way to help you. If you don't go, I'll give them your phone number. You'll have to come forward."

The woman laughed. "You think I used my phone? This is one of Connie's phones."

Angela wanted to grab the woman and shake her. "You have to talk to the police. I can't help you."

The line was quiet.

"Are you still there?"

The woman had hung up.

SEVENTEEN

ANGELA POUNDED HER HAND ON THE STEERING wheel in frustration before pulling a piece of paper from the glove box. She made a few notes. What was wrong with this woman? She knew she could be in danger, so why did she refuse to help herself?

If this woman was Connie's lover, Connie might have had other female lovers. The list of suspects just doubled.

Angela knew she had to call Danny or Det. Lane, but wanted time to think. Talking to Danny would be easier since he was her law enforcement officer. She drove to the store and grabbed a shopping cart before starting down the aisles.

Susan had given her a list of people. There was Mrs. Theresa Bradley, who had been so bitter toward Connie. Maybe she wasn't jealous of a husband or boyfriend. She might be envious of Connie's success. Or Connie involved her in a scheme and had double-crossed her. Angela had to get back home to re-check the list. She hadn't fully considered all the females on it.

She finished her shopping before calling Danny from her car. He picked up on the fourth ring and sounded distracted. Angela told him about the phone call. She gave him the phone number, explaining it was supposed to be a phone Connie owned. She also told him she suspected the woman might be Robert Durham's secretary.

"Det. Lane thought you might help by picking up any information at meetings, but I don't like you receiving calls at home."

"It was on my landline," Angela informed him, "so she probably found my number from the phone book. I'm listed there. Anyone can find me." She hoped it was true.

Danny continued. "Someone knows you're asking questions." He paused. "She found Connie's blouse at her gate? That could mean the killer had or has access to Connie's home. The blouse is evidence."

"I told the woman to take it to the police right away. I don't think she will because she said Connie had a relationship with a cop. The woman doesn't trust them. She thinks the cops will accuse her of the murder or that one of them killed Connie."

"I'll give this information to Det. Lane. If any other information pops up, or the blouse turns up, don't do anything, don't even touch it, just call me. Okay?"

Angela chewed her lip. "Danny, do you think a cop could be involved?"

"You have no idea who or what kind of woman this is that called you, Angela," Danny warned. "Even if Connie had an affair with a cop, it doesn't mean a cop killed her. Don't jump to conclusions."

"Have you found anything new to help Jack?"

"We're on it, Angela. Is that everything you have to tell me? I don't mean to be short with you, but I'm at home, working on some other information we received. I'll give this information to Det. Lane. I have to go."

Angela had nothing else to share, but she felt much better after talking to Danny. It sounded like they were still seriously investigating the case. She knew Danny would make sure Det. Lane would do something with this new information. Now, she knew they must have doubts about Jack's guilt.

Her conversation with the woman opened up some questions for Angela as well. Like, who would have access to Connie's closet? Angela shook her head. Almost any lover.

THE NEXT MORNING, ANGELA WAS READY TO LOOK AT HOUSES with Lilly. She might get some information from Dwayne Palmer about Connie's lovers. She went upstairs to give LJ a goodbye kiss.

"Lilly will be here in a few minutes. I'm going with her to look at houses."

LJ turned from his screen. "Is she moving?"

"I think she just wants to see what's out there." It wasn't a complete lie. "The old house she lives in is big without her husband Harry, who passed away over a year ago. I'd imagine she gets pretty lonely." That was probably true.

"Let me know if you see anything interesting. There might be something I can add to this software program."

"Absolutely." Angela went down to the kitchen to clean up the breakfast dishes. She'd just finished when Lilly pulled into the driveway. She grabbed her jacket, called goodbye to LJ, and jumped in Lilly's car.

They gossiped about the refuge on the drive to Fremont.

"Looks like Ed is interested in one of the other volunteers," Lilly said. "Her name is Melody. I dare say she is causing him to act like a schoolboy."

Angela smiled. Jack told her Ed had been alone for a long time. It was good he found someone who shared his interests at the refuge. "He's distracted. That explains the unwashed pots and unlabeled seeds," Angela said. She explained to Lilly how angry Jack had been with him.

"Jack ought to know better than to be cross with Ed, especially since he's putting his life on the line for his lady friend. A little hypocritical, I'd say. Here we are." Lilly put on her blinker. She pulled up in front of several model homes. The first home had a small office in its garage.

A young woman greeted them, inviting them to look through the floor plans.

"Is Mr. Palmer here?" Angela asked.

"He's unlocking the other houses now. He'll be right back."

They picked up brochures detailing the floor plans, running their hands over the carpet, cabinet, and countertop samples on display.

"A two-bedroom, two-bath might fit my downsizing plans," Lilly commented to Angela, "I want to see all the models just in case."

Angela winked, giving Lilly a broad smile. "Good idea. Take your time."

Dwayne breezed in the doorway. He was in his usual attire of a polyester polo shirt, flared-leg pants in light blue, and white patent leather loafers. He was so 1970s. "Angela, good to see you. You're interested in one of my homes?"

"Actually, this is Lilly Weathers, my friend. She's interested. I'm just tagging along."

Dwayne took Lilly's hand in both his as he leaned into her. Angela recognized the typical Dwayne sales schmooze. He always managed to have his hands on a woman, one way or another. "Have you looked through the samples? Are you ready to take a look at the homes themselves?"

Lilly smiled brightly. "I sure am."

They walked through a door into the first of several homes, giving Lilly his full attention and discussing his properties' superior construction and design.

Angela followed. "Do you know anything about the Ottawa River mitigation the LECOS are pushing? I'm supposed to comment on an environmental assessment for a project near the river. I'm trying to figure out what else is going on."

Dwayne glanced back at her, frowning. "I don't have any work in the Ottawa River area. Not this year. Can't help ya."

He led them through the minimally appointed, single-story home. "What do you think of this space, Lilly?" They walked through a large living room, dining room, and kitchen space. No one had bothered to stage any furniture here to improve the presentation. Placing a chair or two in the room might have made it more interesting.

"This open concept allows you to enjoy family gatherings or keep an eye on a ballgame while cooking."

Angela jumped in. "Well, it helps to know you don't have any work there. What did you think of the last LECOS meeting?"

Dwayne didn't respond. He was watching Lilly in hopes of making a sale.

"It was one hell of a meeting, wasn't it?" Angela continued. "Susan couldn't control it. Of course, you heard about Connie's death, didn't you?"

"Hell, yes, I heard about it." He turned to look at Angela, his eyes wide. "Terrible thing to happen to her. The paper said someone from your refuge murdered her. I can't believe it. She was such a sweet thing."

Angela hid her impatience by taking a breath before responding. "No one from the refuge murdered her. The paper is incorrect. They got it wrong."

"Oh?" He returned his focus to Lilly again and led her into the kitchen. "We only install high-end finishes and appliances in our homes. What do you think of the flooring? Of course, we have several options for you to choose from, including under-floor heating."

Angela bit her tongue. She didn't want to waste too much time defending the refuge. She followed them through the house.

"I thought I heard they arrested someone at your refuge," Dwayne said over his shoulder. "I guess I misunderstood."

"They arrested an innocent man." What else could she say? She chose to deflect. "I heard Connie had a lot of boyfriends. I wonder if the killer was a jealous lover or something. What do you think? You seem pretty savvy when it comes to women."

Angela's compliment hit the mark. He turned away from Lilly and looked at Angela with a knowing smile. "Oh, yeah, I think I know a few things about women," he winked at her. "You know, I could see someone getting jealous over her but enough to kill her? I don't know. If it were me, I'd kill the guy she was doing it with, not her."

"Do you know who she was doing?" Angela asked, using Dwayne's terms.

He chuckled. "Well, Connie was pretty open about dating men who belonged to other women. She had brass, for sure. Someone must have decided they didn't like it."

"Well, that's just it. As open as Connie was about everything, no one knows who she was dating recently."

"I don't know." Dwayne puffed out his cheeks and blew air through his lips. "People might know things. That doesn't mean they'll name names. That's different. People run their mouths off about a lot of stuff until they think there's trouble brewing. They don't want to be involved."

He turned back to Lilly, leading her into a hallway. "We build our homes with wide hallways. They make the whole house feel larger. And, of course, we have the same custom cabinets in the bathrooms as in the kitchen. Do you like the carpet here?"

"Lovely." Lilly turned and put her hand on Dwayne's arm. "Did you ever date this woman Connie you're talking about? I've seen pictures of her in the paper. You would have made a striking couple," Lilly said.

Dwayne put his hand on Lilly's shoulder. "You know, I asked her out once. She told me she was in a serious relationship, though I'm not sure she wanted to be with the guy. She didn't act like she wanted to say no if you catch my drift." He winked at Lilly.

"Oh, my. Yes, I do understand. I'd have difficulty saying no to you if I were younger," Lilly said straight-faced, opening her eyes wide.

Angela nearly choked. Dwayne ate it up, pulling Lilly's arm through his and smiling at her.

Lilly continued. "She must have been in a bad situation."

Dwayne nodded. "Could be. You never know with a woman like her. She attracted trouble."

Angela's eyebrows shot up. "Was Connie in abusive relationships or something?"

He was silent a moment before he went on. "No, not abusive. I mean, well, you know, Connie came on to me pretty heavy sometimes, like she was lonely or sad. Like the guy wasn't taking care of her needs, you know?"

The smirk on his face made Angela's stomach turn—Dwayne's version of sympathy.

Dwayne continued. "Of course, I know better than to take advantage of a woman involved with someone else. A woman like Connie needs a lot of handling. I have too much going on to get tangled up with another man's business, especially when his business involves a high-maintenance woman."

Dwayne went back into salesman mode, leading Lilly into one of the bedrooms. "This home has two bedrooms with large and private bathrooms. Optional jetted tubs if you like."

Angela tapped his arm. "You never asked Connie who the guy was?"

"Oh, no, never thought it was important." He was waiting to see if Lilly liked the two rooms.

Lilly asked, "Is there a powder room, or will my guests have to go through one of the bedrooms to use the loo?"

"On the other side of the house. It's tucked away in the short hallway to the attached garage next to a laundry room."

They spent the next hour touring the other homes. Lilly was marvelous at charming Dwayne. Clearly, Dwayne's vanity biased his view of Connie, making it easy for someone like Connie to manipulate him. Angela noticed Lilly enjoyed doing the same. He'd make an easy patsy.

"What do you think of the houses, Lilly?" Dwayne asked when they finished.

Lilly shook her head. "I don't know. They're all lovely. I need time to think about this. I know my home is too large for me now, but I'm still not sure what I should do. May I keep your brochures, Mr. Palmer?"

"Sure, and Lilly, call me Dwayne." He smiled as he once again cupped both her hands in his. "Call me if you want to see something in Port Clinton."

As we pulled out of the driveway, Lilly snorted. "I hate it when someone talks to me like I'm an old lady. Really! I'm barely sixty-two! The way he held my hands like I was ancient was offensive." She mocked Dwayne's words. "And Lilly, call me Dwayne. Who told him he could call me Lilly? Rather full of himself, isn't he?"

Angela laughed. She turned to take a good look at Lilly. "He was putting on his best salesman pitch for you. By the way, what was the bit about if you were younger, you'd have a hard time saying no to him? I nearly choked. You were sure putting on an act yourself. You had the man in the palm of your hand."

Lilly laughed out loud. "Oh, come on. How was I supposed to react? He sure thinks highly of himself. I couldn't help but play along. I hope I was able to extract more information for you." She checked her rearview mirror, frowning. "Truthfully, his homes are pretty ordinary. I don't like seeing the same flooring and cabinets in a kitchen used in a bathroom. The finishes are okay but not very high-end. It was clear to me even though I haven't been out much. I was disappointed. I heard he built some nice homes over by Perrysburg. I'd hoped these would be smaller versions of those."

"You must be talking about River Gardens. Yeah, he's given several sales presentations on those. From what I saw in his slides, they are unique and expensive," Angela said. "Nothing at all like the homes we saw today."

"Probably a bit out of my price range, you think?"

"I don't know. We could get Dwayne to show us some of those if you'd like."

"Getting a tour of River Gardens might be fun. Do you really think we'll learn more from him?"

Angela shook her head and looked out the side window. "Well, I should prepare better questions if we see him again. I winged it today. I learned more about Dwayne than I did Connie." *One thing was for sure. If he was involved with Connie, he did her bidding. It wasn't the other way around.*

Eighteen

Lilly drove a few minutes in silence. "Instead of going straight home, how would you like to get something to eat in Port Clinton? It'd be nice to chat. We could plan our next step in this investigation."

"Investigation?"

Lilly raised her eyebrows, glancing at Angela. "What do you call it?"

Angela nodded. "I am sort of poking around. What do you have in mind for lunch? Seafood?"

Lilly beamed. "How about some good old-fashioned hamburgers? There's a burger place in Port Clinton I like. They have the best milkshakes!"

Angela's stomach growled. "I'm starving, and that sounds great. Especially the part about the milkshakes."

Instead of heading home, they caught Highway 2 east, making their way to Port Clinton, situated on Lake Erie's south shore. It was a tourist resort town with shopping opportunities and marinas.

"I started the searches on the list of names you gave me," Lilly said. "Nothing you probably don't already know, but I'm still working on it. Now that we're partners, can you bring me up to speed on what you know?"

Angela gathered her thoughts. Lilly could be a great help. Angela told Lilly the information she'd collected but stopped short of filling Lilly in on the phone call from the unknown woman. She didn't want to pull her in too deeply or endanger her. Still, it was good to have Lilly's help today with Dwayne. Someone Angela did not fear. She seriously doubted a goofy guy like Dwayne would murder Connie.

"I'm trying to work out Connie's connections with developers like Dwayne, who worked on projects with her. Even though he was involved with Connie, it doesn't seem as though he had anything new planned with her. He certainly didn't feel any animosity toward her."

"You're kidding," Lilly scoffed. "Those two working together? Despite what he said, I don't see him as the type of man who would attract a woman like Connie."

"Exactly what I thought," Angela gazed out her window, "Yes, they did work together frequently. I just don't know in what capacity."

"They must have gotten something from each other," Lilly said. "They both strike me as people who would only do good things for the environment for profit. I can't see how Jack had anything to do with them. Like you, I didn't know he knew Connie, so there may be quite a few things we don't see."

"Jack only knew her because she was dating his boss. She was afraid of someone. That's why he tried to help her by giving her a gun. How was he to know how stupid his actions were?"

"I know Jack may be many things, but stupid isn't one of them," Lilly said. "She must have had a good story. It couldn't have been anything else. Jack loved his wife, bless her soul. Besides, Connie wasn't his type. Jack's not a philanderer or a murderer. He has a big heart for anyone in a bad way."

Angela watched as corn and soybean fields flew past. Green shoots were still only about a foot high, but it was only June. By July, the soybeans would fill out, and the corn would shoot to the sky, along with the heat and humidity.

"Do you know whether the police might be looking at anyone else?" Lilly asked. "Or are they convinced it's Jack? They should check out this Palmer fellow if he had business dealings with her. I'd bet her death had something to do with these development projects."

Lilly stopped speaking while a red sportscar passed her, doing way over the speed limit. "Too fast for this road. Crazy people. Where was I? Oh, I remember reading about some drama with one of the developments a councilman in Toledo was backing strongly. The project would destroy some important habitat along the Maumee River. Environmentalists challenged him about his support from every direction, but he held firm. The *Toledo Blade* looked like a tabloid for a while, filled with the story of the council member getting divorced. It was the first time I read about Connie King. She was allegedly involved with the councilman I just mentioned. No one had any proof, just gossip. I can't remember his name. By the time his wife left him, his political career was ruined."

"Gilbert told me about it. From what he told me, there were others. That may have happened while River Gardens was under development. Yeah, Connie had a lot going on in her life, and now she's taking down our Jack." Angela balled her fists. "Damn it, Lilly. Even in death, she's ruining lives."

"It looks that way," Lilly responded.

They stopped at the burger joint, ordering burgers, fries, and chocolate milkshakes made from hand-scooped ice cream. They stuffed their faces for the first few minutes, then settled down to a slower eating pace.

Angela wiped her hands on a napkin, sipped her shake, and leaned back in the booth with a sigh. "I'd like to take you into my confidence. I don't want anyone else to know what I'm about to suggest."

Lilly stopped chewing, looking at Angela with her eyebrows raised. She wiped her mouth. "My lips are sealed." She pressed her lips together so hard it made Angela laugh.

"Danny is working on the case with the Ottawa County detective. He has asked for my help. Sort of. They want me to tell them about unusual things that happen at meetings. Things like that. I gave them information about all the groups Connie was involved with. If I remember anything relevant, he's asked me to let him know. I can't interfere with their investigation, but I can do more to help them. More than just standing by and waiting for things to happen."

"Like what we did today?" Lilly asked. "Do you have other activities in mind? I already started looking at the list of names you gave me. If you give me the companies involved, I can expand my search to do financial checks on them. I have a few tricks up my sleeve to find more information."

"That sounds interesting, but it would be difficult for me to explain how I happened to learn that kind of information at a meeting." Angela leaned forward on the table. Lilly leaned in toward her.

"I don't know how I could do more. I go to meetings where I associate with a lot of the same people Connie knew," Angela said in a low voice. "If I ask a few questions like I did today with Dwayne, I might be able to shed some light on something to take some of the heat off Jack. I might even discover other people who'd have a motive to kill Connie."

"You'd have to be careful." Lilly finished her meal. She wiped the frost from her metal milkshake canister before pouring the rest into her glass.

"I don't want either of us to end up hurt or dead. Someone killed once and could do it again, especially if provoked." Angela finished her milkshake, sucking air with the straw.

"I did learn a couple of new things about his relationship with Connie today. Things Det. Lane might find useful." She nodded as if making a decision. "You might be able to find out stuff I can't. Except for Dwayne, no one knows who you are. If there's an opportunity, you can sit in on some of the meetings I attend. Don't acknowledge me—just listen. What do you think?"

"I'm in. It sounds like fun. Let me know the date and time for the next meeting, and I'll be there." She looked around, pushing her plate away. "I'm stuffed. How about a cup of coffee? The place isn't busy, and I could use some caffeine now."

"Perfect."

Lilly called the waiter over. They both ordered coffee as he cleared the table.

"I know you said you've never bought a house before," Angela said, changing the subject. "Didn't you move around quite a bit in the Air Force? Are you serious about buying something or just looking to help me?"

"I don't know. Right now, I'm sizing up my house. I have a ton of stuff I need to clear out. I'm sorting through things. I guess I was looking forward to some feminine company today. Hanging out with Jack and Ed every weekend is a bit much since I spend all week at the refuge with them. It's time for me to broaden my circle of friends. Looking at houses today has made me think about selling my house. In the meantime, we can keep looking at open houses whether I decide to sell or not. It's fun." She smiled.

"Yes, we can keep looking. Aside from cross-examining Dwayne, it was fun to get out with you."

Lilly smiled. "Thanks for inviting me along today. I guess I'm just not sure what I should do. A lot of my friends are scattered across the country. I don't have much family left. None who live here anyway. I have the refuge, but I want something else." She looked out the window. Angela let the quiet grow between them, giving Lilly time to have her thoughts.

When Lilly spoke again, she was more resolved. "I know one thing for sure. I don't want to stay in my big old house alone. It's not like Harry and I ever planned to live there forever. We were stuck in a rut. We'd always talked about moving to another part of the country. I want to have new adventures. I'm not dead yet."

The waiter brought the coffee. They sipped the excellent brew quietly, sharing another comfortable silence.

Lilly dropped Angela off just after two o'clock. She popped into LJ's office. He was still on the computer. "Have you eaten?" No response. "Want me to make you something?"

He nodded absent-mindedly. Angela went downstairs, made two tuna fish sandwiches for him, poured a cold glass of milk, and put it on a tray. Then she pulled him from his work to chat with her.

"You have my full attention," he said through a mouthful.

"There wasn't anything new in the houses we looked at today you would want to add to your program. Dwayne could probably use your help with some designs." She laughed. Angela told him about her trip with Lilly. She didn't bring up her conversation with Dwayne. LJ took a large gulp of the milk, shoving the rest of the first sandwich into his mouth. Angela saw him glance at his computer.

"What are you working on?" she asked.

"I've inserted a sizing tool. The user enters certain square foot measurements. The program computes the scale of the house and automatically sizes stairwells or other structures to fit. If the stairwell or structure doesn't meet standard codes, it prevents the procedure. I'm trying to add a self-help step to correct the issue for the user, you know, how to change the scale of a project to fit stairs." He took another bite of his second sandwich and chewed.

"Too bad you didn't see anything new today." He looked at his computer screen, again, completely distracted. Angela left him at his work. She called Danny from downstairs.

Danny answered on the first ring, and she told him about the house-hunting trip she took with Lilly. "From what Dwayne said, it looks like Connie had problems."

"Good point. I'll give Det. Lane the information."

"Okay, but keep me informed, will you? I'm worried about Jack."

"I understand, Angela. I'll touch base with you next week."

She hung up, feeling pretty good. The more information she found, the more likely she would get Jack off the hook one way or another.

THAT EVENING, ANGELA AND LJ WENT OUT to dinner at one of the seafood restaurants in Port Clinton. She grabbed LJ's hand as they walked in. "This restaurant is my favorite. I can pig out on great food. I get to dress up, too."

LJ smiled. "I agree on both counts." LJ chose one of the tables on an outside deck jutting out from the shoreline over Lake Erie. A light breeze ruffled the tablecloths. Wind chimes tinkled somewhere.

Angela smoothed her dress after she sat down, tucking it slightly to keep the breeze from turning into a Marilyn Monroe moment. She reached out and touched LJ's hand. "You sure are in a happy mood tonight. You must have made a lot of progress on your project."

A waitress appeared promptly, taking their orders and pouring Catawba wine.

"The project is finished. I'm a week early on the deadline. That means I have another trip to Chicago next week to review the results with the client. Because I finished quickly, this contract will include a bonus with my final check. How do you like them apples?"

As LJ talked about his next project, Angela was distracted by the beauty around them. Lake Erie was restless—small whitecaps formed on its surface. The light of a full moon pushed a jagged path across it. The movement of water gave her a sense of disquiet. After a glass of wine, she wanted to forget all her worries.

Their food arrived, and LJ was laughing about something. Angela pulled her attention back to him. Afterward, they each took another glass of wine and strolled along the shoreline board-walk in front of the restaurant. Leaning on the wet, wooden rail, she listened to the wind, putting her arm through LJ's. A raft of waterfowl floated past them, their dark bodies clustered together, bobbing in the waves under the moonlight.

LJ was far away, so she took advantage of the quiet between them to let her thoughts consume her.

What if the Sheriff never cleared Jack? Would Connie claim her last victim? What was Lilly doing tonight? Was she alone?

Nineteen

The next morning, Angela met Gilbert at the office. She rode out to the marsh with Gilbert to look at the levee maintenance work the crew had done.

Gilbert was a great supervisor. The crew kept the levees mowed frequently enough to prevent the growth of shrubs. Without constant mowing, the roots from the bushes created holes in the dike. The holes invited burrowing animals to dig dens. Regular maintenance kept wildlife from destroying the levees' function to hold water to create habitat *inside* the diked area.

When they finished the levee work, they would start spraying to control purple loosestrife on the edge of the marshes. Loosestrife is pretty but has no wildlife value. It quickly takes over, crowding out other beneficial plants. Pearl had mapped the size of areas with the highest purple loosestrife infestations. Area mapping would make it easy to monitor the effectiveness of the spray treatments from one year to the next. It also made it easier for her volunteers to find the areas to spray with herbicide.

Angela watched Gilbert talk with the crew. He worked well with his staff, who respected his knowledge and expertise. As he walked with them, he indicated several areas of concern, one of which was the end of a pond that had suffered severe erosion from wave action. Gilbert instructed his crew to order more fill dirt, landscape fabric, and rock to armor those areas.

As he got into the truck with her, Angela told him her startling discoveries about Connie. Was it something he knew about? If so, he might enlighten Angela about Connie's relationships. "Did you know Connie was bisexual?"

Gilbert laughed. "Whoa! What the heck are you saying? Are you kidding me?"

"No. Did you know?" she asked.

He stared at her for a few moments with raised eyebrows.

"What? I didn't make it up."

Gilbert started the truck while she told him about talking to the unknown woman, careful to omit details surrounding the perfumed blouse Danny asked her not to disclose. Angela realized how easy it was to talk to Gilbert about anything.

"I just find it hard to believe," he said. "Connie never said anything about having feelings toward women. Why would your caller make something like that up?"

"I don't think she did. I think Connie was involved in a con game, taking both sexes to the laundry." Angela shrugged. Connie took the clothes off their back, more or less. "I wonder what Connie's bank account looked like."

"Beats me, but she always dressed nicely and liked doing expensive things. She liked other people to pay for everything. Hell, she didn't just like it. She expected it." Gilbert turned toward her. "Angela, I can't believe she was bisexual. I mean, it's no big deal if she was. I guess I feel stupid because I never knew."

"There was more to Connie than most people knew. You didn't pick up on that at all?"

Gilbert sighed. "No. I didn't. I'll do some checking around. Does Danny know what you're doing?"

"He does. He asked me to help." She looked away, not wanting to explain further. "Jack didn't murder Connie. I don't think Det. Lane or Danny are convinced of Jack's guilt. The problem is that the only evidence they have points to him. I can't let this drop. I don't care who killed her, as long as the police know it's not Jack. So far, I've given them information they would never have found on their own."

Angela looked at Gilbert. "And if you're going to check around, let Danny know. He's working from his house this week."

When Angela returned to the office, she went to see Pearl. She was working with Jim on data entry. Slumped in an office chair, Jim's tall frame stretched under the desk at an angle, his jeans tucked into his duck boots. He wore a headset to listen to music as his fingers clicked on the keyboard at lightning speed while he viewed the datasheet page on the desk. His blond hair was a stark contrast to his dark brown eyebrows, highlighting blue eyes. His button-up sweater reminded her of Mr. Rogers.

Angela was glad to see Jim had recovered from the discovery of the body. He'd only missed a day last week. It had been less than a week since they found Connie, but it felt much longer. Angela fist-bumped him when she came into the room. "Do you have drawings you'd like to share? We have a volunteer recognition display board in the front office. Let's frame some of your works and put them on that board to highlight you as a volunteer. I think people would find it interesting. It would also begin to establish your name as an artist."

Jim smiled. "I'd love that."

"I'll talk to Sally Griffin when she returns. Think about pulling a few pieces together you'd like to show."

Pearl was at a table on the other side of the office, using a computer with a larger screen to create a distribution map of the areas surveyed for frogs. Color-coded data points indicated the different frog species. The map visually interpreted the raw data to show where the largest populations of frogs, by species, were found on the refuge. This map would be an invaluable tool for future habitat management decisions. Angela was impressed.

"I didn't know we did all that. The maintenance guys will finish the levee by the end of the week," Angela said. "Will you have the herbicide in time to start spraying?"

"No problem," Pearl glanced at her. "I put the order in last week. They said it would be here in ten days. They should call me soon for a pickup."

"I approved your order for grass seed and plants, too. Good luck with this. Jim, will you be helping out?"

"Yeah, since Jack isn't here, Ed is taking over the greenhouse. I'll lend a hand a little longer. Have you heard any more news about the murder? Do they have any solid evidence on Jack?"

"I'm afraid they have enough to hold him. They need more time. I'm hoping they find new evidence." She shook her head. "I'll go check in with Ed."

It was good to know Ed had stepped up to take on Jack's responsibilities. She found him outside the greenhouse, where he had just finished putting together a bench.

"Try it out with me, Angela. It's pretty comfortable." He patted the space next to him. "This one will go out on the trail by Pool One."

She sat next to him. "Great job. I'm glad you're here today. I haven't had a chance to chat with you. I hear you have a girlfriend."

Ed beamed. "She volunteers for Sally, your Visitor Services Chief. Her name is Melody Parker. We've gone on a couple of dates now." He blushed slightly.

"Cool. What's nice is that you have a common interest here on the refuge." Angela looked away. She sensed Ed was too shy to say much more about Melody. "Thanks for covering for Jack. This whole situation is a mess. He was just trying to help Connie. Now he's trying to help another woman." It occurred to Angela that Jack attracted broken women to him. Was she one of them?

"Yeah. After our fight at Lilly's, he sat down and told us the whole story. Jack said he was an emotional mess when he met the King woman." Ed looked into the woods. "He told me lots of women can't seem to settle with a man. They go from one to the

next. Jack thinks Connie King wasn't necessarily a bad person—
she was just looking for something. Unfortunately, she didn't know
what she was looking for, so she never found it. Instead, she went
too far. One of those greedy people who never get enough."

"I think you guys are kind. I'm not sure Connie deserved your
charity."

Ed turned back to look at Angela. "Jack was a soft touch for
such a tough guy. I guess I am, too, depending on the situation."

Angela could see Jack had been an easy target for Connie. A
chance relationship could end up taking his life along with hers.

As if sensing her thoughts, Ed commented. "I guess you think
he was pretty stupid. I think Jack thought he could save her. You
know, I saw her once after Jack tried to help her. She was with the
other woman on the land trust. What are they called? Lions? She
looked pretty happy and not scared at all."

Angela put her hand on Ed's shoulder. "I don't think Jack was
stupid. I'm just surprised he was so compassionate toward her.
You said you saw her with another woman. Are you talking about
Susan Worth with LECOS?"

"That might have been her name. I'm not sure. She came to
meet with you last year during Wildlife Refuge Week. Anyway, I
remembered her."

Angela described Susan. Ed confirmed it was the same woman.

"Susan was Connie's business partner." Angela was disappointed. Susan not only had an alibi for the time Connie was
murdered, but she was the one who counteracted Connie's inflam-
matory statements, excusing her for being passionate. Susan was
never involved with the developers. Like Theresa Bradley, she was
connected to the Toledo City Council, had a stellar reputation,
and was known for her ability to work with a diversity of people.
She was active in community welfare programs and had taken on
co-chair with Connie upon the Mayor's request. She was also well
known for other charitable endeavors through the years.

Unfortunately, Connie had managed to pull the wool over

Susan's eyes. Angela wasn't close enough to Susan to presume to open them. "Was she with anyone else?"

"No, just the woman from LEOS or LECOS, whatever you called it. They were laughing a lot. It looked like they were good friends." He couldn't tell her much more, so she changed the subject. They ended the conversation by talking about the greenhouse.

Susan had said she didn't socialize with Connie. She was closer to Connie than she'd admitted from what Ed said.

Even though she wasn't a likely suspect, Angela put Susan on her list. In any case, she'd do a little more checking on her.

TWENTY

Tuesday morning, Susan called to give Angela information about Connie's funeral. The family would gather at a funeral home in Monroe, Michigan, where Connie's brother lived.

Angela would attend in uniform to show support for Susan.

"I think it'll be a nice touch to show Connie's connection with the environmental community," Susan responded warmly. "Thank you, Angela. I really appreciate it."

After Susan called, Angela picked up the phone again. She couldn't let go of confirming who the unknown woman who had called her was. She repeated the calls she'd made the previous week. She hoped she could recognize the woman's voice if she answered. When she called Robert Durham's office, there was no answer. Angela would try later. She went onto the LECOS website to look at photos. There were several pictures of meetings. Connie was in almost every one of them. Remarkable.

Angela looked at people's expressions in the photos, trying to find hidden meanings in a glance or a gesture. There wasn't anyone glaring at Connie. And, there was no sign of any woman looking at her flirtatiously.

Okay, don't be stupid.

She put her thoughts aside and made a few calls to reach some of the people on the list she hadn't contacted earlier. After several calls, she didn't learn much more.

Either no one was interested, or no one wanted to be connected to Connie in any way. Who could blame them? Connie's death was a merciful release if they had anything to hide. Angela could relate.

With a click of the mouse, she closed the website. Out her window, a group of people walked toward the front door of the building. Something had them animated. The door opened to loud voices and the argument that brought them indoors. Wearing backpacks, they had binoculars hanging from their necks. Birders. They must have found something new. She decided to go to the lobby to see what it was.

When she entered the room, they had just asked Kate if the refuge had a certain bird book they could use to look something up. Kate directed them to Angela, who led them to the resource library in the adjacent room.

Two of the birders were arguing about a sighting. The rest of the group listened while they flipped through their bird identification field guides.

Ah, the fine art of birdwatching. Folks who didn't do it believed it must be a relaxing, if not an utterly boring pastime. It was a competitive sport for some people. Birders kept lists of sightings. Some kept a life list that included every bird they'd ever seen. They were always looking for a new sighting. Some people tried to accrue as many sightings as possible each year, competing with others and themselves to beat the previous year's record. Today, the argument was about what species of flycatcher they had seen.

"Couldn't you see the difference in the length of the beak?"

"It was just the lighting. There was no difference in the length of the beaks. They were both Willows."

"I'm telling you, one of them was an Alder."

One of the people in the group spoke up. "I did hear a *fitz-bew* call."

The two birders arguing gave the woman a wilting look, and she moved away from them sheepishly. Angela invited them to sit. No one listened, so she returned to her office. The argument continued, as it likely would all day.

The funeral was on Friday morning. Angela attended the service with Gilbert, who insisted they sit in the back of the room. As they went to their seats, Angela looked around at everyone. Connie's brother hadn't made arrangements for a reception afterward, so this was her only chance to learn about the people who surrounded Connie.

"Did you see Jack this week?" Gilbert asked.

"Yeah. He's not thriving. That's for sure." Angela had visited Jack again on Wednesday. He wasn't talkative. She knew the jail environment was getting to him. He was in dire need of some time in the outdoors. It made her all the more determined to clear him.

Angela nudged Gilbert. "Does anyone look like they're related to Connie?"

She received a baleful stare from Gilbert as he mouthed, "Like, I would know?" There were a large number of people at the service.

"Susan's boyfriend, maybe?" Angela nodded toward Susan, standing with a man she did not know.

Angela received a shrug from Gilbert and a frown. "I'm not interested in who is here, Angela," he whispered. "I have a lot of work to catch up on when I get back to the refuge. I hope you don't think I'm insensitive, but you made me come."

"You didn't meet any of her family when you went out with her?" she asked.

Gilbert shot her a "You have to be kidding" look.

"Okay, but you are my assistant manager, second in command. It's appropriate we both represent the refuge. It has nothing to do with your past relationship."

Angela took another look around the room. She was very interested in who was present.

Susan wore a dark brown dress with black trim, black shoes, and tan gloves. Who wore gloves anymore? Somehow, they suited Susan. She was so proper. The cut of her dress was simple yet expensive. Susan didn't seem to be uncomfortable even though it was warm. In fact, she looked cool as a cucumber. The man with her appeared distant from Susan. She held his arm. A possible boyfriend? Someone from the city council?

Connie's ashes were in an elegant golden urn, befitting Connie's lifestyle. The memorial service lasted over an hour while her family told stories of her childhood. Her parents talked about a loving daughter who always called and shared holidays. Two friends from high school talked about an ambitious, shy teen who wanted to become an actress.

Angela found it hard to visualize Connie in this family picture. This version of Connie was a Big Sister who had mentored two young women through high school, helping one win a full scholarship to college. It surprised Angela that Connie had maintained her friendship with high school chums. Her brother talked about a big sister who helped him with homework and with girls. Connie remembered her parents' birthdays with handmade gifts and expensive dinners.

This was not the Connie she knew.

Connie's mother was well dressed but not in Connie's cutting-edge style.

Where did Connie get her looks? Her mother was short and stout, with graying brown hair. The father might have offered more genetic possibilities, but his complexion was dark. His build was square and muscular, similar to that of his wife. This man had muscles born of hard work.

Angela couldn't find a trace of the fair-haired sliver of a woman in either parent. Nor could she see evidence of old money. They looked like reliable, middle-class people. Her brother Donald bore a strong resemblance to his father. Could Connie have been adopted?

Gilbert leaned toward her. "Do you know anyone here? I mean, other than Susan?"

Gilbert's observation was a good one. There was no one from any of Connie's environmental groups.

When the brother spoke, he was distraught and had difficulty controlling his emotions. She'd try to catch him at the end of the funeral to offer condolences. He might tell her something she didn't know in this emotional state.

Someone brutally killed Connie and dumped her in a ditch. Someone murdered the Connie that Angela knew, not the Connie she heard about today. There had to be someone else in this room who knew the person Angela knew. She'd start with the brother. He had to know something he wouldn't share at a time like this.

Looking around, she saw Det. Lane standing at the back of the church during the service. He appeared to be watching everyone. When the service ended, Angela looked around. Det. Lane was nowhere to be seen.

She caught up with Connie's brother as he was leaving. "Donald King?"

He walked away from the building, crossing the grass lawn to a car parked on the street. When she called after him, he turned and came back toward her. "Yes, what can I do for you?"

"I'm Angela Martin. I worked with your sister on a number of occasions. I'm sorry to meet you for the first time under these circumstances."

He just stared at her.

"I was with the deputy when he found her on the refuge."

Some acknowledgment came to his eyes. Still, he said nothing.

"I'd like to talk to you about your sister and share some stories about her work with us."

He answered with anger. "Connie did a lot for you guys out there. Why did your volunteer kill her? I can't make sense of it. The cops have him. I hope he burns in hell."

Angela answered a little too defensively. "I'm not sure they have the right man." She decided not to elaborate. The guy was angry enough.

Donald King looked past Angela toward Gilbert. His face became red with fury. "What the hell are *you* doing here? You have nerve showing your face!"

Gilbert said he had never met any of Connie's family members.

Angela turned to Gilbert when Donald pushed past him toward another man. Donald threw a punch. The guy ducked, clipping his aggressor with an uppercut to the jaw. Spit and blood splattered the sidewalk as the blow knocked Donald sideways.

Gilbert pulled Angela back, stepping in front of her. "Who is that guy?" she asked.

"Bill Jackson. Connie's ex-husband. I didn't see him earlier." Gilbert pushed her farther away to prevent Angela from getting hit.

Det. Lane appeared with another police officer from out of nowhere. Donald stumbled to stand. Gilbert held him while the uniformed officer blocked Jackson from advancing.

"You have no right to be here," Donald shouted.

"I think a husband has every right to attend his wife's funeral."

"Ex-husbands have no rights." Donald pulled free of Gilbert's hold. He straightened his jacket.

"We were never divorced," Jackson said with a broad smile as he dusted off his clothing. "Connie didn't want to bother. I was fine letting it ride."

Bill Jackson wore a well-tailored suit that fit his trim physique well. The gray fabric was smooth with a slight sheen. A gold tie clasp with a sparkling diamond stood out against the black shirt and tie. Angela raised her eyebrows. Maybe her story about finding a tie clip in Connie's belongings wasn't far-fetched. This man, like Connie, knew how to dress to attract attention. Silver-gray hair at his temples gave him a distinguished look. Angela could easily see Grace Kelly or Connie on his arm. He was a class act.

Until he spoke.

"Your sister was a whore."

"That's a lie! She was a good wife to you. You used her. You made her make deals for you when she didn't want to. She tried to please you. All you gave her was your abuse."

"Dear brother, I never hurt the woman in any way. It was the other way around. She got what she wanted from me before she left."

Donald lunged forward. Gilbert reacted in a flash to restrain him.

"Don't you dear brother me. It took Connie a long time to get over what you did to her. You ripped her heart out. Then you dumped her for another broad who did your bidding. Connie is the only reason deals came your way at all . . ." Donald stopped. He looked around as if, for the first time, realizing other people were listening.

He turned back to Jackson. "Get lost. I'm warning you," he said as he stepped forward.

Det. Lane blocked him. "I think this conversation is over. I'll be contacting you, Mr. King. Mr. Jackson? I have some questions for you now." He flashed his badge. "Step over here, please."

Jackson smiled, tipped his head toward Donald King, and walked away with the detective.

Almost everyone who had attended the funeral was gone. Connie's parents stood near a car on the street, waiting for Donald to join them.

"Well, that was one way to end a funeral," Angela said. Susan joined them. Angela learned the man was Susan's brother. Something else she didn't know about Susan.

"That awful man," Susan commented. "What was he doing here?"

"He said he was still Connie's husband," Angela said.

Susan raised her eyebrows. "I wouldn't take his word for much of anything. The man is a liar."

Angela had no response. Gilbert pulled her away to their vehicle. "I have some work to finish this afternoon, so we better get going."

The drive back to the refuge didn't take long. Traffic was light, and Gilbert was talkative.

"I think when I die, I'd like my loved ones to skip the formality of a funeral. Instead, everyone should get together. A barbecue would be great. The topic of conversation should be good music, nothing else. I think a mariachi band would be nice." He looked over at Angela, grinning.

Angela shook her head. "Funerals aren't for the dead. They're for the living. What you desire won't play into it too much." She looked out the window. "I sure learned a lot about Connie today. I had no idea what she had going on in her life. Do you think Bill Jackson was lying about his marriage to Connie? Do you think he's hoping for insurance money or something?"

"I have no idea. You heard Susan say he was a liar." Gilbert put his blinker on to turn into the refuge driveway. "Connie was never predictable or honest, either."

Gilbert parked at the office.

"A mariachi band? Really?" Angela smiled.

Twenty-One

THE NEXT MORNING STARTED BRIGHT AND SUNNY, but another storm was blowing in fast.

Other than Kate, everyone else was in the field finishing fieldwork before the weekend started. Angela returned a few calls before going for a walk. She had a lot on her mind. The funeral saddened her. Angela needed a good stretch of her legs.

The wind blew hard, pushing her forward as she walked along the levee toward Lake Erie. The sky was full of clouds. Instead of the biting cold she had expected, the air was wet, cool, and fresh. A squall line was headed their way, with a colder air mass on its heels. With fury in its girth, the warmer air would pass through first.

Ducks flew up into the air, landing quickly back on the water once she passed. They hugged the shoreline to stay out of the wind. It helped them to conserve energy. Angela heard the calls of Canada geese over the gusts of wind.

Lake Erie looked like the ocean during a wild storm. The water changed from green to blue-green with white caps dancing on its surface, everchanging and fantastic. Angela couldn't immerse herself enough in this landscape. Like the desert, it drew on her spirit.

Trees draped with thick leafy coats, the color of lime to dark green, with a touch of yellow, lined the open pools of water. The sandbar willows clung to the shoreline, grasping their branches around themselves protectively. Although branches creaked in the forceful blasts, they wouldn't break. They had survived many nor'easters. A squall was no match for these woodlands.

Tree sparrows danced in the shrubs near her feet. An immature bald eagle stood on a snag sticking out of the water as the wind ruffled its feathers, exposing patches of white.

Angela's feet flew before her, pushed out from under her by gusts of wind that snatched at her pant legs. She was at the northernmost end of the trail when she looked up to see Tony squatting near the edge of the lake. He stood up.

"Miss Angela. Enjoying yourself?"

Angela walked over to stand by him, partly to hear him over the wind and partly to let his body block some of it. "As a matter of fact, yes, Tony, I am."

"Nothing like a good storm to clear the air," he turned to look directly at her, "and the mind."

His perception startled her. "Yeah. How about you? Are you checking some traps or something?"

"Oh, no. I'm just looking at the wildlife. There's a good balance of plants and open water in the pond behind us. It's going to bring a lot of birds to it. The 'rats are doing a good job. Pearl wants to close this unit to trapping this year. Good idea. She'll probably have a few years to wait before she reopens it."

Angela nodded. The air was brisk. As she stood there, the cold began to seep through her clothing. "Can I ask you something, Tony?"

"I think so." He frowned at her. "Free country, but I might not have an answer."

She smiled. "Do you ever see people around the refuge, on the marshes, doing things that don't fit? Like someone dressed in a suit or nice clothes out on the trails?" Angela shook her head. "I can't seem to say what I mean."

"I know what you mean." He turned away and raised his chin, gazing out onto Lake Erie. "Over by Darby. I see people there sometimes. One man wears pretty white shoes, so I know he ain't there to take a nature walk. He's been over by Darby a couple of times by himself. Most of the time, he has another fella with him. Regular looking guy. Yesterday, I saw him there with a city slicker."

The only man she knew who wore white shoes was Dwayne Palmer. He was most likely planning something if he was sneaking around the edge of the refuge. Was he finishing something Connie started? Who was the city slicker?

"Can you describe any of the men?"

Tony shrugged. "I didn't think much about it. None of them is my kind." Despite his lack of interest in them, he described Dwayne Palmer in great detail, and Angela was sure she recognized Donald King as the 'regular' looking guy. His description of the city slicker had to be either Bill Jackson or Robert Durham. They both had similar dress styles when suited up. But it wouldn't be Bill Jackson if Donald King was there.

Tony continued. "I guess I seen the guy with white shoes at least two or three times this month. He's going out on a piece of land next to Darby. Do you want me to keep track of him, Miss Angela? I could, for you."

His smile was warm, and there was a new twinkle in his eyes. Yes, Tony would probably love to track a person like he did the animals in the marsh.

"No, Tony. What you told me is enough. I have the picture." He nodded. "I guess I better get back to the office. Would you like to come in for a cup of coffee?"

"No, thanks. I'm enjoying the weather." He smiled.

"Then I'll leave you to your business." She turned and leaned into the wind to keep her balance, forcing her feet forward, one after the other. A few steps later, she turned to wave at Tony to say goodbye, but he was gone.

Dwayne Palmer, Donald King, and possibly Robert Durham? What the hell was going on? Det. Lane needed to know about this. Donald behaved as if he didn't know Connie's ex-husband was in town. Tony told a different story. If it was him. More likely, it was Robert Durham Tony had seen.

Waves struck the rocks along the shoreline, spraying her with mist. She hurried her steps. Finally reaching the office, she held her face up to the sky, letting the weather flow over her. Taking one last look at the marshland behind her, she reluctantly entered her brightly lit office.

Angela called Danny to give him a brief update on the funeral, describing who attended and the fight between Bill Jackson, Connie's ex-husband, and her brother, Donald King. "Det. Lane took Jackson aside to question him. I'll be curious to know what he learned."

Danny said, "Interesting. I'll let you know if he mentions anything to me. Not unusual to hear good things about the woman under the circumstances. People don't air their dirty laundry at funerals. I've tried to follow up on her lifestyle. Nothing hits. Other than rumors she dated a lot of guys, she was pretty private about parts of her life."

"No wonder. Connie made deals. Some of those relationships, casual or not, had to stay private, or she'd never get anyone to trust her." She paused. "I did learn something new today." She told Danny what Tony had told her.

"I'll pass it on to Det. Lane. It might mean nothing, though. I think there's some property for sale east of the refuge. I don't think any of those men had a motive to kill Connie King."

Unless she got in their way somehow. "Did the Detective follow up on the woman who called me?"

"Yeah. Durham's secretary denied calling you. If she won't talk, there isn't much we can do," Danny said.

"I'm leaving early today," Angela said. "I'm going to the jail to see Jack. Try to cheer him up. I'll try again to make him tell us the name of the woman he's trying to protect."

"Let us know what you find out."

Angela barely made the 4:30 pm appointment on time. She was only allowed fifteen minutes. Jack still wouldn't give up the woman's name. Angela didn't have the gumption to argue with him. She tried to cheer him up as much as she could. Ed and Lilly had also been in to see him during the week. His age was showing. It only made Angela more determined to find out who killed Connie.

On the way home, she stopped at the beach in Port Clinton. She didn't want to go home yet. The second storm arrived with cold rain. There was a sharp edge to the wind blowing in. This time, Angela walked until she was too tired to go any farther. She turned back toward the parking lot, her short hair blowing all around. Birds darted in and out of the shrubs and trees beyond the sandy beach.

She was sure the answer to who killed Connie was more straightforward than she was making it. It had to be closer to home. Was she spreading the search too far? Wasn't murder usually committed by someone the victim knew well? Wasn't it generally for love or money? There were just too many suspects. Knowing Dwayne Palmer was skulking around the refuge boundaries concerned her. Dwayne was up to something. Had he killed Connie to keep his plans secret? What kind of plans would be dangerous enough to make him murder someone? It didn't make sense. If Dwayne was working on a new deal, Connie was likely involved. What about Susan? Was she up to something? She had to find out more about Susan.

Angela arrived home, driving through the rain, to find LJ asleep in his recliner with a half-eaten sandwich and a glass of milk next to him. She covered him with a throw, picked up the dishes, and headed to the kitchen. Angela finished his sandwich with some cheese, standing at the sink, washing it down with a soda. She fed the cats the milk before heading upstairs for a bath. LJ came up while she was bathing.

"I shut off the lights downstairs. What do you say to an early night?"

"Sounds good." But when Angela's head hit the pillow, sleep was far away. She lay awake for some time thinking about all the crazy relationships people have. How many could result in the kind of passion or fear that killed Connie?

Time was passing. Jack was still in jail. It had been eleven days since they found Connie. Depressed that neither she nor the police had made any headway toward finding Connie's killer, she rolled over and stared at LJ for a while. Could she commit to LJ like Lilly did to Harry?

She rolled over onto her back, staring at the ceiling. Whenever a car went by on the street outside, the headlights would shine through the blinds on the window. The streaks of light would move from one end of the room to the other in a progression as the car passed. Something about that linear progression depressed her.

Lilly talked about having wonderful memories. Now, she wanted to have new adventures—make new memories. Angela was excited for her. Perhaps a little envious?

When Angela finally slept, visions of jealous wives chased her with clubs, guns, and knives. In her dream, her hair was long. It whipped across her face in the wind. Angela woke during the night to the sound of tree branches scraping the house. Poe, her cat, was on her pillow, twitching its tail in her face as it snuggled around her head.

She slipped out of bed quietly, wrapped a robe around her, and crept downstairs.

After she made a cup of cocoa, she sat on the front porch swing in the dark. Protected as she was by the porch, the sound of the wind in the trees was exhilarating. The rain was gone, and the storm rolled its way farther south. Angela watched the branches of the trees sway overhead.

There was much more to learn about the circumstances that led to Connie's murder. What was frightening was that the murderer might know her if he ran in Connie's circles.

The unknown woman caller had figured out she was investigating. Who else might have picked up on it? Dwayne Palmer? She was sure he was up to something. There had to be a way to follow up on Tony's story.

She sat until her cocoa grew cold, and the moist air chilled her to the bone. It was time to get some sleep.

Twenty-Two

ANGELA WOKE UP MORE TIRED THAN the day before. LJ was up before her and had started coffee. They ate breakfast while she told him about the funeral.

"Connie was secretly married? There could be any number of motives for her murder." He leaned back in his chair, holding his cup of coffee. "Have you told Danny?"

"Yes. Of course. Det. Lane was there, so Danny probably knows much more than he's telling me."

They decided to take the day off from weekend chores to enjoy themselves on Lake Erie. A drive to Port Clinton highlighted the brilliant sweep of tree-lined soybean fields. The storm left behind a rain-washed landscape that was fresh and green. The sun sparkled on droplets of water, decorating the trees with fairy lights.

They drove out to the point of Catawba Island to the ferry port. With no wind, Lake Erie was a sheet of glass. The ferry ride to Put-in-Bay on South Bass Island was smooth, with herons flying just above the surface of the water as they traveled to and from nest-building activities on the islands.

Instead of renting a golf cart, the usual mode of transportation on the island, they rented bicycles. They spent the day exploring shops. It had been a while since Angela had ridden a bike. She tired quickly, discovering muscles she hadn't used in a long time.

They sampled the local wines and foods while pedaling from one end of the island to the other. It was one of those glorious, sunny June days on Lake Erie. Sunshine warmed Angela's skin while light breezes kept the air temperatures cool. Tiring as it was, they enjoyed the exercise, pedaling their bicycles in the shade of trees, passing vineyards.

It was sad this verdant atmosphere was so short-lived. They were into summer now, almost July. Within a few short months, the lush, leafy umbrella would begin to pick up the warmer hues of autumn—yellows, reds, and browns.

They stopped to rest in the shade of a tree along the roadway. "I've been thinking about all this life around us, LJ. About the passage of time. About getting old and dying."

"Well, that's cheery. Why in the world are you dwelling on sad thoughts when we're supposed to be out having fun?"

"I'm just thinking about how Connie died."

LJ sighed. He threw his head back with his eyes closed. The road they'd traveled wound up a steep hill. They were lying in the grass on their elbows, watching the world pass by below them.

"I can't help it," Angela said. "I've never been close to this kind of thing before. How does it feel to confront the weakness of our hold on life, knowing we have to give way to it?"

"You think too much sometimes." LJ fell back onto the grass.

"Did Connie let go easily? It didn't look like she put up a fight. Why not? Why did she just sit there? Let someone shoot her, point-blank, in the face?" Angela got goosebumps.

LJ sat up. "What you need is some good strenuous exercise to get all these ideas about death out of your head. Race you to the top of the hill and back down, now!"

He jumped up and onto his bike, leaving Angela in the dust. She jumped up and, try as she might, couldn't catch up to him. He was already coming back down the hill just as she was near the top.

"You better catch up, or I'll eat dinner without you!"

Angela didn't bother with the top of the hill. She turned right there. They raced to the bottom, laughing all the way. She pushed thoughts of Connie and death out of her mind. Instead, she focused on the physical exertion of pedaling. She let it clear her mind, allowing herself to relax. Finally, she could enjoy the rest of the day with LJ.

Having spent their energy, they ate dinner in a small steak house with a few glasses of red wine before bicycling a wobbly pattern back to the ferry terminal. The sun was setting over Lake Erie as they boarded. Its warmth, mixed with the engine's vibration, further relaxed them.

The wake in the rear of the ferry reflected the golden sunset in drops of amber that splashed upward as the boat picked up speed. Passengers watched great egrets, great blue herons, and cormorants winging their way low over the surface of the water to return to their roosts before nightfall. Several species of gulls dove over the ferry as people tossed food into the air for them to catch. Angela heard their muted calls over the roar of the ferry engines.

"Are you in the mood for a movie when we get home?" LJ asked.

By the time they left the ferry, Angela's leg muscles were sore. They drove to Fremont, a few miles south of their little town of Oak Harbor, to purchase a movie at the big box store. Walking into the bright, harsh, fluorescent atmosphere only a superstore can offer, Angela passed the pharmacy when she spotted Susan in one of the aisles.

"Susan." Startled by Angela's abrupt appearance, Susan jumped. Angela ignored LJ's mumbles.

"Hi, Angela." Susan was sniffling and rubbing her red nose with a large wad of tissue. She appeared to have a terrible cold. "I'm still looking for something to calm my allergies. My usual stuff isn't working."

"I can help you. I suffer from allergies sometimes, too." She stood beside Susan, perusing the shelves. "The funeral was nice, but I'm surprised I didn't see more committee members there."

"Oh, a lot of people were busy. Donald King, her brother, may not have reached out to them, I guess." Susan wiped her eyes.

"It was nice to see all of her family there." Angela paused. "I'd never met any of them before. Did you notice no one in her family looked like her? I didn't see a resemblance in anyone."

"That's genetics for you." Susan started to move away.

"Did you know she was still married? That was a surprise to me."

Susan gave Angela an irritable shake of the head. From the corner of her eye, Angela could see the exasperated expression on LJ's face.

"I told you we worked together on LECOS," Susan said. "I didn't know much about her private life. We never socialized. I had no idea who she dated, and I didn't know she was still married. If Bill Jackson was telling the truth."

She never socialized with Connie? Angela remembered Ed saying he saw them together, laughing like old friends. She wondered why Susan was distancing herself. Maybe she should push her buttons a little. "So, the two of you never socialized? Did Connie have any other women friends?"

Susan stiffened. "We never hung out together, Angela. Ever. I never saw her with other women. Why are you so interested in who Connie or I socialized with?" She rubbed her nose roughly.

Susan was lying to her. Was she distancing herself because she learned what kind of person Connie was? LJ had walked away and waved at Angela from down the aisle.

"You should let the police do their work," Susan continued.

"I am letting the police do their work." LJ was signaling to her from the central aisle.

"I understand. This murder has been a shock to all of us. It's too bad I wasn't in town when it happened. I keep thinking I could have done something. We did have dinner together a couple of times." Susan shook her head. "I guess I feel guilty. I should have been involved with Connie more than I was."

Ah, now she admits she did spend some time with Connie. Was she worried Angela knew something?

Susan took a breath. "I was out of town when your volunteer murdered her. I told you I was in Michigan. My brother invited me to his son's eighteenth birthday party. He was accepted at Yale and will start in the fall. His parents are proud of him, and so am I. It was time for a family celebration."

Susan had an alibi that Det. Lane could check. Angela didn't doubt it was true. "Connie met someone out there, but it wasn't Jack. Do you have any idea who it might have been?"

"How many times do I have to tell you? I didn't know her well. I'm sorry I'm not being very polite. I don't feel well." She picked up a box of allergy medication, peering closely at the label.

LJ was practically jumping up and down now. "I'm sorry, Susan. I'd better go. I hope you feel better." As Angela walked away, she made up her mind to learn more about the relationship between those two women. Even though Susan had an alibi, she might be hiding something important. LJ beckoned her, obviously irritated.

Angela crushed him with a kiss. His impatience disappeared. His smile told her the night was still young.

Twenty-Three

Angela woke to the smell of coffee. Finishing breakfast before her, LJ went back to his computer, leaving Angela alone. While she ate, she looked through the Toledo paper. A newly constructed housing development in Perrysburg, touted for its nature trails, was having a ribbon-cutting ceremony and an open house later in the day. The developer was Bart Linden.

"Well, well. What have we here?" The ceremony didn't kick off until two in the afternoon. She could ask Lilly to join her since she wanted to house-hunt anyway. She picked up her phone.

"I'd love to," Lilly said. "I can drive over, so you don't have to backtrack to pick me up. What time do you want me there?"

"This thing kicks off at two. The man of the hour is one of the developers, Bart Linden. I'll try to learn more about Connie while I'm there. Why don't you come a little earlier? I have Donald King's address. I want to drive by his place. I'm curious about where he lives. Connie had an extravagant lifestyle. I wonder if he does, too."

"Sounds good. I also have some background information on Bart Linden to share with you. I was saving it for Monday." She paused. "I probably can't afford anything in Mr. Linden's development, but it will be fun to look."

Angela finished her morning chores. While waiting for Lilly, she called Danny to tell him about the day she had planned.

"Be careful with questions." He paused. "Why are you interested in Bart Linden?"

"I just want to see his development over there. He was very friendly with Connie."

"I think you've given us enough information. You don't have to involve yourself any further."

"Lilly is going with me. She's house-hunting and looking for ideas. Besides, I want to see what kind of business Linden does with our partners." Angela knew she was treading on thin ice, but she wouldn't let Danny deter her. She had a professional interest in the type of work Linden did. She didn't mention she'd drive by Donald King's house on the way. No sense in getting Danny in an uproar.

Angela told LJ about their plans for the day before she headed out with Lilly in her SUV. There was another nor'easter edging in with a prelude of winds and overcast skies. Both women had their raincoats with them.

"I hope this storm holds off until after the ceremony today," Lilly said. "It would be a shame to drive all the way there just to turn around. Now, about Bart Linden. You remember I promised to do some research on him? He was involved in a scandal involving a housing development on the Ottawa River. It was years ago. The project went bust because someone found contaminants on the scene. Our Mr. Linden claimed to have cleaned the site, but several PCB samples showed up when a contractor hired by LECOS did another check. Environmentalists, namely LECOS, accused him of fraud because he claimed he had completely cleaned the site. He lost a lot of money over it. Connie King accused Linden of corruption and undue influence on local regulators, suggesting he'd bribed someone to say the site was clean. I don't think anyone ever produced hard evidence that the PCB samples actually came from Linden's building site. It didn't matter because LECOS had blasted Linden's credibility. Linden didn't fight the charges and suddenly dropped out, probably due to public pressure. About that same timeframe, his brother was picked up by the police when he started an argument with Connie in a bar. She was with a developer named Robert Durham, and Linden's brother assaulted him. Bart Linden bailed him out. Later, Durham dropped all charges. That's it. I couldn't find anything else."

"Mr. Linden might not be squeaky clean?" Angela asked. "Good work, Lilly."

"Well, there's mention of him occasionally in business deals, which are all pretty low-key. No other scandals. Other than the one incident with his brother, there's nothing on his private life except that he's single."

It took Angela less than an hour to get to Monroe, Michigan, north of Toledo. She filled Lilly in on the funeral, giving her all the details about the fight she witnessed afterward. By the time she turned onto Donald King's street, the branches of silver maples were already dancing in the wind from the upcoming storm.

Donald King lived in an upscale older neighborhood with widely spaced homes on a wide street. The house was a farmhouse style, with a front porch topped with dormers. It was the epitome of the American dream home. Like the other homes on the block, someone kept the front lawn well-manicured. The one difference was the bed of vivid red peonies by the front porch. They were a bit unruly in their size and color. Someone in this house had needed a touch of drama amid the order.

"The peonies are an amazing touch, aren't they?" Angela asked. "It makes the house stand out from the rest on the street."

Lilly nodded. "Very pretty, but the house is a bit too country for my tastes. I like modern architecture with native plantings in the landscape. It's obvious the man has money. This neighborhood reeks of the stuff."

"Let's get out of here. Someone's likely to call the cops on us for loitering. My old car stands out in this neighborhood." Angela made a U-turn in the street.

"Donald accused Connie's ex-husband of corrupting her. Do you think he's telling the truth?" Lilly asked as they drove out of the neighborhood.

"At some level, I think his pain is genuine."

"From what you told me about the funeral, I think it's possible Donald truly loved his sister," Lilly said. "Why she lived the way she did when surrounded by so much love is confusing. Then again, if his accusations about Jackson are true, it might be how she learned to get what she wanted from men."

Angela nodded. "I didn't think of that. Connie's differences from her family could be more than just her looks. If Donald King associates with Dwayne Palmer, we might also question his ethics."

It was time to switch gears. The next stop was Perrysburg. Angela's strategy was to mingle with the crowd, say hello to Bart Linden, and chat him up about the development. He was intelligent, so he'd be suspicious if Angela asked too many questions.

Twenty-Four

"**I**SN'T RIVER GARDENS IN PERRYSBURG? Why don't we drive through it on the way to Linden's shindig?" Lilly suggested.

"Yeah," Angela said. "We can see what Dwayne Palmer is supposed to have developed." The neighborhood was a little out of the way, but they plugged it into their mapping app and made the detour. The houses were mini-mansions with sweeping mature landscapes. Four-foot high, wrought iron fencing lined almost every front yard.

"It sure doesn't look his style, does it?" Lilly commented. "I can't believe the man who showed me those other homes did this development."

The entire neighborhood oozed wealth with large homes on oversized lots. Every housefront had tall columns.

Lilly pointed out statuary was everywhere. "A little ostentatious, don't you think?"

The only noticeable nod to environmental concerns was the use of native plants. Angela's favorite part of the development was the streets. The twenty-five-mile-per-hour streets wound through wooded areas that ended in cul-de-sacs. No square grid system here. There didn't appear to be any public access provided to the waterfront. Angela was a little disappointed.

However, after seeing River Gardens, they were excited to see what Bart Linden had created. Passing Hood Park and the statue of Commodore Perry, Angela drove through the center of Perrysburg, nestled on the banks of the Maumee River.

They entered an area with large, wooded lots connected by winding roads similar to River Gardens. That is where the similarity ended. While the homes were large, they appeared more modest, without the lavish addition of sculptures. Instead, metal, glass, and concrete created more modern exteriors. Each home had plenty of windows to allow an abundance of natural light inside. Lush naturalized, well-placed landscapes added to the luxury of the development.

Even though they were early, there was a well-dressed crowd already present. Flags marked walkways leading up to several homes. Since each house included a minimum of a half-acre lot, they would have to do a lot of walking.

There were four models to choose from. Prospective home-owners could also choose any custom plan approved by the developer within certain size and material limitations. The developer would fulfill construction on a lot of their choice. All the homes had impeccable yards with native shrubs, trees, and other plantings. There was very little grass, unlike River Gardens. On closer inspection, Angela noted that on every window was a frame holding black vertical cords spaced at four-inch intervals. The design was ingenious because the cords did not disturb the view from inside the house. They would prevent bird strikes, saving the lives of thousands of birds over time.

Every oversized house within the exclusive street exuded taste. The homes were an example of well-designed charm that only large amounts of money could buy.

Angela and Lilly looked at each other, raising their eyebrows. These homes catered to the very wealthy. It was unlikely that middle-class salaries could begin to touch them. Angela refused to feel out of place.

"Looks like River Gardens," Lilly said. "But much, much better."

Bart Linden walked toward them. His dark hair was cut in a long style from the 80s, showing a little gray at the temples. His face was well-tanned, indicating he spent a lot of time outdoors.

He removed what must have been reading glasses. "Can I help you, Angela?"

"I don't know, Mr. Linden. We thought we'd see what you offered in your development. I've heard so much about this place in our meetings. I hope you don't mind a couple of lookie-loos."

He smiled. "Look and enjoy. Just don't tell me you've found more tie clips." He smiled. Angela knew he'd seen through her ploy.

"No, no tie clips." Angela returned his smile, ignoring his sarcasm. She followed Lilly to walk through a two-story home as distant thunder rumbled. Sheet lightning lit the horizon over the trees.

A couple of hours later, they finished touring the last home and were back under the canopies around the tennis court, enjoying ice-cold lemonade. Bart Linden was at the podium giving a speech. The Mayor of Perrysburg cut a ribbon. Angela spotted several other developers in the crowd. She assumed the rest of the people present were interested in purchasing homes.

The sky had grown darker. Wind whipped the tablecloths, sending a few napkins flying. Thunder rumbled ominously. As the pair mingled, Bart Linden approached them again.

"Did you enjoy the home tours?" he asked.

"Yes. I'll never be able to afford these homes on my salary," Angela laughed, "I guess it's nice to see how others live." She waved her arm toward one of the homes. "The window treatments are a great idea. I also appreciate your use of native plants. Your mix of species will help wildlife. Using natives will also save the home-owners a lot of money in water bills later."

Linden nodded his head. "I'm glad you noticed. I tried to retain as much natural woodland as possible around each home and blend it into the landscape with native plants. I've always hated how houses get pasted into the surroundings without considering natural aesthetics."

Angela listened to him talk about his plans for other developments. Some of them sounded familiar.

"I noticed how similar your development is to the River Gardens project Dwayne Palmer completed." She shrugged. "Were you involved with that?"

Bart Linden stiffened. He took a deep breath before he responded. "Look, I need to get something straight with you. Now's as good a time as ever. I've worked the past five years to rebuild relationships Connie King single-handedly destroyed in a couple of weeks. Working with LECOS, Dwayne Palmer stole the River Gardens project out from under me."

Before Angela could say anything, Linden continued. "I'm going to give you some history. You may already know this, or you'll find out. It happened a long time ago and is public information now. I think it's time for me to clear the air with you."

He looked around, took Angela's arm, and pulled her out from under the canopy, away from people. Lilly followed. Despite saying the information was public knowledge, he didn't act as if he wanted anyone to overhear what he said.

"If you've seen River Gardens, you know we had a phenomenal development plan. But you only saw part of it. Dwayne Palmer cut costs from our original plan in more ways than one. The houses are big and fancy, but besides the street layout, he didn't do much to improve the environment."

"There was going to be more?" Angela snorted. "How many mini-mansions can you build?"

Ignoring her, Linden explained. "The city originally zoned the land for industrial use because of all the contaminants on the site. After a lot of hard work, they agreed to change the zoning if I could clean it all up to the level required for residential construction. It took a lot of money and sweat. We planned to develop a community of high-density housing with small businesses set back from the river while still offering views of wetlands. We planned walking trails throughout restored woodlands, with kayak launches on the river. Restored wetlands with tree-shrub buffers would catch any runoff from the property and filter it before it made it to open water. It would be a green community where a middle-income home buyer could live, work, and play. Beyond that, homes like the ones you saw here, not that trash Palmer built at River Gardens, would be placed strategically to allow a more natural aesthetic. Overall, we had planned a diverse community of incomes."

Bart Linden was one smart cookie. His plan would have mixed middle and upper classes along with businesses to benefit everyone. She would have liked to have lived there—if the housing had been affordable as Linden had suggested, which she somehow doubted. What did Bart Linden consider middle class?

Angela came back to his comment. "How could Connie steal from you? I don't understand."

"Several years ago, my brother Ted attended a Chamber of Commerce dinner with me. Connie was there, so I introduced them. She became interested in him. Connie glued herself to his side. My brother was a blue-collar contractor. He had no clue what type of woman Connie was. She reeled him in hook, line, and sinker. I tried to dissuade him. My brother only saw a smart, blonde beauty who said she loved him. I knew better. My brother was head over heels. He wouldn't listen to me, so I met with Connie once over dinner to find out what she was up to. I thought I could buy her off. It was a mistake. She didn't go for it. In fact, she laughed. Then she threatened to tell Ted what I had done. I let it drop, hoping she'd fade out of his life. I should have known better. Connie coaxed information out of Ted. She found the plans for what we called The New River Frontier. She wheedled information from my brother about a merger with a New York-based company." He paused for emphasis. "A big company in New York."

Angela raised her eyebrows. The New River Frontier?

"As you may know," Linden continued, "historic glass manufacturing left a lot of lead pollutants in this area. We had already removed contaminated soil and replaced it with clean fill. We were given the go-ahead from the City to put out bids for construction."

He paused as another rumble of thunder shook the ground. "We knew how sensitive the local enviros were about developing riverfront property. We intended to clean and restore additional wetlands adjacent to the project. We had designed trails to provide public access. Your agency had a large role to play in issuing Section 7 permits for the endangered species on the site. It was a good project that would have built great public relations capital for everyone involved. The homes would sell at a nice profit. Without warning, Connie went public with a soil test report of contaminants on the property. She accused me of bribing public officials to get permits. She said things that weren't true and convinced some politicians we were lying."

Lilly nodded at Angela. It was similar to the information she'd found.

"Before we could investigate or prepare a response, the enviros, led by LECOS, went after us, accusing us of paying off local officials to look the other way while we buried contaminants under clean fill. We might have withstood it and proved those LECOS people were wrong, but the New York company freaked out. They backed off, canceling the merger. That company was our main funding source. Losing their backing cost us a fortune. Too late, my brother realized what Connie had done."

He took a breath. "Connie dropped him like a hot potato. He was miserable. In the end, he's my brother. I let it go. He never meant to hurt me. It's taken several years for him to get over it. Now he's back at contracting and steers clear of dinner parties." He smiled.

"It sounds like you or your brother had good reason to be angry with Connie." His brother had certainly been angry enough to attack Robert Durham.

"Sure, we might have been prime suspects for her murder if she died four years ago." Linden shook his head. "I could have killed her with my bare hands. My brother couldn't do anything to improve the situation except get over it. I've recovered, my brother has recovered. Life goes on. I can't say I cried any tears over her death. She must have betrayed someone, the wrong person or persons, one last time."

"Why are you telling me all this now?"

"I don't have anything to hide. I assure you we will work together in the future. I have big plans for the southern Lake Erie shoreline and the Ottawa River watershed. This development is only the beginning. You and I will travel in the same circles. I had to clear the air. Dwayne Palmer did not create the River Gardens concept. I did. I intend to do it as originally planned this time, only on the Ottawa River."

Angela had nothing to say. He must have invested heavily in his dream project to spend time explaining himself to her. Bart Linden was paving the way for future relationships. He had enough motive to kill Connie, but she didn't believe he did.

Linden started to walk away but turned back. "We work with a lot of environmental groups. You should be careful with those LECOS people. You can't trust them."

Angela frowned. Linden was out of earshot when Lilly tapped Angela's arm. "He sure unloaded a deluge of defensiveness. It fits in with what we know from my research. The question is, do you believe he's innocent?"

Angela was watching Linden as he mingled with the crowd. "I think he's truthful about rebuilding a relationship with the environmentalists, including me."

She looked at Lilly. "Otherwise, why tell me his story? Did he kill Connie? My gut tells me he's a businessman. Smart enough to avoid the same mistakes he made the last time. So, I don't think he'd need to resort to murder. I still think whoever killed Connie did it for personal reasons. The part about River Gardens being his idea, his project? I believe that completely. Everything fits. Just look at this place." She waved her arm toward the development. "Too bad Dwayne Palmer went cheap on his version."

"No kidding. After what we looked at today and what Dwayne showed us the other day, I'd say they were light years apart in concept." Lilly sipped her drink.

"It's not just the high price or quality of the finishes. The design of this place is sophisticated. That's something Dwayne distinctly lacks."

Suspicion of Bart Linden was gone. They finished their drinks, leaving their glasses on a tray.

A bolt of lightning cracked through the sky, followed by booming thunder. The ground shook.

"The storm has arrived," Lilly shouted. They ran for the car as the rain poured down.

TWENTY-FIVE

Angela drove toward home slowly. The light faded as the rain battered the windshield. Lightning flashed across the yellowing sky. Angela found herself crawling along at thirty on a fifty-five-mph highway. Unfamiliar with the road, she worried someone might rear-end her.

Lilly turned on the radio to see if there were any storm warnings, but road noise and rain battering the car's roof made it impossible to hear. She turned it off. Sitting in the passenger seat, Lilly huddled into her sweater. The tension was thick. Angela finally pulled off to the side of the road to let the storm pass. Lilly was visibly relieved.

"I'm going to call Susan," Angela said as she reached for her phone. "I'd like to hear her side of this story about River Gardens."

"Do you think she can give you a more objective explanation?"

"Susan Worth was the only other person close to Connie. If I'm not mistaken, River Gardens happened about the same time Susan came on board LECOS. She should have a good idea of what happened. She'll give me Connie's side of it if nothing else."

Angela knew Susan lived in Oregon, a little town southeast of Toledo. They'd pass right by it going home. Angela had picked Susan up for a meeting once. She pulled out her cell phone. Still no bars.

"I can't get a connection on the cell. What do you think if we swing by Susan's house on the way home?" Angela asked. "We can use it as an excuse to take a break from driving in the storm."

"Sounds good to me. You can tell Susan I was nervous driving in this rain. She might buy it better that way."

"My only concern is if Connie was involved with all this trickery, how could Susan not have known about it? Connie had to have shared it with her." Angela frowned. "It's tough for me to believe Susan thought it was okay. I mean, Susan has a reputation for honesty. Of course, Connie might have shown her only what she wanted Susan to see or know. Connie was a chameleon. In any case, I have to be thoughtful about how I approach her."

Angela knew Susan was the epitome of discretion. Diplomacy came with the territory when you ran with hotshot politicos. Angela wasn't sure she'd be surprised to learn about Connie's connections with the developers.

By the time Angela pulled onto the highway again, traffic had thinned, but visibility was worse, and Angela had to drive slowly. The rain didn't let up. On the contrary, the farther east Angela went, the harder the rain fell. Gusts of wind made it challenging to keep the car on the road. Flashes of lightning blurred Angela's vision, with thunder crashes that shook her to the core.

She pulled up in front of Susan's house an hour later, relieved to shut the engine off. She relaxed her shoulders from the driving tension.

"Our story about nerves isn't far off the mark. Wow, I'm stressed." Angela said. "I've been gripping the steering wheel so tight my hands are sore."

Lilly was listening as she looked out of the rain-streaked windows at the modern Victorian-style homes built in the late eighties lining the streets. "Susan might not be wealthy, but she isn't scraping by."

Susan's well-groomed yard had a buckeye, the state tree of Ohio, on one side of the walk and a sugar maple on the other in a traditional arrangement. While nice, the neighborhood wasn't as affluent as Donald King's.

"Being on the city council and an environmental consultant for Toledo must be financially rewarding," Lilly commented. "I think we all went into the wrong business."

Angela nodded. Lilly's observation hit the mark.

The rain continued to pour down, drenching Angela when she ran onto the porch. The house was dark. She rang the bell, only to hear it echo in the stillness. She waited for a while before trying again. No luck. She ran down the steps and followed the driveway to the back of the house. Blinds covered the windows in the rear. No car was in the driveway behind the house, so she peeked in the garage windows. The garage was empty. Angela dashed back out to her car, dripping.

"We've missed her. I can call her from my office this week." She looked through the windshield. "This storm isn't going to let up. We'll have to crawl home." Angela was also a little relieved Susan wasn't home. She'd had enough confrontation for one day.

As soon as Angela pulled back onto Route 2, the rain fell harder than before. Lilly turned the radio on full blast to listen to weather reports. There was flooding in some areas around the refuge, and a tornado watch was in effect.

"No wonder I couldn't get a cell signal. The farther east we go, the worse this storm is getting. If it goes to a warning, we'll find someplace to pull over to wait it out." Angela said.

Lilly agreed. "Let's just try to get home."

It took over an hour to drive the short distance back to Oak Harbor. They said little to each other along the way. Once they made it to Oak Harbor, Lilly would stay at Angela's house until the storm had passed.

They arrived at Angela's just after five. Danny's SUV was parked on the street behind another car. They hurried in to find LJ sitting at the dining room table, drinking coffee with Danny and Det. Lane.

"What's going on? Is anything wrong? Did you catch the murderer?"

Danny gestured to a chair, "Whoa with the questions—we have some of our own. You sure picked a bad day to look at houses. There've been tornado warnings since three. Didn't you hear any of them?"

Lilly and Angela looked at each other. "We didn't have the radio on until we came up on the storm. The weather wasn't this bad in Perrysburg." Angela pulled a chair out for Lilly, introducing her to Det. Lane as she did so. "Has there been a change in the case? Is Jack clear?"

"No, to both questions." Det. Lane sat back, looking relaxed in the hardwood chair.

"A woman was found dead yesterday," he continued. "She didn't show up for work Friday. She was supposed to go out with a friend Saturday night. When her friend went to pick her up, she found the front door open. Someone strangled the woman to death in her kitchen."

The lead weight of dread settled in Angela's stomach. "Who was she?" Lightning flashed outside. Moments later, a house-shaking boom shook the windows.

Det. Lane leaned forward in his chair. "It was the woman who called you. Her name was Deborah Simmons. We found a blouse reeking of perfume in a plastic bag hidden in the garage." He looked at Angela.

Lilly gave Angela a questioning look.

Danny chimed in. "They also found your phone number, without your name, on a slip of paper on her refrigerator."

"She promised she was going to call you. I told her I couldn't help her." The enormity of the situation hit Angela. The woman was Robert Durham's secretary. She had denied talking to Angela when the police contacted her.

Det. Lane continued. "Ms. Simmons was hit on the head with a cast-iron skillet. To make sure she was dead, the killer stepped on her back and used a pendant the victim wore on a leather cord around her neck to strangle her. Forensics is going over the place. By the way, the blouse we found is well-made, not something you'd buy off the rack. Expensive. We'll trace the designer to find out which stores sold it. We'll see if it's connected to Connie King. At this point, we have only your word that the woman told you it was Connie's blouse. We also found a computer in our search. We've already started going through her emails. She knew a lot about Connie and named a few of her friends."

Angela sank into a chair. Lilly put her hand on Angela's shoulder.

"I can't believe it," Angela said. Angela knew she could put herself in danger by investigating, but she never thought someone else could get murdered. She should have tried harder to get the woman to contact the police. Now, the woman was dead. There was no going back. She looked at Lilly. It was time to pull her out of this mess.

Danny spoke. "We're here to tell you to be careful. You've helped the case by talking to people. The person who killed Connie has shown us they will kill again. With or without Jack's help. You can be sure of that. The dead woman had the blouse before she called you and might have already been a target. I don't think it had anything to do with you. At this point, making yourself a target could put others in danger."

He glanced at Lilly. "Det. Lane believes she called someone to try blackmail. He's following up on that. The point is that you might tip someone off or force the murderer's hand. You need to stop everything now."

Deborah Simmons knew what Angela was doing when she called. Bart Linden did, too. Angela wasn't as smart as she thought she was.

Det. Lane spoke again. "However, thanks to your tip, I've done some digging. We found evidence of insider trading in the stock market related to real estate construction in this area. This new information raises the stakes substantially. If Connie became involved with corporate developers, helping them win bids, their businesses would flourish, and stock points would increase. Knowing who might win bids could gain someone some hefty profits. The kind of crime we're dealing with goes beyond local land or environmental issues. Connie's activities included blackmail, stealing corporate secrets, and real estate fraud. Now we know possible insider trading. She had access to information about developments along the southern Lake Erie shore she shouldn't have had. We're beginning to learn she wasn't loyal to her customers, either. She certainly wasn't loyal to you because she's implicated you in some of her deals."

"What? Implicated me? How?" Beads of sweat formed on Angela's forehead. She felt dizzy, like she might faint.

"In her correspondence, she indicated to potential investors that she had received information from you. She was banking on your credibility. She didn't accuse you of anything but inferred you were part of her planning."

Bart Linden's words rang in Angela's ears, how the same brush painted all the LECOS partners after his ordeal with Connie. She thought he was paranoid. Now, she felt the ghostly brush strokes against her skin. Connie had used Angela's credibility to further her schemes. Heat rose up Angela's neck, creating a rosy bloom on her face.

"Have you spoken with Bart Linden? I think it confirms what you told us." Angela repeated Linden's accusations about Connie duping his brother. While Angela spoke, she realized Connie used her, too. Her anger escalated further.

"Do you think someone will come after me now?"

Danny leaned forward at the table. "We don't know what to think. You told me her boss had been one of those guys Connie associated with."

"Yeah, Robert Durham. She accounted for her boss on the night Connie died. In any case, doesn't all this lead your suspicions away from Jack?"

A small branch broke off the maple in the front yard and scraped across the window as it fell into the yard. Angela jumped. Looking out the window, she tried to calm her nerves. "I just want to know if you still think that Jack is a murderer."

Det. Lane frowned at her. "There does appear to be someone else involved. Some people are willing to lie, Angela." Det. Lane's tone was intentionally sarcastic.

"Some of your associates are not what they make themselves out to be. Someone close to you was using the information you gave them. You'd be surprised what a little inside knowledge can do. Jack might work for any of them. He may have been spying on you, using your friendship. It's time for you to step out of the limelight before something happens."

"I don't believe Jack did anything. If Connie was doing all this, where does that put Susan?"

"We honestly don't know." Det. Lane shrugged. "Oddly enough, Susan hasn't been mentioned in Connie's email traffic. She wasn't even the recipient of any of it. As a matter of fact, there are only one or two emails to or from Susan in her account. Either Susan wasn't involved, or Susan was cautious."

Det. Lane stood up. "We're going to keep investigating. I shouldn't have let you get this involved." He shut his notebook and put it in his pocket. He asked Danny to step outside to confer with him for a few minutes.

LJ had remained quiet until the men left. His eyes fixed on her. "Angela, I know what you're thinking. Please stop getting involved with this business. Do what Det. Lane asked. I don't want anything to happen to you. It sounds like the killer knows you or is someone you know very well."

She reached out, putting her hand over his to appease him. "Okay. I know you're worried. I'll be all right. I won't talk to any more people, I promise."

He didn't look convinced. Angela turned to Lilly. "I'm sorry I brought you into this mess. I don't know what I was thinking."

Angela stepped out onto the front porch, interrupting the two men talking. "I believe Jack is innocent. There is no way to prove your suspicion that he was working for someone else. He has no reason to commit these crimes. I hope you can see that by now."

Det. Lane narrowed his eyes. "We will investigate, Ms. Martin, and uncover the facts. You will have to trust the process. If your friend Jack is innocent, the facts will show it. We intend to uncover a killer. Do not say anything about this to anyone."

"You still have Jack in jail. How could he have committed this murder? You have to let him go. Whoever killed this woman killed Connie."

"We don't know anything of the sort. Our detectives are questioning him now. He may know something," he said. "Please, don't make me charge you with obstruction of justice. Stay out of it."

The two men strode off the porch. Danny promised to call her later. Angela stood out on the top step until Lilly and LJ came out to get her.

"What did you talk to them about?" LJ asked.

"I want them to clear Jack. They want me to stay out of it."

"Angela, you have to let Jack take care of himself. He has a lawyer. The police have a murder to solve. Clearing Jack is their problem, not yours. Besides, it sounds like you could be the next victim. Let them do their work. No matter what happens, you have to live with the facts."

Twenty-Six

URING THE NIGHT, SEVERE WINDS, NEAR TORNADO strength, hit the south edge of Lake Erie. The storm took the roofs off several old barns and blew down large trees. Angela watched the news while eating breakfast. Storm chasers had gone out in force to track every wind eddy.

LJ was sipping coffee. "The things you told me about that housing development near Perrysburg have given me a few ideas for my program. I'll work on those today."

Angela nodded. She was glad she could help him with his work occasionally. Right now, she was concerned with the damage that might have occurred on the refuge. She wasted no time finishing breakfast before racing out the door, giving LJ a peck on the cheek on the way out.

The damage was evident as Angela approached the refuge. Tree branches were everywhere. At a nearby residence, an uprooted tree had smashed a car. A few small trees lay broken next to the refuge entry gate. Angela drove around them only to find more branches tangled with other debris littering the parking lot. The maintenance crew was already firing up the heavy equipment to clean up.

Work pushed the recent murders from Angela's mind for a little while as she and Gilbert inspected the buildings. The damage was minimal, with only a couple of broken windows in the shop and a few roof tiles missing. The greenhouse was in good shape because it was sheltered from the winds by the equipment barn.

Gilbert assigned one of the maintenance crew to repair the shop damages. The other two gathered chainsaws to clear the roads within the refuge. While one drove a pickup truck, the other followed in the front loader to move larger trees.

While the maintenance crew tackled roads, Angela helped Gilbert throw sawhorses, Closed Trail signs, saws, and other equipment into the back of the truck. They went out to check the hiking trails. They wanted to unblock them and, more importantly, make sure no widow makers or loose branches hung in the canopy that could fall on someone. They also checked for levee breaches. The refuge would have additional work if neighboring properties flooded during the storm.

Once a work plan was in place for all the staff, the murder of Deborah Simmons hit Angela again full force. The woman should have called the police, not her.

Angela studied the side of Gilbert's face as he drove. The idea of Gilbert dating Connie bothered her. He was too smart to fall for her tricks. Wasn't he?

She turned back to watch the road ahead, refocusing her thoughts. "Lilly and I went to Bart Linden's open house yesterday. Linden is a developer I've met at several meetings. Mr. Linden gave me a scathing assessment of Connie. Can I ask you a question? I need some clarity."

Not waiting for him to respond, she continued. "Of the people I know, you were the only person outside Susan who knew Connie well. I need to know if you agree with Linden." She repeated Linden's story. Gilbert listened quietly, a frown forming on his face.

"From what you told me, I think Linden might be telling the truth. I didn't tell you that Bill Jackson, Connie's ex-husband, called the refuge after the funeral and left a message for me. When I called him back, he thought I was still dating Connie since I was at the funeral. Anyway, we met at a bar this weekend. We had a long talk." Gilbert glanced at Angela.

"He didn't seem too upset about her death. Bill said Connie laughed in his face when he asked for a divorce. Said she took him for everything he had before she left. I'm not clear how or why he stayed married to her. I think he hoped he'd recoup his money somehow. Blackmail? Who knows, maybe he had an insurance policy on her."

Angela's eyebrows raised. Det. Lane would check all of that, but she'd mention it to Danny just in case.

"According to Bill, she took his money. Then she dumped him," Gilbert continued. "He didn't challenge her because she had too much stuff on him at the time. Old news now. I told Danny about my conversation. Still, while it all seems to fit her personality, some people don't know *how* to tell the truth. You shouldn't take anything anyone tells you about Connie as an absolute fact."

Gilbert didn't remember anything about the River Gardens development project because he wasn't involved with the open space folks.

They spent the rest of the morning checking levees and trails. The levees had received heavy wave action that caused erosion everywhere, coupled with wrack lines where debris had washed in on the waves. Trees with broken trunks, branches, and uprooted trees littered the woodlands. One tree was plucked up from the earth and flipped upside down, with its roots forming the new canopy. They had to stop several times to clear large branches from the road. Bald eagle nest sites, once nurturing centers, now lay in shattered heaps on the woodland floor. Angela would ask Pearl which of them had been used by eagles this year.

The woodlands were a grotesque, misshapen wonderland. With each broken branch or fallen tree, new habitat possibilities were born in the wake of the storm despite the damage. The once well-groomed and manicured small patches of the forest now stood in shambles, but Angela didn't see destruction. She saw the creation of true wildness. The broken wood became a sponge to hold moisture, allowing the slow process of rot to begin. Last night's single storm had created thousands of new homes. Fungi and insects would burrow their way to the heart of the battered wood. They would bear offspring, providing food sources for other animals. Flying squirrels and owls would find homes in the broken trunks. The only investment required for the newly created real estate was time.

They cut a few downed trees, clearing them from the trails. Gilbert placed sawhorses with closed signs on them where necessary. They checked Cedar Point Refuge and Metzger Marsh Unit before traveling to the Darby Unit. They found several trees fallen across roads. All in all, the storm had limited its destruction to the woodlots.

As a developer of natural homes and landscapes, the refuge had fared well. Angela was pleased. This storm restored some of the ecological elements of the landscape that man had undone. As a result, these areas would look much different in ten or more years. They would certainly be much healthier.

When they returned to the office, Gilbert set to work with the maintenance crew to clean up around the shop. Repairing the trails would take a week or more to complete. Angela called the regional office to give them a status report.

Pearl came into her office during lunch. She asked Angela to help her check out eagle nests.

"We already checked the one at Cedar Point. It was still intact. The adult eagles were present. We saw a nest down in the Ottawa Unit when we passed through. I was going to ask you which ones they used this year."

"The two that still had fledglings in them were Cedar Point and Metzger," Pearl said.

"I'll go with you to Metzger. Given the mess we found up there, it'll take both of us with good eyes."

"The Metzger pair had three eaglets this year," Pearl informed

Angela. "Before this storm, all three eaglets were fledging, a rarity for bald eagles. I hope they made out okay."

When more than two eaglets hatched, survival was difficult for all of them. Often, one of the three died from being out-competed for food, or the other eaglets attacked the smallest one.

They drove out to the inner Metzger levee and surveyed the damage. The violent storm had ripped through this stand next to the lake, destroying most of the large trees in its path. They lay like vanquished giants, broken in every direction, splinters exposing naked inner wood.

Angela looked for the nest where Pearl believed it had been, but she couldn't tell exactly where that was now. Everything looked different. The newly created habitat Angela had rejoiced over earlier came with a cost for other wildlife. Together, they considered the jumble of treetops lying in the water below the dike where they stood. They walked along the levee in chest waders and searched for a place to enter the swampy woods to look for downed young.

The three fledglings had been in the nest last week. Pearl had recorded the two adults repeatedly flying over the wetlands, searching for food to feed their voracious babes. The fledglings, so close to leaving the nest, might have survived. If injured, they could lie hidden below the tangle of wood.

They skirted a fallen tree only to find more fallen trees ahead. The nest should have been close, but they couldn't see any signs of its remains. The wind blew the already weakened trees still standing, and they creaked in protest at the continued harassment. Venturing too far into the woodlots, through darkened waters, was dangerous.

Scanning the debris with binoculars, they listened for any calls the birds might make. It was possible to pass within a foot or two of a nest or injured birds without seeing them. They clung to the hope the adults were alive and wouldn't abandon the area. If the fledglings had survived, the adults might try to reach them.

In answer to their prayers, an immature eagle flew up from an obscured limb and hastily beat a retreat. It called repeatedly as it circled east, flying low among the broken trees. It appeared uninjured. Their hopes soared with the bird. If one immature eagle had survived, then others might have, too. Within a few moments, an adult bald eagle flew low over them, following the eastward path of the immature.

The trees still standing creaked around them as the wind grew stronger. With renewed optimism, they continued the search. They climbed in and out of the broken wood, tentatively stepping into the dark water when necessary. After searching for about thirty minutes, their spirits were dropping when another immature eagle, frightened by their approach, flew to a branch in a nearby, undamaged tree. It settled clumsily on the limb where it observed the two women. Although the eagle appeared distressed, it was without visible injuries.

Angela heard the call of another eagle in the woodland. Neither she nor Pearl could locate it until an adult flew over them. It disappeared in the jumble of the fallen wood. A few minutes later, the adult and the youngster struggled out of the tangle and perched on another low branch.

"I think we've done as much as we can," Pearl said. "Let's get out of here before we cause more injury with our presence."

Angela was relieved there were no rescues needed today. The three fledglings had survived. It was a miracle. Satisfied with the good fortune of the eagles, they took their departure as quickly as they could.

The two women slowly climbed back around the jumble of branches until they reached the levee. When they made it back to the truck, they removed their waders. As Pearl turned the vehicle around, they spotted the two adult eagles on a snag at the edge of the woodlands. The sun shone on their white heads.

"What a sight to see," Angela said. Next year, the adults would face building a new nest from scratch. The huge nest the monogamous pair had constructed and added to each year for the past five years was gone. They had their work cut out for them.

Ed and Lilly had joined the maintenance crew with a few other volunteers to help clean up around the shops. Pearl dropped Angela off before going to Cedar Point.

"How did you fare through this storm?" Angela asked as she approached.

"I had a little damage. Nothing to worry about," Ed replied. "Lilly came out of it fine. I stopped to see how Jack's place fared. He only lost one tree. We decided we'd come over to give you folks a hand."

"Always appreciated," Angela said as she waved at Lilly across the shop lot. "What would we do without you guys?"

After hanging up her raincoat and putting her waders out to dry, Angela went inside to enjoy a cup of microwave-warmed coffee. The break didn't last long. After finishing a cup, she donned her rain jacket again before returning to help the crew with cleanup for the rest of the day.

Everyone went home on time, wet and exhausted. Tired, Angela locked the gate as she left the parking lot. She usually loved this time of day, alone after everyone was gone. The work done each day always left her with a sense of accomplishment. Today, however, she felt a touch of fear. The raw power of nature showed how little control people had over their lives. The insignificance of humans in the path of something as overwhelming as a windstorm was humbling. Angela's body ached. She was glad the day was over.

The ditches along Route 2 ran full with muddy water that had drained off the land after the storm. Angela drove carefully on the flooded roads. The drainage tiles tapping the farm fields looked like buried fire hoses sticking out of the mud, with water shooting out of them at high velocity. The highly engineered landscape in this part of Ohio continually fought the onslaught of water. Would it ever be possible to allow Lake Erie to stake its claim on this land again?

Angela might have doubted it in the past, but after seeing the changes made by this storm, she knew anything could happen. Humans could reshape and scar the land to their detriment. Nature would always win.

The light faded as Angela drove home. She thought of Gilbert's handsome face. It was easy to forgive Jack for falling for Connie's charms. Angela knew Gilbert deserved mercy, too.

What about Bill Jackson? Was he a victim, like he said? Or did he turn Connie into the woman Angela knew?

When she got home, LJ was in his sweats, asleep in his chair. He'd spent the entire day cleaning up the yard. It was work he wasn't used to doing. Angela didn't disturb him. She was too tired to talk. Leaving him in his chair, she went to bed.

TWENTY-SEVEN

A LIGHT, STEADY RAIN CAME DOWN THE next morning, drenching Angela before she reached the office door. Her frown went deeper than a facial expression. It had been a full two weeks since Connie's murder, and the clock was ticking. The longer the investigation went on, the less likely the police would clear Jack.

The weather matched Angela's mood. She stomped off as much water as she could before going inside. Peeling off her gear, she hung it to dry, then grabbed a cup of coffee. The taste told her Sally was back.

Sally Griffin, the Chief of the Visitor Services program, made great coffee and always had a pot brewing while she worked. Angela was sure Sally pumped pure espresso through her veins using coffee as a thinner to prevent clots. She was hyperactive, slightly plump, imaginative, always cheerful, and, from time to time, a little catty. Her black, short, curly hair allowed her to show off the exotic collection of earrings Sally liked to wear. When she traveled, she always came back with at least one new pair.

Angela flipped her quarters into the kitty, silently thanking Sally for the delicious throat-warming jolt before heading back to her office to check her email. Sally had been on vacation, and

Angela realized how much she had missed her. She'd have to catch up with her later in the day to ask about her leave.

Danny left a note to tell her he'd received her message about checking on life insurance policies taken on Connie. He was patrolling all day and would talk to her later. He also said they were still looking into the murder of Deborah Simmons. She pushed it out of her mind as she dug into the stack of work on her desk, trying to concentrate.

Pearl popped in. "I've analyzed the frog survey data you guys collected. Preliminary data suggests frogs are becoming more abundant on the refuge. Some species you heard, like the Blanchett's cricket frog, have been on a steady decline for some time. I'm impressed. They're beginning to show a rise in numbers, at least locally. The green frogs are increasing, too."

Angela leaned back. "It might be a sign the marshes are cleaner and healthier. Have you talked to any of the folks at other sites to see what they're reporting?"

"Most of the other field stations are seeing the same results we are."

It was good news. Pearl compiled the data for a group in Canada that collected all the surveys throughout the Great Lakes for a master database. The information was evaluated on a regional scale to learn the overall health of the Great Lakes. Looking at the larger geographic area also knocked out some of the errors often found in small data sets encompassing smaller areas of land.

Angela buried herself in her paperwork until Gilbert entered the office with his coffee mug. His hair was windblown and wet. He smelled of fresh air.

"We're getting a lot of rain. The guys are repairing the trail surfaces now. They've finished the cleanup around the office. They've fixed everything in the shop." He paused to look out the window. "With these storms coming in like this, we won't get much mowing or disking done for a while. We'll be busy repairing levees, though."

Angela looked up and gazed out the window, too.

He sipped his coffee. "Good coffee. Nice to have Sally back." He smiled, looking back at her. "The guys are repairing an old portable pump. They might be able to get it up and running so we can take the water down in Pool 1. We'll have more levee work next summer if it gets too high. I'm also a little worried about Metzger Marsh. The outlet gate has been getting jammed in the open position. Every time it jams, we lose a lot of water. We have to keep an eye on it. I'd hate to see Metzger return to the condition it was in four years ago before we could make it hold water. Before you came, it dried out and filled in with willows."

Angela nodded. She'd seen the pictures. Gilbert continued to look out her window. She waited. He had something on his mind. She could tell by his chatty mood, how he was standing, and the tension in his neck muscles. His body language spoke volumes. Something was weighing heavily on him.

Angela figured that if you paid attention to someone you worked with long enough, you'd learn their nuances. It was easy to pay attention to Gilbert. At least Angela knew a little about him, maybe not as much as she should, but she could read most of his moods.

He straightened up and looked back over at her. "I've been working on the web page. Have you looked at it?"

She sipped her now cold coffee. Gilbert always got restless when he had to stay in the office to do paperwork. Whatever was on Gilbert's mind was going to stay there. "It looks awesome. I especially like the changing photos. What are you doing to the web page today?"

Gilbert shrugged, "I have some small things to do. I was going to ask you if you had any notes for the Manager's Corner to post."

Gilbert needed some serious work to do. He had a pile of paperwork on his desk. He must not have any upcoming deadlines because he wasn't ready to settle into it yet.

"I do have a couple of things. I want to feature our volunteers a little more on the site. We could start with Jim's reason for volunteering at the refuge. We could feature his artwork if he allows us. Let me check my email, catch up with Sally, and chat with Dave," she said. "Then we can go over the web page to discuss some new items. In the meantime, check out a few web pages of refuges on the West Coast. They have some good ideas we can use. We should also link the Friends newsletter to our website."

His face lit up.

Sally was conducting an in-class field trip today. Kate was at the post office, mailing some boxes before she came into work. Angela would catch up with Sally later. She popped into Dave's office to see how things were going around the refuge.

He had been working on a grant to acquire new kiosks, benches, and boardwalks for the public trail areas in the marshes. The kiosks had themes that tied together, making the overall message more exciting. He had worked hard to put together the project. Angela was curious to know whether or not he had heard anything about the grant yet.

He swung around from his desk with a smile as big as she'd ever seen. "I just heard about the grant this morning. It looks like we'll get the whole amount. We can complete the entire project by National Wildlife Refuge Week next September. The contracting office is ready to put our work descriptions out on bid for the boardwalks and interpretive panels."

"Let's look at your diagrams again to refresh my memory." The maintenance crew would build the kiosks in-house to save money. They would use recycled plastic that didn't leach chemicals into the soil or marshes. The whole project was a welcome improvement to the existing rotting platforms made of wood. A volunteer had designed the cast bronze birds and frogs to mount on the new walkways.

Before Angela met with Gilbert, she grabbed another cup of Sally's coffee. He'd gone through the Internet looking at web pages of refuges. After typing "Friends" into the search engine, he found dozens of websites for other groups. Some pages were more interesting than the Fish and Wildlife Service standard format.

A northeast wind had picked up force. They could hear it buffeting the building. The portages would be full as the wind drove the rain southwest, pushing Lake Erie inland.

Gilbert looked up at Angela. "Instead of staring at this computer, let's check the Metzger Gates. If a log or anything else is stuck, I could use your help."

They grabbed their lunchboxes and headed out into the storm. Angela wanted to see the tide gates in action. They were designed to allow a certain amount of water into the unit, but not above a specific height, protecting the inland areas around the wetland from flooding. The gates closed once the water levels reached a certain level within the unit.

The gates worked the same way for outflows. During heavy rains, water entered the unit from the surrounding lands through drainage ditches. When the water level inside reached the limit, the sensors at the gate determined if the water outside was low enough to allow drainage. If so, the gates would open to allow outflow. If not, the unit had heavy armoring along both sides of its levee to protect it from wave action. A pair of overflow weirs near the gates reduced some of the high-water impacts.

It was a sophisticated system that worked well for the most part. Occasionally, a log or something could jam in the gate. Angela wouldn't complain. No system was foolproof. With the increased amount of broken wood in the wetlands since the storm, jams were more likely.

Driving down the back road to Metzger, they passed several refuge wetland units. Waterfowl cloistered in groups close to the opposite shorelines to find shelter from the winds. On the near shore, waves washed up onto the riprap lining the units, splashing onto the levee road. Occasionally, the wind grabbed a wave and flung it across their path, drowning the windshield. They drove slowly.

Gilbert once again seemed to have something weighing on his mind. He wasn't in a bad mood, just quiet. Few men made Angela feel as comfortable as she did with Gilbert. The man was easy to be around, even when he wasn't at his best. It was curious. What was it about him that had that effect?

Gilbert glanced at her and caught her looking at him. She didn't look away.

"There was another woman murdered this weekend," she said. Gilbert shot a surprised look at her. She continued. "Det. Lane still thinks Jack could have killed Connie. I argued that if Jack was in jail, how could he kill someone else? They still won't let him go."

"Who told you about another murder?" Gilbert asked.

"Danny. On Sunday, after the open house, I told you about." She paused. "What I didn't tell you was Danny and Det. Lane were both at my house when we got home. Anyway, it looks like I have to back off. Other things are going on. They said I could complicate things."

"I'm glad to hear you're backing off." He gripped the steering wheel tighter. Angela noted his white knuckles. "Let the police find the killer, Angela. You've done enough."

"It sounds easy to just let it go, doesn't it? I understand why they want me to stay out of the way, but I have to help somehow. I just don't know what I can do without causing a problem for them now."

"I think the police are doing everything they can. It's only been a couple of weeks. Geez, Angela, give them some time."

"I've heard if the police don't solve a case within the first few weeks, it's not likely to be solved. We know they started on the wrong foot by arresting Jack. I don't think they can do this without help. I'm not saying they don't know their stuff, Gilbert. I do know that I can get more information with my connections."

He just stared out the windshield without responding. He grumbled something Angela couldn't understand and gripped the steering wheel tighter.

When they reached the Metzger levee, the full brunt of the winds hit them. Waves crashed onto the levee, sending muddy spray across the windshield repeatedly. The wipers left pale streaks of brown on the glass. Lake Erie was a shallow lake for its size, reaching an average depth of thirty-five feet throughout most of its body.

When the winds kicked up enough to raise waves of eight to ten feet, they stirred the lake floor, creating muddy, chocolate-colored water. The shallow waters allowed the wind to displace its energy into waves. Because of this, more shipwrecks occurred on Lake Erie than on the other Great Lakes.

They parked behind some trees, out of the full brunt of the wind. They sat for a while, eating lunch and watching the brownish surface of Lake Erie try to reclaim her swamps.

They didn't speak about murder anymore. Angela glanced at Gilbert, who was staring straight ahead. She couldn't study his face, but his body language told her he wasn't happy. He must have sensed Angela was watching him because he spoke without looking at her. "Be careful, Angela. Just be careful. You could get hurt or, worse, killed."

Gilbert spoke so softly that Angela barely heard him. "I'll be fine, Gilbert," she said with a nonchalance she wasn't feeling. "I don't think this wind is going to let up. Do you? We should take a look before it gets worse."

The wind buffeted the truck, shaking it ferociously. Gilbert opened his door first, and getting out of the vehicle, they zipped their raincoats up, pulling their hoods over their heads. They bent against the wind as they walked to the catwalk, crossing over the gates. Looking down, they saw the difference in the water level between the lake and the marsh was at least three feet, with the marsh being lower. The gates were in the closed position as they should be. Everything was working well. The interior lands on the south side of Metzger Marsh were protected from flooding, from this marsh anyway. That was the limit of refuge responsibility.

The wind whipped the hood on Angela's jacket off her head. She jerked, trying to grab it to pull it back on. Gilbert grabbed her by the shoulders. She reacted without thinking and pulled away, causing her to stumble back against the catwalk rail, falling backward over it. Gilbert's fingers gripped her shoulders as he held her at arm's length, pushing her down against the railing. His quick movements frightened her. Looking into his face, she saw what looked like anger.

Twenty-Eight

Angela regained her balance. Gilbert stared at her for a few seconds before letting go. Then, he walked back toward the truck. Getting in, he slammed the door shut and started the engine.

Angela was surprised and frightened. She looked behind her at the gates. The waves of water were pounding against them on the lakeside. She was within inches of the swirl of water below.

Why had Gilbert jerked her like that? He'd almost toppled her over the rail. At first, she'd been a little shaken. Now she was angry. Stomping back to the truck, she shook water from her coat before opening the door to climb in. Gilbert was looking straight ahead as if in a trance. He put the truck into gear when Angela stopped him.

"What the hell was that all about?" she yelled.

He had pulled forward but slammed on the brakes.

"You scared the crap out of me," she continued. "What were you doing, trying to push me into the water?"

He looked at her as if what she said didn't make sense. "What in the world made you think I'd push you into the water? What are you saying, woman? Has all this talk about murder warped your mind?"

She just stared at him until he blew out a short breath. He hit the steering wheel hard with his hand. Although his voice was quieter, it held the knife edge of anger. "I saw you jerk. I thought you'd slipped. I tried to keep you from falling. Someone should shake some sense into you if you think I was trying to hurt you." He turned to look at her. "I didn't mean to scare you, Angela."

He pulled himself up, looking her in the eye. He no longer spoke softly. "Ah, hell, yes, you should be scared! You don't know who you're dealing with or what you're doing. What do you mean, you'll be fine? Connie got herself murdered. Now, another woman is dead, too. We don't know who's doing this. We can't all protect you, Angela, not all the time, and you damned well don't seem to want to take care of yourself. What is wrong with you?"

His tirade ended. He continued without softening his voice. "Everyone worries about you. I worry because I care about you. You frustrate the crap out of me with the way you think you can solve everyone's problems. Like you're some sort of crime-buster who can fix the world all by yourself." With that, he put the truck in gear and executed a U-turn. He stopped again before shutting off the engine.

His outburst dumbfounded Angela. Why was he so angry? Didn't he understand she was only trying to help? She did this for Jack. For everyone else on her staff, the sheriff might blame. She had to protect the refuge. That was her job.

What did he mean when he said he cared for her? Angela could hear the wind gusting outside the truck, shaking it with an occasional blast.

"Why did you stop?" she asked.

"I have something else to say to you. I've applied for another job, Angela." He sat, staring ahead through the windshield, not looking at her. Her heart plummeted. "I made the first cut. I'm on the list for interviews. It's time for me to step up, improve myself—to move on. Now, I'm afraid to leave you or the refuge. It's bad timing."

Her heart leaped into her throat, and blood pounded in her ears. Tears were suddenly dangerously close. Gilbert had applied out without telling her.

He paused. "I have to go. It's time. I can't stay here forever.

Now, this murder investigation has made me rethink everything. The refuge needs me now." He finally turned to look at her. "You need me."

The look in his eyes struck her to the core. She had to look away. What had she seen? Whatever it was tore through her chest and shredded it.

Her mind was reeling. Gilbert had just said he was leaving. His words rang in her ears. Feelings that she had refused to acknowledge threatened to explode to the surface.

Angela wrapped her arms around her waist, holding herself tightly. She never thought she'd have to face these feelings. She thought she was safe. Could Gilbert read her reaction? She couldn't let him know how deeply his leaving would hurt her. Hell, she never knew. As usual, she was just comfortably skating along like nothing would change.

A relationship with a man like Gilbert could tear her apart like it ripped her parents apart. She'd care too deeply, too much, and it frightened her to consider it. She still felt the pressure of his grip on her arms. It reminded her of the strength of a man who worked with his hands and muscles for a living. She wanted to hold on to that feeling. She desperately wanted more.

She turned to stare out the side window, leaning against the door, pulling her body away from him. Angela couldn't let him see her face. She didn't want to ruin the friendship they had.

Then, the voice in her head reminded her nothing is free. What would she give up for Gilbert? If he even felt the same way about her? He said he cared, but that was because they were friends. Besides, it was wrong to date a subordinate. If she broke that rule, would she ever see another promotion or manage another refuge?

Anger erupted in her for everything she could never have. Gilbert was her subordinate. She was his boss.

She looked back at his profile, at his handsome face.

Her career was the only thing she could control. It was hers. No one could take it from her. She couldn't jeopardize everything she'd worked for or base her life on emotions. Blurting out those feelings now might lead her somewhere . . . or nowhere.

And then there was LJ. She was in a relationship that didn't frighten or threaten her independence. It was comfortable. Even though they lived together, there were no strings. No ties. Just enough passion. Enough.

She should have seen this coming. She should have recognized Gilbert would have to leave sooner or later. He had a career to follow like she did. She let things go the way they were without discussing his career.

"You're leaving?" she choked on the words. She could hardly breathe.

Gilbert looked at her. He looked confused, but Angela knew it was time to take control. Like she always did. Reaching out, Angela softly touched his arm, feeling his muscles tighten. Her voice sounded calm in her own ears as if it came from someone else. "Of course, you made the cut. You're way overdue for a promotion."

He turned away and closed his eyes. Was he relieved?

She looked at his beautiful profile. Angela continued, feeling stronger with each word. "You deserve to move up. I'll help you in any way I can." Angela wanted to get back to the office. *Please, Gilbert, just shut up. Don't say another word. I can't bear it.* The office was a better place to be than the side of a lonely road on a windy, turbulent day. There she could shut herself away behind a door.

Angela watched his face change, taking in her words and the meaning he believed was behind them. She knew it was a lie. She'd told it well.

When he finally spoke, his voice was soft again. "The job is out west. I'll let you know when I have an interview." He was calm. "I didn't mean to frighten you. I'm sorry. Please, I just want you to be careful."

He started the truck, and they drove back to the office without speaking again. Angela stared straight ahead through the windshield, controlling her thoughts.

Careful? She was always careful, even when, without knowing, she was moving forward into danger, into God knows what. A weight rested on her chest. She forced herself to breathe.

The words she'd said to Gilbert rang in her ears, her cheerful tone mocking her over and over again. *I'll help you in any way I can.*

She was out of the truck in a flash with her empty lunch bucket, walking toward the office, holding her head high. Her feet felt like lead. At the door, she looked back. Gilbert was nowhere in sight.

Angela knew she had to make sure Gilbert had an alibi for both murders, if for no other reason than to assure herself he was clear of trouble. Going to her desk, she checked his travel paperwork. According to what he had turned in, his alibi held for Connie. If she had to produce evidence, she could. Did he have an alibi for Deborah Simmon's murder?

As she got up to shut her office door, Sally Griffin came in to give Angela a report on her day and a brief review of her vacation. Angela pulled herself together, bringing herself back to the present.

"Are you okay? You look like someone died."

"A lot on my mind with the murder. Don't worry, I'm okay." Angela lied. "Can we do this tomorrow?"

"Sorry. I forgot about that woman. Sure, we can talk later." She stopped at the door. "I see Lilly came back."

"Yes. It's good having Lilly around. I've missed her. The refuge is helping her regain some interest in life."

"That's what friends are for." Sally smiled and left her office.

Friends. How many friends did she have here? Gilbert was one of her best friends, wasn't he? What were they to each other now? Would she lose a friend? A good friend? Her body ached to the bone.

Danny tapped on the door, poking his head in before entering. "There's no news today about the case. I drove through the complex. Everything is safe and sound." He smiled. "I'm headed out. I'll keep you posted if anything comes up."

Safe and sound. The words echoed in Angela's head.

SEVERAL HOURS LATER, ANGELA SHUT EVERYTHING DOWN. Once again, she was the last person out. She carefully set the alarms, locked the doors, and shut the gates. Gilbert usually stopped in to say he was leaving. He hadn't come by today.

"Enough self-pity. Stop it," she said out loud. No one heard.

After so many years of being a Deputy Refuge Manager, Gilbert had finally decided to step up to the plate to become the boss. Angela should have known this day would come. What did she expect? Did she think things would go on the same way forever? Of course, Gilbert was on the certified qualifications list or cert, what he called the cut. He had more experience to do this job than Angela did. She'd been a Refuge Manager for over ten years and had an excellent reputation for running a refuge. She was able to get a lot of work done with minimal budgets. That usually meant maintaining a pretty high level of morale, which was easy to do when good people worked for you. Impossible with the wrong people. She'd had her share of those.

Gilbert had contributed to her success at this refuge, and he deserved a shot. Angela would give him a good recommendation. She had to enjoy doing it.

He would leave. Angela didn't have to like that.

It wasn't until she turned onto Route 2 that Gilbert's words about safety rang in her ears. She spent a lot of time alone in the office, making herself vulnerable to people who might want to harm her. She had to be more aware, especially after Gilbert left. Many things had changed in this one afternoon—would she ever feel comfortable in the same way with him again?

What Angela wanted was a hot bath.

Pete and Poe met her at the back door, along with the delicious smell of lasagna. LJ had cooked his favorite dish. He put the bubbling pasta dish on the stovetop, turned off the oven, and headed upstairs while Angela tended to the cats, who rubbed her legs while she fed them their evening snack. Angela rubbed their heads. Picking each one up in turn, she hugged them to her chest.

She went upstairs, where LJ was shutting down his computer. He met her with playful kisses on her face and throat. All at once, the fears of the day washed over her. She quivered in his arms. All she wanted was to make love to LJ. To feel his arms around her, holding her. Surprised by her passion, he carried her into the bedroom.

Twenty-Nine

Later that night, a hot bath further soothed Angela's body and mind. Then, in sweats, she met LJ downstairs. They ate at the dining room table, enjoying the meal with a new music CD he'd found. The blues softly filled the room, fitting her sad, satiated mood. LJ was in another world, which was fine with her. She didn't feel like making small talk.

Were there things she didn't know about him because she never asked? Never looked? No. He was LJ, a computer programmer and squeaky-clean guy. She was sure of that.

A hollow spot settled in Angela's stomach despite the meal.

Sinking into her thoughts, she analyzed Gilbert's words out on the levee. When he'd said he was leaving, Angela's heart shattered. Her mind exploded in pain with the rhythm of her heartbeat making her want to cry out. What had happened? Where did those feelings come from?

Angela had never felt that way with LJ. Those feelings ran too deep. She had never looked for a relationship requiring that much. Why had her heart betrayed her? Angela had carefully avoided the pain her parents could not. Why was this feeling so out of her control? How could Angela consider anyone else but LJ? She felt like she had cheated on him, even now, just thinking about Gilbert.

Angela focused on loading the dishwasher. While LJ went back to his computer, she drank a cup of chamomile tea while searching through her eBooks for something to read. There wasn't anything to hold her attention. She went to bed early, emotionally drained. The tea helped her to drift off to sleep.

THE NEXT MORNING, ANGELA STOOD IN LINE at the bakery section of the small grocery store down the street from her house. Only a few donuts remained by the time she reached the front of the line. Luckily, Angela was looking for bagels, not donuts. Before checking out, she also picked up some cream cheese, strawberries, and bananas to add to the repast.

She felt a lot better this morning. She'd have an open discussion with Gilbert about his job search. He shouldn't feel uncomfortable telling her he wanted more from his career.

As she pulled out of the parking lot, the car pulled hard to the right. Damn. She pulled over, getting out to look at her right front tire. She had a flat. Did she run over something? She was lucky a gas station was nearby where she could drop the tire off for repair. She spent the next half hour changing it. Throwing it into the trunk, she looked down at her filthy uniform.

She had a couple of meetings later in the afternoon, so she had to change before going to work. She called the office to tell Kate she'd be a little late. After dropping off the tire, she walked home for a fresh uniform. LJ was off to pick up some computer supplies in Toledo. There was a message on the house phone.

A muffled voice said, "Next time, it'll be you." She couldn't tell if it was a man or a woman. The sound was gruff. What was it about? Was it something for LJ from one of his clients? They often left cryptic messages that made no sense to someone not involved in a computer video game. She didn't erase it.

Angela walked back to the gas station. The kid who worked there was talking to the owner, Jess Williams, in excited tones when she walked in.

"We'll just ask her now that she's here," Jess said. He handed her two pieces of metal. "Got any idea how these found their way into your tire?"

Jess dumped the tip of a knife blade and a flattened bullet into her hand. Angela heard the voicemail message again in her head. Someone left that message for her. Angela's knees went weak. Jess helped her into his office to sit in a chair. Then he gave her some water. She called Danny on her cell phone to tell him she was at the gas station getting her tire fixed because someone had flattened it. He told her not to let anyone touch the pieces of metal.

She looked at the pieces in her hand. *Well, too late for that.*

When had this happened? She didn't recall seeing anyone near her car, and the tire was in good shape when she left home. Someone did this while she was inside the store. Driving even the short distance on the flat had ruined the tire rim, requiring the mechanic to replace it with a new one. Danny arrived along with Det. Lane and Dep. Hill. They took the tire, bullet, and knife tip to check them forensically. After everyone had handled everything, there was little hope of finding much evidence.

"What happened?" Danny asked.

"From what I could see," Jess explained, "someone tried to give her a flat by shooting her tire. People think that will cause the tire to burst. It usually only causes a slow leak. When that didn't produce the desired results, they must've decided to cut holes in the tire. They jabbed it into the wall of the tire several times. They broke the knife on the rim. You can see the gouges in the rim, too." The kid working for Jess pointed at the marks on the inside of the rim. "And you can see where the bullet hit the inside of the rim."

Det. Lane had more questions for Angela. She explained where she had parked at the grocery store and how long she was inside. Dep. Hill headed to the store to canvass the area to see if anyone saw or heard anything.

Det. Lane pulled out his notebook. "Did you see anything strange before your tire went flat?"

"No. I backed out, went to the driveway, then pulled out. The steering wheel was hard to turn. When I accelerated, it pulled hard to the right. I stopped. That's when I discovered I had a flat. I didn't see or hear anything suspicious." She paused. "There is something else. When I went home to change clothes, there was a weird message on my phone."

Det. Lane looked at her as she continued. "A muffled voice said, 'Next time it will be you,' or something like that. I couldn't tell if it was a man or a woman. It didn't sound threatening. I thought it might be some strange message for LJ about one of the video games he's involved with. He gets a lot of those. You can listen to it if you like."

Angela took them to the house, where they heard the voicemail. Det. Lane confiscated the machine. Angela plugged in the corded phone that LJ kept around when the power went out or when he was testing old computer lines.

Det. Lane warned Angela not to say anything about this to anyone at work. She wondered what she would tell LJ about the phone. Did they suspect someone else at the refuge? She agreed to keep her mouth shut.

She made it to the office a little after nine and gave the excuse of a flat tire without the drama. It turned out to be the right time for everyone to have a coffee break. The staff and volunteers helped themselves to the goodies Angela had brought. Gilbert was acting like his usual self. Had she imagined everything the day before?

Gilbert brought her up to speed on the work the maintenance crew had finished on the levee repair. With the little extra money left, he ordered some additional riprap rock armoring for problem spots on other sites.

Sally and Angela grabbed their cups of coffee to chat in Angela's office. Sally regaled Angela with stories about her vacation, making her laugh until she cried. She was a hoot to spend time with if you enjoyed sarcasm because her humor had a sharp edge. Sally had gone to the Ozarks in Arkansas to explore old Indian ruins. The excursion itself was a serious endeavor to study an archaeological site. Sally was fascinated with ancient ruins. However, the entire trip, with the trials and tribulations of logistics, was funny.

She shared her adventures with kooky guides and the difficulties of understanding the dialects of Arkansas. "I couldn't understand what anyone was saying half the time. It felt like I was visiting a foreign country."

Sally asked about Connie. Angela filled her in, omitting the info about the second murder or her flat tire. "I just hope they're doing enough to clear Jack, Sally."

Sally's response surprised her. "Oh, Angela, you always think the best of people. Connie was a slut. Our friend Jack isn't the dear old soul you seem to think he is." She sipped her coffee and cradled the mug near her chest. "Do you really think he's innocent?"

"Yes, I do." Angela couldn't believe her ears. Sally should be the one person to defend Jack. She'd worked closely with him all this time. Angela thought they enjoyed an amicable relationship. "I've known Jack long enough to be certain."

"People aren't always what they make themselves out to be. You have to understand that. They show us one face, Angela. The face we see is of a helpful, community-minded volunteer. Unfortunately, it's not always a true or full picture of them."

"Is there something specific about Jack you aren't telling me?"

Sally sipped her coffee again and leaned forward, placing her cup on the desk. "Jack is a man with passions. I've seen him when he is furious. I can tell you that he can be quite volatile. I've also seen him when he is hurt. He may seem like a tower of strength to you, Angela, but his emotions run deep. I think he could hurt someone if he thought they had betrayed him or threatened someone or something he cared about."

"That could be true of any of us, Sally. I don't take my passions or trust lightly. If someone betrayed me, I'd be hurt and possibly angry. It doesn't make me, or Jack, a murderer."

Sally nodded. "Well, I hope you're right."

The break was over. They both returned to work. Angela found it difficult to concentrate, especially when she looked out the window and saw Gilbert walking with the maintenance crew.

Angela's instincts about Gilbert's integrity had been spot on. She'd buried the idea of being attracted to him. She didn't want to deal with it. She didn't think she was making the same mistake with Jack.

After work, instead of going straight home, she drove to Crane Creek State Park to walk the boardwalk. There was a break in the weather. Although it was partly cloudy, the rain had stopped.

Several cars were in the parking lot. Crane Creek was a hot spot for birdwatchers. A well-built boardwalk led people over the swamp and through woodlands to put them close to birds. Crane Creek placed the impacts of people in a single, well-built, well-kept facility. As a result, visitors had a quality experience with quality facilities, which is how it should be.

Lake Erie held a mystique comparable to the mystery and wonderment she felt for the desert. She'd always loved the desert for the play of light across the land. Here, the light played across the depths of the water. Both had open stretches of space where her mind could stretch to the horizon.

She was still enjoying the changing light play over the marsh when she spotted Tony. He was in chest waders, walking through the wetland, stopping now and then to bend over, probably checking a trapline. When he looked up, Angela waved at him. He acknowledged her with a tip of his hat. She could see his smile even from a distance—a smile that changed his face entirely.

He continued his slow progress. Angela looked away for a moment to follow the flight of a great egret. When she looked back, Tony was gone. Searching the tules, she couldn't spot him. How did he get out of sight so quickly? The man was an enigma, appearing in the oddest places and disappearing like magic. She couldn't remember how many times she'd spotted him when she hiked around the marshes. Somehow, he was always around.

What did anyone know about Tony? When Angela first came to the refuge, she'd taken a trapping course to learn how to trap. Like using fire to manage habitat, trapping was a wildlife management tool that helped increase or reduce the vegetation in waterways. It was a tool she had never used before. She wanted to understand how to use it wisely.

She'd learned from her instructor that the LaRoche family had trapped furs in Canada and the Great Lakes area for generations. Indeed, the LaRoche family descended from French royalty. The more current descendants had Algonquin blood from marriages over time. It was interesting to think of Tony as royalty or Native American. She certainly could see he had inherited some of his skill set. He loved what he did. She doubted he would choose to do anything else. He did it better than anyone else in these marshes.

Or was she wrong about him? How many people Angela dealt with daily had mentioned him at one time or another? She hadn't thought about it at all. Now, she was sure Connie had winked at him once.

Angela stood up straight. That was several months ago. Tony had walked into the office when Connie and Susan were on their way out the door. She had greeted him like a long-lost friend.

"Tony! How are you? Where have you been keeping yourself?" Connie had asked.

Tony smiled and removed his hat, stepping up to her. *"You should know I've been minding my own business, as usual, Miss Connie. What else?"*

Angela thought it was an unusual comment, but Tony put his hat back on and walked to Pearl's office without saying another word. Now, the portent of his words rang in her ear. *You should know I've been minding my own business.* What did Tony know about Connie?

There were at least a dozen people on the boardwalk. There were as many more on the beach. Angela removed her shoes and socks to wiggle her toes in the sand. Angela nodded at the other people as they passed. Although the sand was ice-cold, it was refreshing on her feet. A stiff breeze blew through her hair, chilling her skin.

She'd have to talk to Danny about Tony. In the meantime, who cut holes in her tire? Someone she'd called? Donald King was pretty much out of the picture, or was he? He was right to be angry about his sister's death. Was there more to it? Was he possibly involved with Connie's scamming of people? Was it a family enterprise?

What about Bart Linden? He said Connie declared the affair was over. The real question was whether or not his brother was finished with Connie. Was he really willing to walk away from such a shameful incident?

Angela shook a clump of sand off her toes. Many of her questions were unanswered.

Someone murdered Deborah Simmons. The blouse connected her to Connie's murder. The damage to her tire indicated she'd attracted someone's attention. She must have touched a sore spot with somebody. She had called too many people to know if the person might be someone she spoke to face-to-face or just over the phone.

The questions were driving Angela crazy.

Danny could speak to Donald King if he hadn't already. Dwayne Palmer might have known Deborah. Could he fill in some blanks about her? He was chatty enough about the women he knew. He told Angela he had developed the River Gardens project Bart Linden claimed was his. She couldn't believe Dwayne was a killer. He just didn't fit.

Angela might not know someone well, but she instinctively knew whether they were truthful or trustworthy. Angela never trusted Connie or considered her an honest person. She realized that she knew very little about Connie King or her many relationships with men, including Gilbert and Jack. That had thrown her for a loop.

She had to talk to Gilbert about his job search. It was time to face the changes it would bring. She'd have to be his friend and keep her selfish emotions out of it. He was ready to leave. He wasn't asking her for anything.

Whatever she did, she couldn't let Gilbert leave her life permanently. She'd have to maintain contact.

A dog ran past her, making Angela look around. Only two other people were walking along the shoreline now. She was alone. She hurried back to the car, locked her doors, and ran the heater to dry her feet. She brushed them off as best she could before putting her shoes back on. As she pulled out of the parking lot, she saw only one other car left in the parking lot. Wasn't she supposed to be more careful about being alone? It was time she took the warnings seriously.

In the safety of her vehicle, Angela relaxed. She'd made some decisions. Gilbert would remain her friend no matter where he was. With that fixed firmly in mind, she turned onto Route 2, tuned the radio to a rock station, put the volume up high, and headed home as the sunset reflected off Lake Erie, casting a bronze glow on the clouds.

LJ wasn't home when she arrived. Angela had just slipped into the tub when he poked his head around the bathroom door. "Hi, Hon. I hope you didn't make dinner or anything because I already ate."

"No. I just made it home. I'll make a sandwich tonight. What kept you so late?" she asked.

He moved a little further into the steamy bathroom. "When you get out of the tub, we need to talk."

Thirty

"**Y**ES, WE NEED TO TALK. I NEED TO TELL YOU some things, too," Angela said.

"Is everything okay? Is this about Jack?"

Angela shook her head while reaching for a towel. "Sort of. I'm fine. Let me get out of the tub."

He ducked back out, leaving the door partially open. Pete and Poe meandered into the bathroom to inspect her pile of dirty clothes, paying particular attention to the sand-encrusted socks. After exploring the smells of Lake Erie, they sat across the room, waiting for her to finish bathing. They were a little indignant. It was unacceptable for her to shut the door on them. Poe snuggled up into her crumpled shirt while Pete stretched across the top of the commode tank.

After a vigorous rub with a terry towel, Angela pulled on her standard evening attire—sweats. She dumped Poe onto his side, tossed her dirty clothes into the hamper, and then padded downstairs, where LJ was waiting with a glass of wine for each of them. She made herself a sandwich while he waited for her to sit down.

"I have great news, I think, anyway. I want to hear your news first. If it's not good, let's get it out of the way," LJ said.

Angela told him about the holes in her tire and the strange phone call. "Det. Lane will return the home phone when he gets information from it."

"Someone destroyed your tire?" His face turned red with anger. "You've been threatened? My god, Angela, what if the person had jumped you? Or shot and stabbed you, not your tire? Do you see what happens when you try to solve everyone's problems? I'm glad you're getting out of all this mess." He wrapped his arms around her. "I can't believe this happened."

She relaxed. It felt good to have his arms around her. She appreciated many things about LJ—traveling, eating at great restaurants, hiking, and riding his motorbike. There was no question they had fun together, but did she love him?

The differences in their careers made them a good couple. LJ never asked her about her job or visited the refuge. His lack of interest was OK with her because it let her leave work at the office. She was interested in what he did but not the details. It would bore her to death to have to do the kind of work he did or talk about it at length.

"What news do you have to tell me?" she asked.

"Eat your sandwich." LJ pushed her plate toward her. After Angela took a large bite of the sandwich, he lifted his wine glass. "Let's toast to a new beginning."

She lifted her glass as well. "A new beginning?" she mumbled with her mouth full.

He smiled broadly, unable to contain his excitement. "I've been offered a job in London. Or Amsterdam, if I prefer. The company wants me to oversee new staff and work closely with a couple of our clients, developing the home design software I've created for small spaces. We're moving to Europe."

Angela nearly choked. *Move overseas?*

"Angie, are you okay?" LJ put his hand on her shoulder.

She swallowed her food and gulped the wine, feeling the burn as it washed down her throat. "I'm fine. I don't understand. You want to move? Why can't you do the job from here?"

He frowned. "This wasn't the reaction I was expecting. You love to travel as much as I do. It would be a real kick to move to London or Amsterdam. I have a lot to learn about European construction. My company wants me to experience living there so my designs will better fit the needs of their customers."

"Can't you just go there for a few months?" Angela knew it wasn't possible as soon as she said it aloud. The look on his face verified it.

"I could take vacation time to visit you," she suggested.

"Angela. My new job is more than just a short-term assignment. The company wants me to spearhead a new division. I could be living in Europe for years."

"What about my career? Refuges are my life. It's what I do. Am I just supposed to quit?"

"I'm going to make plenty of money. You could explore all the natural sites of Europe to your heart's desire. If you want a job, I'm sure you could do the kind of work you do anywhere."

Do my kind of work anywhere? What the hell?

"LJ. I don't think you understand. What I do is preserve American wildlife. It's about preserving American lands and natural resources, our natural heritage. I'm proud of what I do." Would she feel the same conserving native species in another land? In Europe, her life would be in LJ's hands, not her own.

Angela stared at him. He looked surprised. She stood up and walked across the room, gathering her wits. Finally, she turned to face him, controlling her voice as best she could. "Maybe it sounds corny to you or something, but I have a passion for my work. It's a calling, not just a birding trip. How is it that after all this time, you do not understand that I love my career? I can't just walk away."

All of the emotions of the last several days overwhelmed Angela and threatened to go on full display. She stood, pulling herself to her full height, taking a deep breath.

He sat back in his chair, staring at her. After a moment, he put his glass down. "If I don't take this job, I'm not likely to get an opportunity like this again. It would mean no promotions, and I'd grow stale or redundant. You have to understand. Computer software isn't a static thing. It's constantly changing. It's not just the software. It's all of the technology in general. I can't afford to get stuck in a rut doing the same thing. This is a big step up for me. Don't you see that?" He was pleading. "I can't believe *you* don't understand."

They looked away from each other. When Gilbert dropped his bombshell on Angela, she knew she couldn't give up her career. There was no decision to make. Now, LJ was asking her to do precisely that. Could she give up her life with LJ? Their relationship had developed because they didn't have commitments. No one had ever spoken of love, marriage, or forever. He loved his career, too. There was no doubt they shared that same drive.

Was this a step toward forever where one of them had to give something up?

Angela held his hands, looking down at him. "I do understand. Better than you may think. It's what makes us who we are. How long do you have before you have to answer?"

"I'm sorry, Angela. I didn't have time. I've already accepted the position."

For the second time in the same number of days, Angela heard the loud slamming of a door in her mind. But this time, she also felt the slap in her face.

"You couldn't wait to talk with me?" Now, she stood over him, shaking her head.

"I didn't think it would be a problem. This is a great opportunity for my career, Angela. You and I are happy together. You can join me." He paused. "I'm not going to force you. It's completely up to you."

You can join me. Why did that sound condescending? Did Angela want to make a life with LJ or not? Why was she being asked to throw everything away? She had two college degrees and almost fifteen years invested in this career. Taking a breath, she reined in her emotions.

"When do you go?"

"Next month."

Her mouth was dry. Her chest was so tight she could barely breathe. "This must have been in the works for a while. You made your decision without even talking to me. Now, you expect me to make mine immediately."

It was a statement, not a question. LJ should have begun this discussion long ago. Angela couldn't believe he was asking her to change her life with a snap of his fingers. She took another deep breath, and as her lungs expanded, the ringing in her ears faded.

"I expect you to at least think about it," he said. "I want you to come with me to explore Europe." His eyes were bright with promise.

The pain she felt right now was that LJ hadn't included her in his decision before he made it. It had little to do with love. Her heart wasn't involved in this relationship. Her mind took control to move them forward.

"Give me time. Let's see how this job goes for you. If it works out, we'll see what happens. At first, you'll want to get settled and concentrate on work. I can visit you as often as possible. I won't leave my career right now. It means too much to me. The reputation of the refuge is on the line because of this murder. I cannot leave now.

"Angela, we'll have a wonderful time over there. Imagine the bike trips we could take. You could get away from all this trouble." He stood, pulling her into his arms. She could see she was crushing the dreams of this man. Did he know what he was doing to her?

"My time with you is always wonderful. You mean a lot to me." She didn't want to fight or argue with him. He hurt her by making plans without talking to her. They weren't on a journey together; they had arrived at a destination long ago when they first met. Now, there were new horizons to meet. He'd made his decision, and there was no sense in carrying on. A new journey was waiting for him.

Angela looked at him, knowing he cared about her, but he'd never said he loved her, even now. He'd move on. "We'll have to see what happens. For now, you have to get ready. I'm excited and happy for you."

"At least you're not ending this," the hurt was evident in his voice. "You know we're good together." LJ went to his office.

Angela's heart ached. Even now, he hadn't voiced his love. Neither had she. Would that have made a difference if he'd told her he loved her? Her mind shifted to a future of living in Ohio without LJ. Without Gilbert. Many changes were happening so quickly. At least she still had the trio of Jack, Lilly, and Ed.

Angela finished her sandwich, poured herself a second glass of wine, and downed it before going to bed early. She had a series of chaotic dreams. First, she climbed into a long, dark cave without a flashlight. She stumbled along. Each time she hit her foot, the pain triggered a tiny spark of light, giving her a brief look at the path ahead. The more pain she inflicted while stumbling, the brighter the flash. Still, there was blackness.

Her dreams shifted to driving on four flat tires and being chased by Canada geese running because they couldn't fly. Next, she was in a tiny raft, tossed about on a very stormy Lake Erie, while LJ and Gilbert, in separate, much larger boats, motored away from her in different directions. She couldn't get either of them to turn back to help her. Angela was yelling at the top of her lungs when a bolt of lightning struck the water. She awoke with a jolt.

THIRTY-ONE

LJ HAD TURNED ON THE LAMP on her nightstand.

"Good morning, sleepy." He sat on the edge of the bed. "Are you feeling okay this morning? You were calling out in your sleep."

She stretched, feeling like she had barely slept. "No. I don't feel well. I think I'll call in today and spend the day in bed. I'm exhausted."

"After what happened to your tire yesterday, I think some rest would be wise. I've been up most of the night. We have a lot to talk about, Angela. Things to work out. I have to get going right now. I have things to wrap up before taking on the new job, so I'm flying to Chicago today. I'll be back by dinner."

He kissed her softly. After he left, Angela locked all the doors. She called the refuge to leave a message on Kate's extension to let her know she wasn't coming in today. She called Danny directly.

"I'll let Det. Lane know you're at home. Call us immediately if anything else happens."

Angela went back to bed.

She awoke in the afternoon, again with Pete and Poe crashing across the bed. They were in a game of chase that was always amusing. She lay in bed a little longer, letting her head come to full consciousness while the cats bee-lined back out the door, tumbling down the stairs. She could hear the crash at the bottom of the steps as they banged into the coffee table. Poe must have caught up with Pete in what sounded like a full-body tackle.

Angela spent more than an hour dressing before walking to the store to pick up a few things for dinner. Cooking, for a change, might put her in a better mood. She wanted to take her mind off work. Angela knew LJ was hurt, but she was more angry than hurt because he didn't consider her when he made his decision. However, she did understand that he couldn't pass up this opportunity for promotion in Europe.

Angela shopped for pot roast, carrots, and potatoes. It was the only meal she knew how to make well. She bought ingredients to bake a cake from scratch. It was worth a try. She took her time walking home—the air was crisp. The sun shone brightly.

The house soon filled with the smells of an old-fashioned pot roast cooking in the oven. A small salad and dinner rolls complemented the simple fare—a sour cream chocolate cake with chocolate frosting for dessert added to the old-fashioned flavor.

By the time LJ came home late that evening, a chilled bottle of wine was ready. "What smells so good? I'm starving."

"We can finish our conversation about our future." Angela filled his plate. After pouring him a glass of wine, she sat down herself. "I've thought about you all day." She was no longer angry with LJ. "Let's face it. It's not like we talked about marriage in our immediate future. We've never talked about forever. We enjoy each other's company immensely. It will be a big change, and I will miss you. Right now, we're on two separate paths."

"I wish you could just go with me," he answered.

"I wish you could stay. We both want different things, but the main thing is that you have to take this promotion. You're right that you won't have another opportunity like this."

"I'm going to miss you more than you know."

"I'd say we're both going to miss each other terribly." Angela smiled. "Let's talk about the things you'll get to experience."

It was time to let go of each other. They both knew it. Instead of crying over it, they spent the evening talking about LJ's future and the fun they'd had over the years. Angela bit back the tears. Yes, she'd miss this man.

THE NEXT DAY, THE LAST THING ANGELA WANTED to do was spend more time in her office. She asked Pearl if there was any biological work she could do. Pearl didn't have anything specific Angela could do, so Angela improvised.

"I'll go check the marshes at Darby to see how the purple loosestrife control is going," Angela said. Pearl appreciated the additional set of eyes on the project.

Some people can spend all their days inside, in the comfort of air conditioning or artificial heat. For Angela, an icy cold wind on her cheeks and frost in the air or a hot sun was preferable to spending every day inside. She'd gladly trade a month of days in her office, with its constant temperatures, for one lousy day outdoors. It cleared her head. She wondered what her childhood would have been like if she'd never felt warm, squishy mud between her toes.

She dropped off her backpack on her desk and grabbed a field bag. The maintenance staff was already at work. Gilbert drove in as she pulled out. Angela waved.

This warm, dewy Friday morning welcomed her with a light mist over the marshes. She could smell the fragrant spice of the woodlands, and the sun was greeting the Western world with a pale, diffused shade of salmon, along with a few streaks of gray. It was a perfect way to end the work week, doing what she loved.

Angela stood on the edge of the marsh, where the hardwoods met the shallow water. An expansiveness filled her, starting in her chest and working its way to the tips of her fingers. Everything she touched, everything she could see, seemed to communicate with her, breathe with her, pull her beyond herself.

Angela donned the chest waders, giving herself a quick covering of bug spray. A few mayflies stuck to her and tangled themselves in her short hair, but she ignored them. She was in the midst of life. Even the whine of mosquitoes was not a deterrent while her bug spray was doing its job. As she stepped through the cattails, she smelled the pungent scent of decaying plant life released under the pressure of her boot.

This rotten-egg-like aroma evoked thoughts about the cycles of life and death on Earth. To all things, an end must come. Right now, it seemed, the end of many things had occurred. It had all begun with Connie.

Is it time for me to leave? There was still Jack, Lilly, and Ed. She thought of them as her family. The marshes were what Angela needed. She loved the wild places along the Lake Erie shoreline. Angela had made the right decision to let LJ move on. There were no wild places she could call her own in Europe or that would fill her heart with a sense of accomplishment.

As painful as it was, a new beginning was near for some. It was certainly true for Gilbert, too. Was there a new beginning some-where for her? Was it here? A breeze carried the light, sour scent of gulls, fish, and mussels. The sweeter smells of thistle, milkweed, and wild cucumber countered. To the left of her, along the edge of the cattails, a great blue heron, almost four feet in height, stood still. Its long neck stretched forward as if in a trance, staring into shallow waters, waiting for a meal to come along. Finally, a fish came within reach. The bird reacted with a swift and lethal blow of its sharp bill.

Flipping its head upward, the heron snatched the fish sideways. Flipping it again, the heron turned the fish so it could consume it head first. The great blue contorted its neck several times, swallow-ing the fish whole. Angela watched as the meal was forced down its long throat. After a few moments, the bird moved forward a few steps with its long, awkward legs and began its vigil anew.

She stood still, listening to a bullfrog thrumming monoto-nously in the distance. A leopard frog couldn't refrain from snor-ing occasionally. A muskrat broke the water's surface in the middle of the pool. When it saw her, it smoothly turned toward the cattails on the opposite shoreline, swimming with its back barely visible. Its tail worked as a rudder to guide it. With a dive and a splash of its rear foot, it disappeared beneath the water, probably into a hidden tunnel leading to a hut somewhere in the cattails.

She worked her way along the marsh in the opposite direction to keep from disturbing the heron. Angela spotted a little bit of purple loosestrife where the cattails gave way to smartweed. Stepping back to the shoreline, she retraced her steps to the truck to grab a couple of trash bags, tucking them inside her waders. She bagged the offending plants before pulling them up by the roots to prevent them from spreading more seeds, tied the sack around the stems, and threw the bagged invasive onto the shoreline.

Potomageton, duckweed, and water milfoil were abundant. Snails and aquatic insects were attached to the plants, feeding on them for nourishment. Angela was gaining emotional sustenance with each step. Pickerelweed and water lotus sent up blooms, creating floating bouquets. Her boots oozed and sucked through the marsh, stirring up gray sediment with each step. An eastern kingbird flew by her, while tufted titmice called *Peter, Peter, Peter.* The piercing whistles of cardinals sounded through the nearby woodlands.

The marsh would mature through the summer to supply abundant food for ducks and geese later in the fall, the season Angela loved more than any other. When autumn arrived, the weather would turn cold. The trees would flaunt their vibrant yellows, oranges, and reds. Now, the lush, green canopy above her intensified the warmth of a summer day. The sky had lost its pink glow. It was now an uninterrupted expanse of vivid blue. The light morning mist had disappeared.

A movement caught her eye. Across the way, she saw Tony on the state land bordering the refuge. He was moving slowly, head down, wearing his chest waders again. The state folks must have hired him to do some work, or he was checking traps. Tony often contracted work with the state to spray for weeds or repair infrastructure like screw gates.

She had to speak with him to clear up her concerns about his connection to Connie. Tony disappeared into the tules. She watched for a few moments, but he didn't appear again.

A great egret, in snow-white splendor, flew over her. It found a spot to land and began its version of a hunt vigil not far from the great blue. Beyond them, Angela could see the refuge boundary's small, white metal sign. The stylized blue goose on it spoke to her. It was more than the marshes here along Lake Erie. She belonged to this refuge.

Angela wandered on, caught up in her daydreams, when she felt the ground slide out from under her. Too late, she realized she'd stepped into a deep trench. It was one of the ditches that led to the main pump to empty the marsh. Caught off guard, she had no time to catch her breath before the chest waders filled with water. Her head was below the water within moments. Angela struggled to get to the surface. It was useless. The water-logged waders pulled her down. She couldn't kick her legs effectively enough to swim. The channel was deep, and Angela hadn't touched the bottom yet. The weight of the waders made it impossible to pull the straps off her shoulders to shed them. The urge to gasp for air was overwhelming.

Thirty-Two

ANGELA THRASHED HER ARMS ABOVE HER HEAD to no avail. There was nothing to grab.

Then strong arms wrapped around her and pulled her out of the water onto the shoreline. Spluttering and coughing, Angela found herself lying face-to-face with Tony.

"Take it easy," he said softly. "Let me help you sit up so you can breathe. There, cough it out, then you'll be okay."

Tony wrapped his arm around her shoulder, holding her forward while she expelled water. He gently pushed her short hair from her face, wiping the mucous from her mouth with the palm of his hand. After a while, she stopped coughing and could breathe again.

"Feel better?" he asked. He wasn't smiling. He watched Angela intently, his eyes filled with concern.

"Yes, thank you." Angela was embarrassed but grateful. "I'm glad you were nearby." She looked at the water. She had panicked. She was glad the pump wasn't operating, or the pull of the water might have claimed her before Tony could reach her. He had saved her life.

She looked up at Tony. "Thank you." There simply was nothing else to say.

Slowly, a smile appeared on his face. He pulled away from her and stood up. "I better help you pull those waders off."

She unbuckled the straps at her shoulders, and he grabbed the boots and pulled. The waders came off with a slosh. Angela sat on the ground in a wet uniform. Tony held out a hand to help her stand. He walked her to her truck, carrying her waders, allowing her to hold his arm to stay steady. Her stocking feet weren't well equipped to walk on the gravel-covered levee.

They retrieved the bagged loosestrife on the way, and Angela sat on the tailgate to let her feet dry a little before putting on her boots. The warm air was muggy. Her stomach grumbled from hunger.

"Are you hungry, Tony? I have a couple of sandwiches in my ice chest. I'd be happy to share one with you."

Again, that warm smile. "That'd be nice, Miss Angela."

She reached for the ice chest and grabbed two sandwiches and bottled water. Then, she cut an apple in two using her Swiss Army knife.

Tony sat on the tailgate beside her. They ate without talking, enjoying an easy, quiet time.

"You sure are deep in your thoughts, Miss Angela."

Angela shook her head. "Just enjoying being alive. Thanks to you." He ducked his head in embarrassment. "I saw you over on the State land. Are you working for them or just checking out new trap areas?"

"Nope. Neither. I just like getting out to see what's here." He took a bite of his sandwich.

Angela looked away, staring into the distance. "Yeah. That's why I'm here today. It helps me think and get things off my mind." She turned to look at him. "Connie King is on my mind today. If I remember correctly, you said you knew her, didn't you?"

"I don't know if I said, but I did know her."

Angela told him about Connie's murder and how the police had arrested Jack. "I don't believe he did it." She chose her words carefully. "How well did you know her? Did you consider her a friend?"

"I wouldn't call her that. No." Tony pulled his head back, looking up at the sky. "I saw her around. She knows some bad people, Miss Angela." He looked at her. "So do I. But they aren't my friends. You knew her. Was she your friend?"

"No." Angela paused. "I see what you mean."

"You gotta know who the bad ones are. You gotta watch them."

Angela nodded. She was relieved that Tony didn't consider Connie his friend. "You told me you saw some men near the refuge. Those men were friends of Connie. Do you remember what they were doing out there?"

"I saw them digging up stuff. At least, that's what it looked like they were doing. One of them had a metal box he carried around. I didn't stay to watch them, so I had no idea what they were up to. I'd've told you if they were on the refuge." He paused. "You know, I met Miss King several times at the state game and fish offices. She took me for an ignoramus, a dolt. That's a bad way to treat people. I guess it makes them feel smart when they aren't."

Angela raised her eyebrows.

"I know you're sometimes unsure of me, but you've never treated me that way." Tony put his hat on. His voice returned to his usual slow, lazy drawl. "Nope. She was a bad 'un. I steered clear of her. Her loss, not mine."

She hadn't noticed Tony's change in speech until he resumed his drawl. Mr. Tony LaRoche wasn't slow—there was more to this man than met the eye.

Tony finished the water in his bottle and handed the empty to Angela before standing up. "I better get going." His warm eyes looked through her. He was a good man. A kinship had formed. Angela had a new friend.

"Thank you, Tony. You saved my life today. I can't say that enough."

"Nothing to say. Glad I was there." He touched his ball cap and walked down the levee, disappearing around a curve behind the trees. Angela stared after him for a while before packing up the remains of their lunch. He was nonchalant about what he'd just done, and it moved her.

She continued to sit on the tailgate, letting her uniform dry as she watched an eagle circle above her. Life was tenuous. In a matter of seconds, it could end. Every moment was precious, and she had to live it to the fullest . . . in her own way. She didn't want a man who didn't consider her when he made important decisions or believed that whatever he wanted was good enough for her. She was right to let LJ go.

Angela wasn't ready to leave Ottawa, not yet. She enjoyed the wonders of her job. The near-death experience she had just had made her realize how quickly life could change in an instant. It also made her realize that she had good friends here.

Angela had much to review about her job, life, and relationships.

Gilbert deserved a promotion. Angela would, of course, help him to succeed.

LJ was good at his job. This opportunity to work in Europe was too big to pass up. He was free to go without worrying about what he'd left behind.

Gilbert popped in right before she was ready to call it a day. "You wanted to talk to me?"

Angela'd forgotten about the sticky note she'd left him when she returned from the marsh. After spending a couple of hours in the reality of the paperwork she dealt with, she was ready for a break. Angela smiled at him as he sat down. She could see he was nervous.

Angela kept her voice even. "I want you to know that I believe you'll make an excellent manager. I admit that I was a little upset, knowing you'll leave. I apologize for my reaction. You're good at this job, and I'll give you an outstanding recommendation, of course."

"Thanks, Angela." He leaned forward, resting his elbows on his knees. Looking down, he picked at his thumbnail. "Look. I didn't mean to yell at you out at Metsger. Forget it, okay? I know you're being polite. You're my boss, and I shouldn't have crossed that line. I'm sorry I didn't tell you about applying out earlier. I should have. I just know there are some good job opportunities out there. I might never move on if I didn't try for them now." He looked up at her. "I was afraid you might get mad if I told you I was looking for a new job."

Angela held his gaze. "I understand. I could not be angry with you for improving yourself. I'm sorry you thought that. Sooner or later, we all move on. We have to. We'll always be friends, Gilbert. I hope you know that."

He took a deep breath. When he smiled, Angela felt warmth spread through her. She hadn't lost her friend.

"Yeah. We're friends. If you ever need me, Angela, you only have to call. I've got your back." Gilbert stood up. "Thanks for the support." He paused. "Did you have a good day off yesterday?"

Angela smiled. "I just needed some R & R. I spent most of the day catching up on sleep. I feel fine today. I think I was a little too stressed about Jack and the refuge. It wore me down."

"It looks like you enjoyed the marsh this morning." He laughed. Angela looked down at her uniform. It was pretty obvious she'd gone into the water.

"Oh yeah. Just a little mishap." She laughed.

"Good. Nothing else worrying you?"

"No." Angela wasn't supposed to talk about the flat tire incident. She sure didn't want to talk about LJ. "Kate said you went to Darby. I didn't see you out there."

Before answering, he hesitated for a split second. Angela caught the pause.

"No, I didn't actually go to Darby. Kate was wrong. I went to Navarre to check the mowing the guys were doing and to talk to the power plant biologist about the bluebird nest boxes Pearl put up. Pearl said she's getting a lot of bluebirds mixed in with the swallows, and we're starting to have problems with raccoons. I wanted to help her by putting cones on the posts to keep the raccoons from climbing up to get the eggs. I let the biologist at Navarre know what I was doing." He paused. "He's looking forward to working with us on another hunt this winter."

The Navarre Unit of the refuge was unlike anything Angela had ever dealt with before. Ottawa was the only national wildlife refuge with a nuclear power plant in the middle of it. The Ottawa Refuge managed the marshes, and the power plant had a biologist who coordinated with the refuge staff. They allowed the refuge to conduct deer hunts on the property, only allowing black powder rifle hunting. High-powered rifles could cause some real security issues for the Nuclear Regulatory Commission.

Deer overran the marsh at Navarre. This year, Gilbert hoped to lower their numbers before they permanently damaged the habitat. He planned to increase the number of hunters by one-third and extend the hunt by an extra day.

Angela looked forward to the fall hunt because it managed the deer herd. At the same time, she was always glad when hunting season ended. The hunt meant a tremendous amount of work, long hours, and some serious people control to ensure that hunters were in the correct units, doing what they were supposed to be doing.

The few minutes at the end of the day spent talking to Gilbert about work felt good. She relied on Gilbert's expertise and respected his opinions. She would miss his camaraderie.

THIRTY-THREE

ON Saturday morning, Angela woke early to do laundry and other housekeeping chores. The phone rang—it was Lilly.

"I have to go shopping to buy supplies for a quilt project. Would you like to join me?"

"Sure. I've always wanted to learn to quilt myself. Maybe you could help me with a small project." Something creative would certainly take Angela's mind off Jack and LJ. It would also give her an outlet for some of her energy. "And there are a couple of antique shops in Port Clinton. I want to stop in to see if they carry vintage watches. I wear them when I go out."

Even though LJ would be leaving soon, getting out of the house without him tagging along wasn't difficult. All she had to do was mention shopping, and she was free for the day, allowing LJ to plan his upcoming move.

Angela swung by Lilly's place. True to her word, she was ready to go when Angela knocked on the newly repaired screen door. "The guys did a good job here. It looks brand new."

"They've worked magic here more than once," she said.

Lilly lived on the outskirts of Oak Harbor, so her home wasn't far from Angela's house. They drove east toward Port Clinton, following Route 2 onto Highway 163. The sunlight sparkled off the water as wind-driven waves broke along the shoreline. Angela wore a light jacket. Although July would arrive in a few days, the breeze off the lake was cool, giving them a great day for walking and shopping.

Two antique stores later, Angela hadn't found any old watches. They moved on to the quilt shops.

"Lilly Weathers! It's been ages since we saw you." Two older women at the first shop greeted Lilly with hugs.

"I know, I know," Lilly said as she pulled them aside.

Angela stepped back to give them privacy. Lilly hadn't been back to the shop since Harry died. Angela gave the old friends time to catch up. She strolled the aisles, glad to be out with Lilly today, creating a new friendship by doing something that had nothing to do with her job. Angela wandered around, looking at fabrics and patterns for quilts. She picked out a simple kit for a throw to show Lilly when she rejoined her.

"What do you think of this one? Do you think you could give me a few pointers?"

A crinkled smile shone up at her. "I'd love to. You've picked a nice one. This pattern will be simple to make with enough complexity to teach you a few things. I didn't know you liked to sew."

"I learned in grade school. Then, in high school, I made a few of my clothes. Not a lot, really, but I did enjoy it."

"I won't need to teach you how to use a machine?"

"No, I'm going to have to find it. I have a portable somewhere."

"That's good. We can start next weekend if you like. Do you have any cutting implements?"

Angela purchased a cutting mat, acrylic ruler, scissors, and a rotary cutter with her kit. Lilly picked out some colorful fabrics, thread, and new blades for her own rotary cutters.

Leaving Port Clinton, they drove past the stately homes along Perry Avenue. They made a side excursion to Catawba Island to see the scenery. Their next stop was in Lakeside for lunch.

They found a table in the crowded restaurant and put in their orders.

Halfway through the meal, Angela saw Ray Silverman, the developer she'd talked to on the phone who'd called Connie names. Everyone on the LECOS and SOS boards knew him. He was known for doing high-quality work. He also advocated for the refuge, which stood him apart from his associates. His name was on only one of the fax lists Susan had sent her. Before he had shown up at the last meeting, it had been almost a year since Ray had attended—until the murder.

Angela waved him over to their table to join them. Angela had promised to stop investigating, but a chance to talk to someone who'd dated Connie was an opportunity she couldn't miss.

Ray was tall, lean, and attractive. Angela guessed he was in his mid-fifties. Today, he wore jeans with white-soled boat loafers instead of his usual suit. Ray greeted Angela with a smile. He had a newspaper in his hand, and his gray hair was neat, cut just below the ears. A well-trimmed gray mustache topped his broad smile. His tanned face was otherwise clean-shaven. He pulled up a chair at the table. "Angela Martin. Long time no see." He called the waitress over to order a beer.

"Hi, Ray. I saw you at the last meeting. I guess you didn't see me." She introduced him to Lilly. Angela couldn't help but notice the spark of interest in Lilly's eye when Angela explained his involvement with LECOS and SOS. Lilly continued to tackle her sandwich, keeping quiet.

"What kept you away from the meetings? I missed seeing you," Angela said as the waitress set a beer in front of Ray.

"Business has been good. I just haven't had time." He glanced at Lilly. "What are you ladies doing today?"

"Just enjoying some good weather, doing a little shopping. A girls' day out." Angela smiled, noting he'd changed the subject.

"Sounds like fun. I'm looking for a new boat. Well, it's more like a fishing yacht. I love to fish and entertain at the same time.

I've checked a few listed in the paper. The ones I wanted to look at are moored in Marblehead." He tapped the folded publication in front of him. "I've seen some real beauties today. Several that appeal to me. I'm going to have a tough time settling on just one."

He was buying a fishing yacht? His business must be doing well. "Are you planning to come back to the LECOS meetings?"

He took a sip of beer. He glanced away before clearing his throat.

"I owe you an apology," he said, leaning toward Angela. "I'm sorry I was rude to you on the phone the other day. I knew about Connie. It brought back some bad vibes."

Angela didn't respond.

"You know that I dated her." It was a statement, not a question.

Angela nodded. "It was some time back, wasn't it?"

Ray shrugged. "It was a while back, but she was part of why I broke it off with LECOS. When we ended our relationship, my business picked up. I've just been too busy for the meetings." His beer arrived. He took a small sip, carefully placing it on a napkin, staring at the frosted glass as water dripped down the side.

Angela sat back in her chair. It was time to cut to the chase. "To tell the truth, Ray, I've been trying to make some sense of her death. I worked with her for a while. I didn't know much about her. I vaguely know that she caused some people a lot of trouble. I can tell you, she didn't always make my life easy. Even so, I don't know why someone would murder her." She was only making small talk. Right?

"You don't understand why? If that's true, the Connie you knew was quite different from the one I eventually knew," he said.

"Have the police talked to you about her?"

"Yeah. I was surprised they didn't seem too interested in what I had to say." He paused. "I shouldn't speak ill of her now. There were probably lots of reasons she ended up the way she did. Connie was a beautiful woman. On the surface, she was smart and funny."

He shifted in his chair. Speaking to Lilly, explaining himself. "I'm an honest businessman in construction. I contract smaller jobs for custom business sites. I make a decent living. I have no complaints."

He turned back to Angela with a warm smile. Angela was sure he was good at sales. He was buying a yacht, after all.

"I'm only successful as long as I'm shrewd in my assessment of what a job will cost before I bid on it," he continued. "I'm too small to risk a lot of money on any venture. I met her at a Chamber of Commerce dinner. She was pleasant to be with. We talked about development in the city and how Toledo was beginning to become a cleaner place to live. That interested me. I'm into re-purposing old buildings, restoring neighborhoods, and going green. She hooked me when I learned she was involved with the environmental movement in the area."

"After that, we dated a few times. About two weeks after we started seeing each other, I went through my mail. I saw some rejections on jobs I was bidding on. I knew I'd put in some pretty good numbers, so I was concerned about it. I noted the company who had gotten the bid, some joker named Dwayne Palmer."

Angela glanced at Lilly. Dwayne Palmer. Again.

"Business continued to go downhill. I wasn't winning many bids. My income suffered. Palmer and another guy, Durham, kept coming out on top. I had no idea what was happening, but I didn't put two and two together until one night, Connie and I were going to go out for dinner. I was running late, and I went to take a shower. I needed another towel. When I came out to get it, I caught Connie on my computer looking through my upcoming proposals. She didn't have time to react. My worksheets and proposals for bids were on the screen."

He reached for his glass, wiping it with a napkin before sipping. He stared at the glass as he spoke.

"Needless to say, I was angry. The woman didn't even apologize. She just started laughing, picked up her purse, and walked out. She commented that, uh-oh, she was busted. I was speechless."

He slumped in his chair. "I saw her attach herself to men at other functions. I didn't have solid proof about what she was doing. If I knew them, I warned them. Shortly after our split, I started winning bids again."

He sat up straight. "That's it. I can only tell you that Connie must have crossed somebody who didn't take it well, who didn't get over it. I wasn't surprised when the police questioned me about her. When I caught her at it, I was too shocked to do anything. I'm not a murderer."

"Do you think she was working with someone? You mentioned Dwayne Palmer. Do you think she was working for him?"

"I doubt she worked for anyone. She set up the deal, found the sucker, and I'm sure someone paid a lot of money for the information. It might have benefitted her to give information to someone along the way. I don't know. We had a good time together. She was warm. She didn't appear to be too interested in money. We never talked about work, hers or mine. We enjoyed the same books, movies . . ."

Angela waited for him to finish. He didn't, so she rescued him. "It looks like Connie took you for a ride. She gave me a lot of heart-burn for other reasons."

Angela had heard enough. "Do you have more boats to look at this afternoon?" she said, changing the subject. He visibly relaxed.

"Only two more. It doesn't matter. I saw one this morning that may be hard to beat."

Thirty-Four

CHATTING WITH RAY WAS INFORMATIVE. He left in a hurry to look at the next boat. Angela and Lilly emerged from the deep shade of the restaurant awning to a hot sidewalk drenched in sun. The day had warmed up. "Ready for a stroll at Marblehead Lighthouse?"

"Sure," Lilly said. "We can walk off some of our lunch. Do you think we can make room for some ice cream later?"

"I like that idea."

"Dwayne Palmer surfaces again?" Lilly asked. "He represented himself as honest. I found it interesting. It is a little curious that he was candid with a stranger. He doesn't know me."

"I agree. He sure didn't hold back," Angela said. "He'd already talked to the police and was direct with me when I called him a couple of weeks ago. I don't think he has any reason to hide anything."

"I know you're supposed to stay out of this, but this information is good. Since Ray already talked to Danny and the Sheriff's office, you might want to let Danny know you ran into him today." She paused. "He gave you a strong motive for Connie's murder."

"Very close to Bart Linden's story. Whew. Connie was busy."

They just happened to be near the ice cream parlor when they finished their walk. While the women enjoyed their treat, they looked through their purchases. Afterward, Angela dropped Lilly off at her house.

On her way home, Angela stopped for groceries for a barbecue. Angela bought potato salad at the deli. At home, she sliced tomatoes and put corn on the cob in foil for LJ to grill with chicken. He enjoyed a bottle of wine while she enjoyed a cold glass of lemonade.

Their dinner was delicious, with ice cream for dessert. It sure didn't bother Angela to eat it twice in one day. LJ filled her in on his upcoming move. Angela could honestly be glad for him. Afterward, they sat on the back deck, listened to the frogs, and watched the fireflies dance, creating a peaceful show against the backdrop of the lawn.

She didn't mind the shift in the relationship with LJ. He didn't seem heartbroken. Were they both relieved?

Angela went back into the house to get ready for bed.

What was Lilly doing this evening? Was she playing cards with Ed, or was he with a girlfriend? Maybe she was starting her quilt project. Sitting in the company of LJ tonight, Angela had felt alone. He had an exciting new life ahead of him. A life she would play no part in. She knew it was for the best, but parting with LJ wouldn't be painless. She did care about him and would miss his company.

Before bed, she checked her emails. She sent a note to Danny to tell him about her talk with Ray. Danny would relay the information to Det. Lane. There were too many coincidences about Dwayne Palmer to overlook. Angela doubted that Dwayne had anything to do with Connie's death, but she was sure he knew more than he was letting on.

SUNDAY MORNING, ANGELA TUMBLED OUT OF BED. Pete and Poe slipped between her legs, wanting their morning breakfast. They didn't often demand space on her lap or shoulder, so she made time to give it to them this morning. LJ was already up, working on the computer and turning over projects to a colleague.

Angela pulled out a book she'd wanted to read for a while. She took advantage of the quiet time with the cats around her. The three of them made themselves comfortable on the couch. Unlike the day before, the sky was overcast and brooding. The cats warmed her, making it a good day for reading. Their demands for attention were endless.

The kitties had finally begun to snooze when the phone rang. Angela reluctantly put the book down.

"Angela. It's Lilly. Dwayne Palmer called and said he could show me some houses this afternoon in Port Clinton. I don't want to monopolize your weekend, but could you join us?"

Angela sat up straight. "Today?" She looked down at her pajamas.

"His idea. If you can't come, I can go alone."

"I wasn't planning on going out today, but this could be fun. Besides, I don't think you should go alone with what we know about Dwayne." She paused. "What time?"

"I told him I'd meet him at eleven. It shouldn't take more than an hour. We could have lunch afterward."

"That sounds great. Where does Dwayne want to meet you?"

"At his Port Clinton development. He gave me directions. If you pick me up, we can go together. I didn't tell him I was inviting you along." Angela could imagine Lilly's smile on the other end of the line.

"I'm sure he'll be pleased to see me." Angela might learn more about how Dwayne's development at River Gardens came together. She threw on clothes, grabbed her purse, and let LJ know she was leaving to meet Lilly in Port Clinton to look at another house.

Just as she passed the Darby Unit of the refuge, Angela spotted Dwayne's truck, with some other cars, on a side road next to the refuge boundary. Her curiosity aroused, she turned around and pulled into the Darby entrance. She parked well inside the gate where no one could see her car from the road, closing the gate behind her. Putting her phone in her back pocket, Angela left her purse in the vehicle before slowly trekking through the woods to the east boundary of the unit.

After she crossed beyond the refuge boundary, she saw several men standing in a small clearing ahead of her. Dwayne was with Robert Durham and Donald King. Dwayne had a metal box with him, much like the one Tony mentioned. She was seeing what he described firsthand. She watched them from her hiding place for a few minutes, hearing bits and snatches of their conversation.

They were laughing about something. Durham kicked a small pink flag that stuck up out of the ground. They walked a little closer to where Angela was hiding. She squatted down into the shadows of the undergrowth, where she could hear their conversation clearly.

Durham picked up a handful of dirt and sifted it through his fingers. "You're sure you've marked all the buried samples? Are you going to be able to find them again? You didn't miss any?"

Dwayne nodded.

"How many?"

"I've placed forty around this piece of land," Dwayne said. "Once I GPS them all in, I'll take the flagging out. We'll put an offer on this piece contingent on an inspection, and when the inspectors find the contaminants, we'll be able to lowball it. I had to be careful with this stuff. I didn't want it to get spread around. It's mostly PCBs, but there's other junk with it. I wore gloves. It's funny how easy it is to buy this stuff when you know who to talk to," he snickered. "Most of the other developers will drop out quickly. They won't want to bother with the potential problem this presents."

"What if the inspector misses finding any of them?" Durham asked.

Dwayne smiled. "Knowing the right people always helps."

Durham laughed. "Especially when you throw a few Ben Franklins their way."

Donald rubbed his hands together. "This property is a prime waterfront location. Once we get the land, we'll come back out, dig up all the samples, and claim we cleaned it all up. The inspectors will re-test the site. We'll get this piece of land for a song and make millions. Durham, are you in with us on this one?"

Durham was all smiles. "You boys have done a great job. Too bad our little Connie isn't here to see this."

Dwayne nodded. "Connie helped me with all the environmental planning, told me how to plant the samples, and who to hire to test the site. She'd done it before, lots of times. How do you think I landed the River Gardens project? We can name this one after her. How does Connie's Cove sound to you?" They all laughed.

The wind picked up from the storm front, making it difficult to hear them. The men walked back toward Route 2. Angela waited until she was sure they were gone.

She leaned against the tree, waiting to hear their vehicles start. She tried to call Danny. There was no signal. Using her phone, she took photos of the flagging. While she looked at homes with Lilly, Det. Lane could get a warrant to search this land.

"Angela."

She swung around to find Dwayne standing in the clearing where he'd met the other men. He was holding a GPS unit in his hand. Damn. She didn't think he'd come back right away. He was supposed to be on his way to meet Lilly.

"What are you doing out here?"

THIRTY-FIVE

THINKING FAST, ANGELA PLAYED INNOCENT. "I saw your car parked out by the road. I decided to stop to chat with you. Where were you? I couldn't find you."

"Well, I'm here," he said slowly.

"What's going on? Thinking about buying this land?" she asked.

He nodded, glancing at the flags on the ground. He looked at her hand, still holding the cell phone. "Yeah, I was looking over this piece of land. It might be a good place to invest in a development project." He stepped toward her. "What were you taking pictures of?"

Angela had to draw him away from realizing what she was doing. He'd be suspicious if she didn't act a little put out. It was time to act like the granola cruncher he thought she was. "I thought you might want to develop this land. I was trying to take a few snapshots of the habitat. This location is right next to the refuge. Development here could devastate the wildlife in this area."

He shrugged. "People want to live here, Angela. As they say, you can't fight progress."

That pushed her buttons. Angela hated that saying. Filling in every square acre with housing along the sensitive lakefront was not progress in her mind. She pulled back her emotional reactions.

It was time to control her anger. Dwayne had her trapped, standing between her and freedom.

Showing a little righteous indignation, she pulled herself up straight and started to walk past him. "The refuge is going to be surrounded by humanity. Wildlife conflicts are bound to happen. A coyote will get shot for crossing a yard or, more likely, for eating a cat or dog. Not to mention all the birds that cats will kill."

He stepped in front of her, stopping her progress.

Angela went on the attack. "Why can't you build in Port Clinton? You can develop lots of property there. People will be closer to amenities."

He raised his eyebrows. "I can see you don't understand the building business. That kind of development is costly because of the price of the land. This area appeals to folks living around Perrysburg and Toledo with higher incomes. People like simple, single-family houses tucked away from everything in this neck of the woods. I'll build small bungalows with private marinas attached. You have to know your market, Angela."

Still trying to get around him, she continued. "Oh, I don't know. It seems like the kind of housing they have near Perrysburg goes over well in Port Clinton, especially along the city's waterfront. There's a lot of space closer to town where a development project like that could happen. I'm not the only one who wants to see this land stay wild. If developers are going to build, it's better to stay closer to the infrastructure. Doing that will use less of the raw land surrounding them. Someone developed River Gardens like that. You claim you did it. It was pretty innovative for you. Why can't you do that again?"

Dwayne stepped into her, forcing her backward. "What do you mean *if* I did it? You don't think I did River Gardens myself?" The smile was gone.

You blew it, big mouth. Angela put her hand on Dwayne's arm. She tried to step to his side. "Oh, I believe you. I didn't mean to make it sound like I didn't. You know how I feel, Dwayne. I'm just dismayed that more development will take place in an area with so much potential for wildlife."

Dwayne grabbed her arm and pulled Angela in front of him. He smiled, putting on his salesman charm, giving Angela goosebumps. "I think you can see there's plenty of room for people here who enjoy being close to wildlife. This area doesn't sit right on the edge of the Lake, but it's pretty close. We're thinking about dividing it into twenty large lots, leaving half of the trees and building only custom homes. Wildlife won't suffer. Closer to the water, there's a place deep enough to allow about ten to twenty slips for boats. These homes will be high dollar value only. This type of development isn't quite like River Gardens. It will make up for the lower-end stuff you saw the other day."

Acting the belligerent environmentalist was getting Angela nowhere. It was time to change tack. "I guess you're right. You know me. I get worked up about this stuff. I'm sorry. I didn't mean to go on the attack. Tell me more about this idea of yours." She hoped she could maneuver her way out of this yet.

His smile couldn't conceal the hard look in his eyes. Angela had to be ready to run for it.

"Walk over that way. I want you to see the views these homes will have." Dwayne pushed her forward. "I'll show you where we plan to build the boat slips."

Still looking for another way to get away, Angela walked in the direction he indicated. She wasn't interested in looking for views. She turned to say something just as a massive piece of wood swept past her face, scraping her shoulder.

Dwayne's face was red and contorted from the effort of swinging the heavy club. Missing her, he stumbled, reaching out to grab her arm. Instead, he pulled the cell phone out of her grasp.

Angela spun around and ran down the dirt trail toward the water. Dwayne picked up the phone before running after her. Too late, Angela realized she was trapped, so she jumped off the path into the woods, pushing her way through the Japanese honeysuckle.

Dwayne couldn't keep up, wearing his usual polyester dress pants and loafers. Angela jumped over fallen logs and pushed through the brush. After a few minutes, she couldn't hear him behind her, but she was a little disoriented. Angela had parked her car at Darby, which should be on her left—the only way to safety. There was no way she could make it back to her car without being seen. She'd have to figure out a different route.

Angela scrambled down into a ditch choked with thick shrubs to hide. Leaves on the ground covered her tracks. She burrowed under the bushes, bumping against an old, hidden concrete culvert.

She crawled inside its shadowy darkness, watching for whatever might be living inside. Even a non-poisonous water snake would be a nasty fellow with which to share a wet hole. Angela yearned for the safety of her refuge now, where she could mentally map her way out of this mess. Why hadn't she ever taken the time to become familiar with the land that surrounded the refuge?

Catching her breath, she scrunched up her knees and listened. Her heart pounded in her ears as she pressed her back into the curve of the damp concrete. She probed her shoulder lightly. Nothing broken.

A branch cracked outside. Angela heard the crunch of footsteps grow louder. Dwayne must have figured out she would run toward Darby. He was trying to cut her off.

She moved deeper into the tube, staying as quiet as possible. Angela could hear Dwayne panting, his breath ragged from the effort of chasing her. He was close.

How did she get herself into this stupid situation? She heard him stumbling through the fallen leaves as he walked past her hiding spot. He lacked backwoods skills, but that didn't change the fact that if she could hear him, he might be able to hear her.

There were small movements in the leaves around her. She was too scared to care what creepy crawlies shared the pipe with her now. Looking through the circle of light at the end of the tube, Angela could see the shadows were getting longer. Her watch display was a few minutes past noon. Was Lilly wondering what had happened to her? By now, she would have called Angela's cell and her house. Everyone would be worried. The problem was that they had no reason to look in Darby. No one would ever see her car unless they came through the gate into the unit.

Dwayne's footsteps moved away from her. He stumbled, and Angela could hear him curse as he started beating the bushes with something. A stick cracked on a fallen tree trunk near the concrete pipe. The branches near the opening moved. Angela froze, holding her breath, mentally pulling herself farther into the hole, into the blackness. She saw his foot as he stepped down into the ditch near her into a muddy puddle. He shook his white patent leather shoe violently. He cursed about ruining his new shoes.

His foot moved away. Angela couldn't hear his steps anymore. He wasn't dumb enough to leave her this way. She wondered if Dwayne had a gun. He could easily wait her out and pick her off from a distance. If he found her in this concrete pipe, he could shoot her. Out here, away from the refuge, no one would ever find her body.

She waited. She could faintly hear traffic from the highway. That helped her with a sense of direction. Her watch now read one fifteen. It seemed more like hours since she dove into this pipe. Faintly, she heard a truck start. Was Dwayne leaving?

Angela waited. Dwayne might try to sneak back into the woods to find her. She wished she'd held onto her cell phone. He must have looked through the pictures by now and realized that she'd heard his conversation. Crap. There was no way he'd give up looking for her.

Time was on his side. Once it was dark, he might have difficulty seeing her but would still be able to hear her movements. If he went to Darby, he'd find her car. Angela decided to wait until sunset. Then she'd take her chances. She knew what lay behind her—water. Was his truck still out on the road? Where was he?

A muscle spasm jerked her right leg. She moved into a more

comfortable position. Angela wiggled her feet and rubbed her legs. It was going to be a long wait.

Twigs cracked and broke several times during the next hours, but no one or anything passed by her. Deer? She couldn't tell. Damn it. Her legs throbbed with pain that would only worsen if she stayed in this hidey-hole much longer. Anger bubbled up in her. When she made it out, Dwayne would answer for what he put her through.

THIRTY-SIX

Angela shivered as she waited. Her mind focused on the lay of the land. Darby was to the west. A marina and a gas station were down the road to the east. What about the edge of the lake? Was there a way to get to the gas station from there? No, that would only take her farther away from help. If Dwayne caught her out in the open, she'd be helpless. If she moved, it had to be back toward the main road, where she had a better chance of getting help if she needed it.

Another half-hour passed when Angela's luck took a radical turn. Her legs were stiff, and she was losing circulation in her feet. The leaves outside began to move as the wind started to blow, causing the tree branches to sway. The storm front had finally arrived. Rain pelted down on the ground. Water ran under her through the culvert. She couldn't hear anything above the creaking trees and falling rain. Scared, she waited.

The stupidity of her fear hit her like the cold water now seeping through her jeans. If she couldn't hear Dwayne, he wouldn't hear her either. For once, she was happy to be cold and wet. Dwayne was wearing the wrong clothes to be out in this weather, so Angela bet he would remain in his truck.

She crawled out of the pipe cautiously. There was no one in

sight. The gray darkness had the feeling of twilight. Crawling from one shrub to another, she took her time moving toward the highway, searching for Dwayne as she went. The rain continued to fall, but Angela was glad to be out of that hole.

She crouched in some bushes as a deer ran past her. It didn't see her. Angela stayed still to see if whatever had scared the deer was coming her way. After a long wait, she moved on.

Angela found her way back to the trail. She crawled through bushes to where Dwayne had previously parked his truck. It wasn't there. Angela could see it farther down the road, parked closer to the Darby entrance. If she went to her car, he would catch her. Angela crawled closer. There he was, sitting in the truck, watching the road.

He turned his head, surveying the woods with binoculars. She didn't move. Dwayne could see through the grayness with a good pair of binocs. Her sweatshirt, soaked with rain, stuck to her skin. The sweatshirt would work in her favor, even wet. The gray fabric would blend with the background and serve as camouflage.

Dwayne continued watching for a few more minutes, then put the binoculars down. He hit the dashboard. Yeah, he was worried. He should be. He'd had one shot at getting rid of Angela. If she hadn't turned around when she did, he'd be driving home right now, free of all his cares.

He picked up a cell phone to make a call. Dwayne wasn't completely stupid. He was probably calling for reinforcements. It was time to get out of this place.

Angela moved away from him in an eastward direction. If she could circle behind him, she could go to the gas station on the edge of Port Clinton. There, she'd call LJ to rescue her. She just had to get out of these woods without getting spotted.

She crawled through the bushes toward Route 163, staying parallel to the road, stopping from time to time to rest and take her bearings. An hour later, she came to a gas station. She didn't see Dwayne in the parking lot, so she stood up. She ran as fast as she could into the store.

The teenage boy behind the counter looked surprised as she entered. She was muddy from her head to her toes, with leaves in her messy hair. She didn't want to scare him.

"My car broke down off the road. I need to phone my husband to pick me up."

The boy stared at her.

"I was in such a hurry to get to a dry place that I left my purse and cell phone in the car. I didn't want to go back for them. I'm a mess. I fell in the mud."

He didn't seem too sure of her, but he took her into a back office where he said she could make her call. Angela hoped beyond hope that LJ was home.

The phone rang once before LJ picked it up. "Angela, is that you? Where are you? Are you okay? Lilly told me you were missing. You were supposed to pick her up to look at houses with some guy. She's worried sick. Do you know it's after five? We're under a tornado watch! Everyone's been looking for you. Where are you?"

"Please, LJ, stop talking and listen," Angela told him what had happened to her.

"Stay put. I'll call Danny. I'm on my way to pick you up now."

"I'll wait in the women's bathroom until you get here. Just knock on the door. Please hurry!" Angela was terrified that Dwayne would come into the station. She didn't think the teenage boy was likely to be much help if Dwayne grabbed her.

She walked toward the front door. She thanked the boy for the use of the phone. While he served other customers, Angela ducked behind the shelves, racing into the women's bathroom.

Luckily, the restroom had two stalls. Angela claimed one for herself. Several women came in and out without seeing her. Finally, someone knocked on the door and whispered her name.

LJ had arrived at last with reinforcements. Danny stood with Det. Lane near the store entrance.

"Oh, my God. I've never been so glad to see you in all my life."

Angela wrapped her wet arms around him, hugging him with all her might.

Danny and Det. Lane went off after Dwayne when she told them what had happened. As the surprised teenage boy watched, LJ led Angela out. Danny would get Angela's car for her later.

LJ had towels in the car. Angela dried herself off the best she could and wrapped them around her. Even though LJ was quite warm himself, he turned the heater on, knowing she needed the heat to calm her shivering. He didn't say a word to her all the way home. Angela knew he was worried sick. She could see he was a little angry, too.

When they pulled into the driveway, he finally spoke. "Angela, you scared me to death. I'm so glad you're all right."

Angela sat for a moment as those words surrounded her. She was relieved that he wasn't spouting words of love. It would have been too much to take. Without responding, she went inside to take a long, hot shower. When she came downstairs in clean pajamas and wet, clean hair, LJ handed her a glass of wine, which she accepted gratefully.

"Tell me everything that happened. You were supposed to stop helping the investigation," LJ admonished her. "But you seem to have caught your man. I want to know the details. I'm relieved it's finally over!"

"I need to call Lilly to let her know I'm okay."

"Already done. Lilly says she'll talk to you tomorrow."

Careful to position her bruised shoulder to avoid pain, Angela sat beside him on the couch and told him what had happened. "It sounds crazy after everything I went through today, but I find it hard to believe that Dwayne murdered Connie. I always felt uneasy around him because he's such a sleaze. I never trusted Durham. I wouldn't put it past him to murder her."

"They were all in it together? Connie, her brother, Durham, and Dwayne? They must have had a pretty tidy little business together. I'm sure they made major bucks running those kinds of real estate scams." LJ sipped his wine. "I still don't get it. Why would Dwayne kill her?"

"I don't know. Something must have gone sour." Angela sipped her wine. "It just doesn't fit. Even after today, I think I'm missing something. Why would Dwayne kill Connie? Did the other two help him? They said they missed Connie and wished she could be there today."

"Well, the other two might not know Dwayne did it."

She shook her head. "One thing for sure, I would never have suspected that her brother was involved in something crooked. There doesn't seem to be any indication that Susan knew about any of this, either. Those three men handed me a pretty smooth storyline." She sipped more wine. "Connie must have fooled Susan as well. There's no way she'd involve herself in this kind of scam."

"I'm just glad we can get back to our lives without me worrying whether or not you'll get yourself hurt."

"We can all work together again at the refuge without other volunteers worrying about having a murderer in their midst. This incident should clear Jack."

Danny called to tell her they were questioning Dwayne at police headquarters. Another officer would bring her car over within the next hour. "It's weird. Some pieces aren't fitting together yet, and we have some loose strings to tie up. It'll take a while to get the truth out of Dwayne."

"I only care about clearing Jack. He's out of it now, is that right?"

"Oh, yeah. That's right. This clears Jack. If you're at work, I'll catch up with you tomorrow."

"I'll be there." Angela hung up. She leaned against LJ. He kissed her hair, stroked her shoulder, and helped her to the bed, where she fell to sleep immediately.

She woke later in the night from a nightmare. Dwayne was chasing her through the woods, shouting, "I didn't kill Connie."

THIRTY-SEVEN

THE ALARM WENT OFF. MOVING THE CATS OFF her chest, Angela rolled out of bed. Ugh. Monday morning. She didn't feel like going to work. Her bruised shoulder had limited movement, but she wasn't sick. Besides, she had to go to work because she might see Jack.

Sally had hot coffee brewing, with the familiar aroma of her special blend filling the office. Angela checked in with Kate, who told her Pearl was on her way to Lansing, Michigan, to attend a meeting of biologists called at the last minute with some Regional Fisheries folks. There were no volunteers in the greenhouse.

Angela settled into her desk just as the phone rang. It was Jack calling to thank her for everything she'd done. The sound of his voice renewed Angela's spirits.

"I'm home, Little Sis. It's wonderful! I have you to thank for believing in me. You don't know how good it feels to be in my own bed, using my shower, and eating whenever I want. Lilly made breakfast. I just hope Ed doesn't eat it all before I get back to the table." He laughed.

"I'm so glad you're out, Jack. What about your friend? Is she still staying with you?"

"She finally found a safe house in Toledo that had room for her.

They called her yesterday morning. Her husband will never look for her there. When she heard from the safe house, she called the Sheriff to clear me, but they were already releasing me. Thanks to you."

Angela was glad the woman had a solution that didn't involve Jack. Angela only wished she'd found it sooner. "I'll let you get back to your friends. Stop by later if you can, huh?"

She hung up with renewed energy, focusing on the flow of the day's business. Things could finally get back to normal. Yesterday faded into the distance as she dove into her emails. Susan Worth called to chat about another meeting and asked how she was. Angela marveled at how fast bad news travels.

"I'm fine, Susan."

"I guess you had it right about your volunteer. He wasn't guilty after all."

"Yeah, this clears Jack. I don't know, though. As weird as it sounds, I'm not sure I can ever believe that Dwayne was involved with Connie's murder. In my mind, some things just don't fit. Danny assures me that Det. Lane will put all the pieces together. I want to believe they caught the murderer."

Susan sighed. "Really, Angela, your imagination is out of control. Your volunteer is in the clear. That should satisfy you."

"I am satisfied. I only wonder why Dwayne would kill a meal ticket like Connie?" Angela paused. "I guess it's hard to believe it's over. Be honest, Susan. Connie fooled you, too."

Susan paused before saying anything. Her voice lowered slightly. "My relationship with Connie was business. You saw how she was able to handle people in meetings. She was a pro. She was able to make things happen when no one else could. She made it easy for me to see the good in her. Unfortunately, she was involved with something beyond the scope of her duties. I feel terrible for her."

Even after everything that had come to light, Susan continued to see the goodness in Connie.

"The next meeting is going to be on the third. It will all be different with Connie gone and this news about Dwayne going public. I'll see you there." Susan hung up.

Angela's mind was in a muddle, trying to piece together the events of the past three weeks. Was it Dwayne who cut holes in her tire? When that happened, she'd only talked to him once. Did he have any idea she was investigating at that time?

Tony LaRoche popped his head into her office doorway.

"How you doin'?"

"Hi, Tony. I'm fine. What's up? Pearl's not here." He pulled up a chair, put his elbows on her desk, overlapping his forearms, and resting his chin on them like a boy. He looked up at Angela.

"Not here to see Pearl," he said. "You sure took good care of yourself out there yesterday."

"You heard about my ordeal, too? Boy, bad news does travel fast."

"I was there. That real estate fella was trying to hurt you." He sat up. "But you gave him the slip and kept out of sight." He snapped his fingers. "Pretty good sneakin', I'd say."

"You were there? You saw him try to hit me? Why didn't you help me? Why didn't you stop him?"

He frowned. "I watched to make sure you were okay. You did fine without my help. It wasn't like you were drowning or something." He stared at her for a split second, then smiled. He was looking at Angela with admiration.

"You did good. If you'd looked like you needed my help, I'd've given it. But you didn't. Nope, not this time." He slumped back in the chair and shook his head. "You sure are something."

Tony was paying Angela a compliment. There was no sense in being angry with him. It was like being mad at a fox because he ate chickens. What action would he have taken if he thought she needed help escaping Dwayne? It was one thing to save her from drowning. Would he have confronted Dwayne? She couldn't believe he had been there the entire time.

The hair on the back of Angela's neck rose. How often did

he watch her in the woods? "You'll need to talk to the Sheriff's office. Please tell them what you saw. It'll help with the case against Dwayne Palmer."

"Mebbe. We'll see." He stood up to leave. "Take care of yourself, Angela. But then, I guess I don't need to say that."

She stared at the door for several minutes after he left. She wasn't going to wait for Tony to talk to anyone. As she reached for the phone to make the call herself, she saw Tony pass the window on his way to the parking lot. He looked a little wild with the sun shining full on his grinning face and unruly hair shooting out from under his ball cap. She was glad he appreciated the refuge and contributed his skills to the refuge trapping program. His assistance was invaluable in maintaining the marshes at a healthy level by reducing muskrat activity. She wouldn't want him as an enemy. She was unsure how she felt to have him as a friend.

She ate lunch with Gilbert. They talked about her ordeal. Like Tony, he was amazed by how she escaped.

"You can take care of yourself," Gilbert said. "I just wish you wouldn't get in those situations in the first place. I'm glad you're okay."

After lunch, Gilbert told Angela he was going to Sandusky for a meeting with the Ohio Department of Natural Resources.

"Oh, by the way," Gilbert said, "I checked with the previous refuge manager on that River Gardens issue. He said all he could remember was that one developer was screwed out of a job. He said someone greased the wheels for Dwayne Palmer to get his bid in. Apparently, the deadline was extended by a day in his favor. He said that Dwayne Palmer was lucky like that more than once."

That corroborated everything Angela knew now.

"I better head out, or I'll be late for the meeting." He stopped. "There's a broken gate at the Navarre Unit. I sent the maintenance crew to repair it."

The everyday work of the refuge was once again upon them. Things would return to normal—no more worry about murderers.

Angela was glad that she and Gilbert could talk to each other.

Sally and Dave came in to tell her they were on their way to a meeting with the Toledo Metropolitan Area Council of Governments. They were taking their personal cars so they could go straight home after the meeting.

Everyone at the refuge had things to do on the same afternoon.

After another hour, Kate left early for some personal time, which she deserved after dealing with three weeks of reporters heckling her. Angela called LJ to let him know she would work late to catch up with stuff she'd neglected while out on the marsh enjoying herself last week.

As she sank back into her reading, the telephone rang. Angela was distracted, but a lousy connection full of static caught her attention. A woman told her that the gate at Metzger had a log jammed in it. She was fishing from her boat and saw the water coming out of the marsh.

THIRTY-EIGHT

DAMN. ANGELA WOULD HAVE TO TAKE CARE of it herself since no one was around. Didn't she just discuss this sort of thing with Gilbert? Today wouldn't be a day to catch up with much of anything.

"Okay, thank you, thank you!" She hung up the phone after yelling over the static. There was no one else to deal with the gate. She grabbed a jacket, and slammed the door shut before locking it on her way out.

She drove through the refuge gate, stopping to lock it behind her since everyone was gone. What a pain in the neck. The winds were out of the northeast, and under these conditions, the water should be pushing itself into Metzger, not pushing it out as the woman had said. With a sigh, Angela knew she'd better check out the situation anyway.

After several attempts with no reply, Angela gave up trying to reach Gilbert or anyone else. It just wasn't turning out to be her day. There was nothing else to do. She had to check it all out herself.

A change in wind direction could be a disaster for the unit. It had happened before. It could easily happen again if the gates were jammed open. If the main screw gate had become unseated again, it would take another month to repair it. It took years to reverse the effects from the last time. If something unseated the screw gate, it could reset itself if you raised and lowered it a few times. That is if you did it right away before the water completely drained.

On the road along the west side of Metzger, Angela unlocked the entry gate by the boat launch canal. After she drove in, she left the gate open so that she didn't have to unlock it again on her way out. She parked on the side of the road near the water control structure.

The electricity was running inside the powerhouse at the weir. She crossed over the grate that spanned the screw gates, peering down into the water. The gates were set very deep, and with the northeast wind pushing the water against them, it was impossible to see them. It didn't look like the marsh was draining, but it could go either way since the head, or water level at the gate, was a little higher in the marsh than outside. Even with the wind, the marsh would drain if the gate was open.

Angela wondered if the caller meant some other marsh. As far as she knew, there weren't any other wetlands in this area with a large water control structure like this. It didn't make much sense. There was no indication of water moving out, and the water was too deep on the lakeside to see a log or anything jammed in it.

Angela heard another vehicle pull up. When she turned, she was surprised to see Pearl walking toward her. "What're you doing out here? I thought you were on your way up to Lansing."

"I was. Before I got too far out of town, I called ahead on my cell phone to double-check the meeting location. There was no meeting scheduled. I received the message about the meeting on my voicemail. I must have gotten the wrong date. I'll check it when I get back to the office. I came back this way to do a little birding over on this end of the Refuge. The gate was open. I thought someone was trespassing. I was almost all the way out here before I realized it was you. Anyway, what are you doing?"

"A woman called to tell me that we were losing water from Metzger. Gilbert is over in Sandusky meeting with DNR, and Sally left for the day with Dave. The maintenance crew is at Navarre repairing another gate. It seems to be a day about gates. No one else was around, so I came out to see myself. Everything looks okay. I better check it out anyway—the wind could be masking something I can't see."

"Do you need help?"

"No, I can handle it. I'll raise and lower the gates myself to check their status. I should be able to see any changes."

Pearl looked relieved. "Good, I can get a little more birding in before we lose the light. Maybe tonight I'll get home at a decent hour."

Angela laughed. "What, no houses to build? Yeah, go on ahead. I won't be much longer myself." She drove away as Angela went to unlock the powerhouse. Stepping into the dark, concrete room, the hair on her arms rose with a sudden chill that only damp concrete can emit. She felt around on the wall until she found the light switch.

Fluorescent lights flickered on, bathing the room in an artificial, gray light, which didn't lend the room warmth. Angela found the switches that powered the gates. The gauges indicated that they were in the closed position. Angela flicked the switch to open them to one foot. That was enough to create a visible whirlpool without losing a lot of water. She could also verify if the controls were reading correctly.

She returned to the grate over the gates and looked down. The sun was midway in the western sky, leaving the space below her in shadows. Crossing to the opposite side, she peered over the railing, still too dark. Stepping off the bridge, she took a well-worn pathway that led down through brushy dogwood to the base of the structure. The path was a sure sign that they spent a lot of time checking the water levels there.

It took her a few minutes to work her way farther down onto the rocky riprap slope. She stepped under the walkway into the shade, where the contrasts between light and dark were absent. Angela could see much better here. The water was moving, causing a whirlpool to form, creating a sucking noise.

The power of the water was immense. Like a kid, she dropped a stick into it to watch it get caught up in the vortex. The current drew it down, and it disappeared. It would pop up on the other side of the weir after traveling through a fifty-foot culvert, continuing until it broke free from the force of the suction and surfaced onto Lake Erie more than fifty yards out.

The head difference between the amount of water inside the marsh and outside wasn't much. But there was enough difference that water would drain when the gate was open. Still, there was no indication of a log jam or the marsh draining. What had the woman seen?

A wad of tissue paper was dangling in a bush nearby. The stuff was everywhere. It made Angela think of the pink tissue in the ditch where someone had murdered Connie. Susan had wiped her nose with pink tissue.

It was a tenuous connection, at best. Susan? She had never seriously considered Susan before because Susan was at her nephew's party in Michigan when it happened. Her brother lived in Ann Arbor. She could easily have returned the same day.

Susan, a political animal, was the only person Angela hadn't seriously considered a killer.

Angela stopped in her tracks. The day Angela called Susan to get contact information, Susan had said something about Jack's gun in the car. How did Susan know about that? Det. Lane had made a point not to release that information to the public. The story in the paper didn't mention the gun at all. Angela didn't notice the admission at the time.

Susan knew how to get what she wanted. Why hadn't she considered that before? Susan dealt with Connie regularly. She had to have known what she was up to. Had Susan found out about Connie's scams and lashed out?

The pieces fit. It all made much more sense than Dwayne Palmer being Connie's murderer. Knowledge of Connie's scams would have ruined Susan's reputation.

When Angela went back to her office, she'd call Danny. Did they have the wrong man, after all?

It's over. Stop driving yourself crazy. Dwayne is in custody. Jack is in the clear.

Still, a woman just lured you out to this gate for no reason at all.

How could she be so stupid? Goosebumps rose as she heard a vehicle drive onto the weir. She turned to start back up the path to see if Pearl had forgotten something.

"Hello, Angela."

Angela looked up, but the setting sun was in her eyes, putting a woman in silhouette. Just as she raised her arm to block the sun, a sharp pain crashed over her temple. Fragments of light shattered her vision. Falling backward, Angela slid down across the jagged rock, branches clawing at her as she twisted to right herself.

What the hell? Her already bruised shoulder took the full impact of her fall. Angela landed at the bottom of the slope, halfway into the water.

Dazed, she tried to regain her balance. She struggled to get up. Some loose riprap rolled into her. Another blow sent sharp, cracking pains across her shoulder and through her head.

"Stop," she yelled. She could hear the sucking noise of the whirlpool in the muddy waters next to her. Angela's vision blurred completely. Someone's hands shoved her backward over the rocks.

Ice-cold water seeped through her jacket and enveloped her body, pulling her down. A high-heeled shoe jabbed her in the side. Angela turned her head. Unbelievably, there it was—a Jimmy Choo-style beige shoe with a spiked heel. *Susan.*

The heel stabbed into her neck and glanced off, cutting a gash in her skin. Angela gasped. Her body slid down. Cold water washed over her face as the foot pushed her shoulders under the water. Angela arched her back, struggling to reach the surface.

"This time, you won't get away from me. The cops will think you fell," Susan yelled.

The cold water brought Angela to her senses. Her lungs were screaming for air, and she could feel the draw of the whirlpool. The vortex pulled at her waterlogged clothing, dragging her into it. But unlike the stick, she was too large to pass through the grates.

I'm going to drown.

THIRTY-NINE

FEAR TRIGGERED ANGELA'S SENSES, BRINGING her head above water. She struggled onto the rocks as Susan kicked her head again. Angela reached up, grabbed an ankle, and heard Susan scream as she pulled hard. Susan, already unbalanced in her heels, fell to the ground.

"Let go, you bitch!" Susan shrieked.

Coming out of the water, Angela held tight to Susan's ankle, pulling herself onto her knees. Now Angela had more control, even though the rocky surface gave her little purchase. Stabs of pain from sharp rocks made it difficult to remain kneeling. She tried to stand.

Susan kicked out with her other foot, catching the side of Angela's face with the heel of her shoe, tearing a gash in her cheek. Angela fell to the side, and Susan hit her with the pipe again. Digging her fingers into Susan's ankle, she reached out to grab Susan's other foot, knocking her shoe off as Susan continued to fight. Angela fell to the ground, holding tight to Susan's ankles.

"You stupid woman! Let go!" a crazed Susan yelled at her again. Ducking her head, Angela hung on to Susan with all her strength. Blows of the heavy pipe rained across Angela's shoulders and back. She had to find a way to get those blows to stop. Her wet coat absorbed much of the impact, but sharp pain tore at her muscles with each thwack. Steeling herself against the pain, Angela focused all her strength on protecting her head while holding Susan down. The attack was so incessant that she was growing numb. How long could this go on?

A wave of fury rushed through Angela. She raised herself up, letting go of one ankle and swinging her arm out. A sharp pain seared through her forearm as it blocked another blow from the pipe. The sound of metal hitting bone filled Angela's ears. The weapon flew from Susan's grip, skittering across the riprap into the water, out of reach.

Angela lunged up the slope, wrapping her arms around Susan's knees. Susan fell backward on her butt, grabbed a rock, and beat Angela across the shoulders and head. Blood ran down Angela's face. She bit into Susan's thigh as hard as she could, burying her teeth in the flesh.

Susan screamed, dropping the rock and giving Angela a chance to grab Susan's arms. With her head tucked, she pressed her body against Susan's, pinning the other woman to the ground. Her boots dug into the rocks as she held the thrashing woman down until she could sit on top of her. Angela's head was pounding with pain. Blood freely streamed into her eyes, blurring her vision.

A second wind brought a new wave of rage. Behind it came a bubble of laughter at the absurdity of it all. *Am I delirious?* Susan is trying to kill her in high heels on a rocky levee slope. It was like being caught up in a deadly cartoon.

Susan bucked, and Angela lost her grip on Susan's hands. Susan clawed at Angela with pink, painted fingernails. Another sharp pain grazed Angela's cheek. A duller pain burst at her scalp as Susan's other fist yanked hard at a hank of hair.

I am not going to let a living Barbie doll murder me.

Muscles trembling with effort, Angela grabbed Susan's hands, pushing them down to the ground, where she held them.

Susan's body went limp for a moment. Angela used the brief reprieve to gain a better hold. "Why did you kill Connie?" she gasped. "She was your partner."

"She was no partner! She betrayed me!" Susan's voice was raw with hurt. "Connie turned against me. She started to cut me out of our deals and had the nerve to blackmail me to keep quiet!"

No honor among thieves. Angela closed her eyes a moment. Jack was caught in the middle. He made a convenient patsy. Innocent Susan was not so guilt-free after all. She was involved all along. Angela wanted to wipe the blood from her stinging eyes, but she couldn't let go of Susan's hands.

Susan thrashed again. For a moment, Angela felt her body lift and her grip slip. She clamped her fingers tight, dug her toes into the ground, and slammed Susan into the ground. Susan's breath whooshed out in tandem with her own.

Susan screamed, "You just couldn't leave it alone! First, the police had Jack, then Dwayne. Why couldn't you stop?"

Susan was raving, but the effort weakened her, making it easier to hold her. "You're all stupid!" she sobbed. "Connie was too greedy."

"You didn't care about the environment at all, did you?" Angela asked quietly. "You contaminated land to get it cheap for your developers. It was just about money. Scams."

"They weren't scams," Susan spat. "Developers got what they wanted. The environment didn't suffer, either. We had it all under control."

Susan relaxed under Angela's grip. "No one was getting hurt. Why shouldn't I be reimbursed for my efforts? No one else worked quickly enough to save those habitats. Not you, not the stupid government. Everyone moved too slowly. The developers knew that and used it against all of you. We just made it happen so that we could share their profits. What was wrong with that?"

Susan Worth, council member, environmental champion, and model community citizen, was a murderer, a thief—a fraud. Susan had been a part of the environmental movement for so long that Angela thought she was above suspicion.

"Connie's murder was all about rage, not a dirty deal gone bad. You shot her in the face. It was brutal."

Susan's muscles quivered. Then, Angela heard a quiet sob.

"I was brutal? I loved her." Susan sought Angela's eyes. "I thought she loved me, too. I understood all her affairs with men because that was part of the deal. She wasn't supposed to sleep with other women. She was leaving me. She said I was an old bore. How could she say that to me? It was hateful. Why did she do that? Why?" Susan pleaded with Angela to answer. Her eyes filled with tears, and she turned her face away.

Angela had to get some help. With newfound strength, she grabbed Susan's hands, raised her off the ground, and wrestled Susan onto her stomach. Susan didn't resist.

Awkwardly, she held Susan's arms behind her back. Lying partway on her, Angela untied one of her boots. She pulled the shoelace out, using it to tie Susan's hands together behind her. Angela was too tired to care if it was too tight. She used the lace of her other boot to tie Susan's feet.

"You were the woman who just called me about the gate?"

"I knew you'd come. I made sure your staff were all somewhere else before I called."

Angela hauled herself onto the weir, leaving Susan on the rocks. She called Pearl from the truck radio. Det. Lane hadn't returned her cell phone yet.

Pearl said Gilbert was already on his way out. "He was in the office when I returned. He was looking for you. I told him you were checking the gates. He's on his way out there to give you a hand."

"Give Danny a call, too. Someone attacked me. I have her in custody."

Pearl started to say something, but Angela didn't wait to listen. She threw the mic back onto the seat and walked down to Susan, who was on her back again, kicking, trying to stand up.

Angela sat just out of reach, watching Susan flop like a fish out of water. Susan's face was bleeding. Her legs were scratched. Her dress was torn and dirty. The image of this woman in spiked high heels trying to kill her on the riprap slope was utterly ridiculous. She thought she could hit Angela on the head with a pipe—that killing her would end her problems.

Susan was mumbling. Angela couldn't understand everything she said. It sounded like she was conversing with Connie, repeating the question, why? It was all about love or some kind of love—the kind of love that killed.

Blood began to dry on Angela's face, making it itch. Her head was pounding. It was difficult to move the arm Susan had hit with the pipe. Was it broken? She was losing the adrenaline that had kept her going during the fight. Pain was setting in. She reached up with her other hand to feel the mat of blood in her hair. It hurt too much to examine the extent of it. Had she dislocated her shoulder? Her entire body felt like it had gone through a crusher. Searing pain overwhelmed her. Angela wanted to throw up. Lie down. Sleep.

Angela's eyes drooped until she heard a man shouting her name. Gilbert and Danny made their way to her. Susan was quiet now—she had quit mumbling.

Danny continued down to Susan's side and untied her, looking at Angela with a quizzical expression when he saw how tightly she had secured them. Susan no longer struggled. Her tear-streaked face was blank.

Angela stood up. "Danny, I'd like you to arrest Susan Worth for the murder of Connie King and Deborah Simmons. I'd also like to add assault and attempted murder to those charges." Angela gingerly touched her head again. "And will someone close the gate before we lose too much water?"

"Good job, Angela." Danny hauled Susan up the slope.

Gilbert held out his arm for her. He leaned in close, holding her arm to support her. He whispered, "Thank God you're alive."

Angela wanted his arms around her, to hold her tight, and never let go.

He didn't.

She tried to throw her arms up, only achieving a shrug. She pushed Gilbert away. "No kidding. That woman is a lunatic."

Gilbert took her arm. "You're all wet, bleeding badly. Your head is a mess. Let me help you up the slope."

She was angry and embarrassed with herself for being fooled by Susan. She was angry with herself for wanting more from Gilbert after she decided to let him go. Angela began to indulge in a moment of self-pity. Gilbert brought her up short.

"Danny told me he warned you to be careful. Why were you out here alone?" Gilbert asked.

"Because everyone thought Dwayne was the murderer, didn't they? Everyone thought the ordeal was over," she said.

"No one told you it was all over," Gilbert raised his voice. "Danny told you he wasn't sure. Didn't it strike you odd that someone called you out here? Why didn't you wait for someone to come out with you?"

Angela felt herself weakening. "Because I told you, I thought it was over. Besides, everyone was gone. There was no one else."

"You should've waited."

"How could I? I couldn't let Metzger get ruined again." She said as tears burned her eyes. She had a job to do taking care of the refuge. Her reputation as a manager mattered to her. Everything was blurry, and her stomach did a flip-flop. Feeling sick, she just wanted to go to sleep.

Angela made it to the top of the slope before she fell. Gilbert's strong arms wrapped around her. Feeling nothing, she was weightless, moving into darkness on a slow-moving wave.

FORTY

SOMEWHERE ALONG THE WAY, FLOATING IN and out, sounds began to enter Angela's brain once again. Feeling throughout her body returned soon after that, bringing with it a dull ache. Then, a warm softness surrounded her. Eventually, the darkness grew lighter until she blinked. She found herself in a hospital room.

She stared at the ceiling, then let her eyes focus on the TV set on the opposite wall. Angela must have groaned or moved because a face appeared above her.

"Angela. Angela, are you awake now?" LJ spoke softly to her.

Don't be silly. Can't you see I'm awake? He didn't seem to hear her. Another man who looked like a doctor walked in behind him. They turned to each other. They were speaking, but Angela couldn't understand their words. Soft gray-green darkness came over her. She blinked to fight it off. Instead, she sank back into its softness.

The next time she opened her eyes, LJ was there. He took her hand and kissed her face. "You'll be all right now. The doctor says you're a miracle in the works. You survived everything that woman threw at you."

She stared at him blankly until she remembered. The attack on the weir. Susan.

LJ held her hand tighter.

"You've been in the hospital since Monday."

"What day is it now?" Angela asked.

"Thursday. Danny had Gilbert following you, but Gilbert had to go to Sandusky. Danny was following up on some leads on Dwayne and Susan. They left you out of sight for only a few hours. That was all it took for Susan to move in on you. You took care of yourself pretty well, Angela, despite it all."

Tony said the same thing to her after her earlier experiences with Dwayne. A movement on the other side of her bed made her turn her head. She winced with pain.

"We questioned Dwayne," Danny said. "While he was guilty of trying to kill you out in that woodlot, or at least assault you that day, he didn't have the right answers to fit Connie's murderer. Or Deborah Simmons', for that matter. Dwayne went after you because he thought you would expose his real estate scam. Susan partnered with Connie, Dwayne, and Donald King. Later, when Connie partnered with Robert Durham, she cut Susan out of all the new deals. That perfumed blouse Deborah Simmons had? A shop in Toledo sold it to Susan Worth. Once we made that connection, we knew who killed Connie King, but Det. Lane needed more evidence. She confessed she found Connie's blouse smelling of a different perfume. Susan was suspicious and followed her the night Connie met Deborah Simmons. When Susan saw them kiss and drive away in Ms. Simmons's car, she got into Connie's car and waited all night until she returned. You know the rest. None of their group suspected Susan of murdering Connie. They figured Jack did it, or Connie'd pissed off a jealous wife. The police are looking into their business dealings now. I'm afraid Mr. Dwayne Palmer will not only serve some time for attempted murder, but he will also face charges for real estate fraud and insider trading, among other things. His buddies will face the same charges."

"We suspected Susan for some time," Danny continued. "We only had some tenuous evidence connecting her to both murders, not enough to nail her, so we kept her under surveillance. The woman was rich from real estate schemes as well as corporate theft. Det. Lane followed a long trail of money. He knew Susan must have killed Connie. He had to find the motive. Her financial records showed a sharp fund decline, while Connie's boosted. They tied correspondence together with other evidence and had the whole story. Neither Connie King nor Susan Worth worked hard to cover their trails. They thought no one would get wise to them. Det. Lane finally had the evidence they needed from the lab, placing Susan at both crime scenes. They were getting a warrant for her arrest the day she attacked you."

Angela interrupted him. "It was all about money and love, Danny. Susan was Connie's lover. Susan expected Connie to see other men, but Connie dumped her for another woman. That's why Susan went crazy."

Danny nodded. "Yes. They were lovers. Det. Lane knew Susan would come after you if she thought you knew something. That's why they wanted you to stop investigating until they could get the warrant. I made sure that Susan learned about your little adventure with Dwayne yesterday. I told her he had been arrested. We all figured if we acted like Dwayne was the killer, she'd leave you alone. For some reason, she still believed you were a threat."

Angela remembered her conversation with Susan that day. *Me and my big mouth.*

LJ plopped down in the chair next to the bed. "You guys didn't tell me anything. I could have stepped in, given you a hand to keep an eye on Angela."

He glanced away. Angela was unable to read his thoughts. "I should have known better than to respond to the phone call. I guess I wasn't thinking clearly. There's no way you could have done anything about this," she said. She reached for LJ's hand. "I'm here, LJ. Susan didn't win this battle."

Angela remembered Gilbert's words. "Thank God you're alive." Even though he hadn't put his arms around her, Gilbert's words had gut-wrenching emotion. Did he have strong feelings for her? Was that what she saw in his eyes and heard in his voice? Was that what she wanted?

Danny continued. "To finish the story, Susan made sure Connie met all the connected people and left Connie to do all the dirty work. Connie figured out the schemes to entice each investor. Once they were on the hook, she leaked bid information to her partners. After her deals went through, Connie severed whatever relationship she had with the injured party."

Danny walked to the end of Angela's bed, tucking a notebook into his jacket. "Which," he continued, "left Susan to mop up afterward. She mended the relationships Connie ruined and garnered partnerships with more companies. Connie also learned some corporate secrets that she took advantage of on the stock market. Susan had no visible connection with whatever deal Connie worked out, which meant Susan had no liabilities to threaten her. With her knowledge and contacts, Susan funneled large amounts of money into a joint account she shared with Connie in Switzerland. Det. Lane checked their local bank accounts. Shortly before Connie died, income in Susan's account started to decline rapidly. Det. Lane has since learned that Connie created a new account in Switzerland for herself. She moved funds from the joint account to it. Susan must have realized this."

"Susan said Connie tried to blackmail her."

"Connie made enough connections to run her scams," Danny said. "She didn't need Susan anymore. She had Dwayne Palmer and Donald King to handle the real estate deals. Their stock market accounts were gaining. The money was piling up, and sometime soon, Susan planned to retire with her nest egg, taking a large chunk of money with her. Connie decided she wanted that money in her nest egg. By cutting Susan out, she could take her share. What could Susan do? She couldn't go to the police."

Angela shook her head. "Connie and Susan were formidable. No one caught on except Bart Linden and Ray Silverman. If Connie hadn't decided to dump Susan, everything might have continued as usual. At least for a while longer."

"Connie left Jack's gun in the glovebox of her car and forgot about it," Danny said. "It turned out to be very convenient for Susan to implicate Jack. Lucky coincidence for Susan—bad for Jack. I have to finish some paperwork, but before I go," Danny reached into his shirt pocket. "I have one more thing for you to see." He handed Angela a copy of a note written in a feminine hand, precise and neat in appearance.

"You're looking at a copy of Susan Worth's confession, or I should say her insanity plea. Det. Lane has the original. Susan thought we'd let her go home if she explained everything. Read it, Angela. It'll give you the chills." Angela skimmed through the paragraphs, seeing what she already knew until she got to the part that explained the attack.

I liked Angela. I'm sorry I killed her. When she told me that she didn't believe Dwayne was the murderer, I knew it wouldn't stop.

Angela handed the paper to Danny.

Danny looked her in the eye. "I'm glad you made it through this. You were lucky, Angela. She would have killed you."

My big mouth. "Susan thinks she killed me, too? She doesn't remember the fight at the weir or her arrest?"

"Nope, at least that's what she claims. You shouldn't dwell on it." Danny tore the confession letter into small pieces and tossed it in the trash can.

A nurse entered the room to tell them they had to go. LJ kissed Angela goodbye, and the nurse checked Angela's pulse. "You need to rest, dear."

Angela agreed. Her body ached. The medication took some of the physical pain away, but it couldn't erase the emotional pain.

She rolled to her side and stared at the trash can. In it lay words that would haunt her.

FORTY-ONE

Angela stayed in the hospital for a week before being discharged with a few simple instructions, such as no climbing, running, or jumping. Okay, that was easy enough. She didn't feel like doing any of those things anyway. Her head was partially shaven, showing off some ugly stitches that she covered with a scarf. It felt like she'd used it for bowling. No rough and tumble activity was all right with her, but she was anxious to get back to work to check on her refuge.

Jack had been busy working in the greenhouse. The first day Angela returned, she found a small potted oak tree on her desk with a note telling her that a little head injury was nothing for a person who was as strong as an oak. Everyone was glad to see Angela back and Jack in the clear. Knowing how much Angela liked potlucks, the staff had arranged one for lunch that day. It would also be a going away party for Gilbert. Angela had picked up a gift to say goodbye to him. It was a new brass nameplate with Gilbert Chavez Refuge Manager written on it.

Angela spent the morning reviewing emails, signing paperwork, and timesheets. She was just about to read a memo from the Director when Gilbert popped his head in the door. "Got a minute?"

She remembered what LJ had told her about Gilbert following her to ensure she was okay. Gilbert deserved to hear how grateful she was that he was looking out for her. She wanted to tell him she'd never forget what a good man he was.

"Come on in. I owe you a huge debt of gratitude and thanks since you were the one watching my back. I don't think I was too nice to you when you came to my rescue."

Angela noted his sheepish smile as he took a seat. "Yeah, well, I guess I blew it, so no gratitude, please. I'm just glad you're okay. I wish I'd been there when you needed me. You did okay on your own, though." His words brought back the image of Tony sitting at her desk.

"Don't be humble. You came exactly at the right time. I know I'm headstrong and not the easiest person to work with. You're a good man, Gilbert Chavez, and I'm thankful you're on my team."

He looked away toward the window.

"Lilly told me LJ is leaving," he said, changing the subject. "That he's going to Europe." He turned and held her gaze. "What about you? Are you going to follow?"

Angela paused before answering. "No. We're parting ways. Amicably. He invited me to visit. I don't think I'll accept the invitation."

Gilbert held her gaze and nodded. Could she let go of her fears? A man like Gilbert might change her completely in a good way. Did she want to take the chance?

"And you? Are you ready for your new adventure in Nevada? Your new boss called to tell me they've offered you the position. Pahranagat, I hope I said that right, is damn lucky to get you. I hope you stay in touch. I can't wait to hear about the place. Maybe you'll invite me to visit after you're settled in."

There. She offered an olive branch. Would Gilbert take it?

Gilbert smiled, and she saw a light in his eyes. "You'll always be welcome, Angela. I'd love to have you visit. We could explore the place together."

Angela looked down at her desk, feeling the blush rise up her neck. "Have the guys finished all the levee work? Are they ready to start spraying loosestrife?"

Gilbert leaned back in the chair. "They finished the levee work and are tackling the loosestrife." He paused. "I had hoped I could tell you about the job before they called you to set a start date."

Angela hoped her smile didn't echo the pain she felt in her heart. "I told them I required at least another month. I hope you don't mind."

"No. A month will be good. I'm finishing up the projects I've been working on, like that web page. Next week, we can sit down and make a list of things to keep me busy until l I leave."

"Your new boss told me he was pretty impressed with you. I told him he should be. Good job, Gilbert. You're going to do well."

"Thanks, Angela." He stood up and walked toward the door. Turning back, he said, "I'm glad you're okay. I wouldn't have wanted to say goodbye to you that way." He held her eye for a few moments before he walked out.

All was good with him. From the smells coming through the door, it was time for lunch. Potluck.

Tony was there, and he pulled her aside. "I'm glad you're okay now. I guess that woman snuck up on you." He looked around. "Those volunteers said your boyfriend is leaving. Does that mean you're leaving, too?"

"No, Tony. I'm not going anywhere for a while." When she said she was staying, the change on his face made her feel good.

"I'm glad. I mean, we just got to know each other. You know? Friends?"

Angela smiled, giving him a brief hug. "Yes. We just became friends, didn't we?" She liked this man. She'd have to nurture this friendship.

After the potluck lunch, she strolled out to the greenhouse with Jack, Lilly, and Ed to look it over. Jack, Ed, and some other volunteers did a great job constructing it, right down to the sprinkler systems and automatic vents.

"Did you know this crazy woman is talking about selling her house?" Ed asked. "She wants to get a travel trailer. Can you believe that? She wants to spend her golden years driving all over the country to other refuges."

"Oh, Ed. It's not that bad," Lilly shook her head. "I can always come home, park in your yard, and hang out for a while." Lilly laughed. "It's not like you'll never see me again."

"The three of you apart?" Angela asked. "I can't see that happening. What would you do without these two, Lilly?"

"See. Even Angela gets it." Jack said. "Why do you want to leave your buddies all alone?"

Lilly put her hand on Jack's shoulder. "Well, I haven't decided to do it yet. The point is that now that I'm alone, that old house is just too much for me. I'm not sure I want to buy another house. Angela knows I've looked. I haven't seen anything that excites me. Buying a motor home or travel trailer might suit me fine. I've looked at a dozen or so, and I'm excited. I'm not in a hurry. I have a lot to do. You aren't going to get rid of me too soon."

She winked at Angela. "And besides, if you want to join me, I'm all for it. The dogs will gladly make room for you." She smiled. "We could have a road trip, and when you get tired, I could drive you to the nearest airport and put you on a plane back home. Come on. It could be a lot of fun." Lilly looked at Angela for support.

Angela bit back the pain and smiled. "I think it sounds wonderful. I hope you let me hang out with you every once in a while. I love road trips. You aren't getting rid of me that easily. I can't wait to spend time with you in your new home." Angela couldn't tell Lilly what she was really thinking, that she didn't want to lose any more friends, but she understood Lilly needed to make a new life without Harry. She understood that more than ever. She still had Jack and Ed.

"Oh, great. Sleeping with two dogs. Just the kind of road trip I'd want to take." Ed shook his head.

Jack smiled at Lilly. "Are you saying you'd be our traveling home away from home?"

"That's it. You could come to ride with the girls and me anytime. Ed, it's not like my dogs have fleas."

The girls were a new addition to Lilly's life. Patty and Windy were two springer spaniels. She had just adopted them from a neighbor. They had purchased the pups and found out, too late, that they were allergic to their hair. They didn't want to send them to a shelter or a breed rescue, so Lilly purchased them. They were the perfect temperament for her personality. They made terrific companions, keeping her active and giving her purpose.

"Don't worry about it right now. It's just something I'm considering. I just wanted to know what you thought," Lilly told them.

As much as she enjoyed the lunch and hanging out with her friends, Angela's head began to ache. Making excuses, she went into her office and shut the door. Angela took some medication for her pain. She closed her eyes to concentrate on breathing, listening to laughter from the front office.

Susan was charged with murder, but she might never make it to trial. Her mental state seemed in the balance. An institution might be in her future. Dwayne Palmer, Robert Durham, and Donald King faced other charges. Angela, Bart Linden, and Ray Silverman might have to testify, but it was far off. Everyone was lining up their attorneys.

Angela wasn't going to worry about any of it now. What was the saying? Not my circus, not my monkeys—something like that. She could get back to running her refuge.

Jack was in the clear. Jack's friend was safely tucked away in a safe house and would find the protection and legal assistance she needed to get through her ordeal.

Gilbert leaving meant she had to review his job description and prepare a new job announcement. Replacing Gilbert wouldn't be easy, but there were a lot of qualified people in the refuge system who would leap at the opportunity to work at Ottawa. No one could replace Gilbert, but she was sure she'd have a good pool of candidates to select from. It would take time to complete the process of advertising the job, waiting for a qualified applicant list, and then interviewing the candidates. In the meantime, she'd take over Gilbert's duties.

LJ could take advantage of the opportunity to work in Europe and start a new branch for his company. Once they made the decision to let each other go their separate ways, Angela felt the joy of giving in a way she'd never experienced. She truly wished him the best.

She would stay at Ottawa Refuge with her friends. She'd have to get to know Ed's girlfriend, Melody. Jim Messinger had said he would continue volunteering for Pearl at the refuge even after he graduated. He loved being 'one' with nature.

She would miss Lilly Weathers terribly, but she would help Lilly find a good truck and travel trailer combo for her new adventure. It would have to be one that could accommodate Angela when she came to visit. Angela looked forward to those road trips. Following Lilly could lead her to some new adventures. Angela would make new memories, too.

There was also Tony. An unusual friend, but he had her back, didn't he? She smiled to herself. He was as much a part of these marshes as the water—beautiful in his way.

Angela's life with LJ had been convenient. It was time for Angela to learn about herself. It was time to learn about relationships and different kinds of love. She could no longer stay safe. She knew now that while it was comfortable being in a relationship like she had with LJ, it wasn't living.

She wouldn't let Gilbert leave her life, but she'd take it slow. It was more than just exploring a new man in her life—she had to explore a new Angela. She still had many fears to overcome.

When Gilbert settled into his new job, Angela would fly to Las Vegas, Nevada, then drive ninety miles north to visit his refuge. It had such a strange name. She pronounced it phonetically in her head—Paw-ran-uh-gut. Gilbert told her it meant Land of Shining Water.

Angela knew the arid desert well. She had learned that Pahranagat was a Southern Paiute name and had spiritual meaning. She knew water was vital to all living creatures. A name like that meant the refuge was about life—about living.

A burst of laughter interrupted Angela's thoughts. Her head felt better. It was time to rejoin the party.

Credit: Lisa Kuhlman

AFTER STARTING COLLEGE IN HER THIRTIES and graduating from New Mexico State University with a Master of Science in wildlife studies, Christy J. Kendall served as a Wildlife Biologist, Refuge Manager, and Project Leader at multiple wildlife refuges across the country with the U.S. Fish and Wildlife Service for twenty-five years. During those years, she grew to love and understand the employees, volunteers, and non-profit organizations who gave their time and money to support conservation. In the genre of mystery and through fictional characters, she tells their stories.

A former military wife, Christy began following her wildlife career after her husband served twenty years in the U.S. Army and retired. Christy has two beautiful daughters, two granddaughters, and two grandsons. She lives with her husband in Washington with a cat named Charlie and a dog named Gemma.

9 781684 922444